PAUL,
APOSTLE OF CHRIST

PAUL,
APOSTLE OF CHRIST

THE NOVELIZATION
OF THE MAJOR MOTION PICTURE

A Novel by
Angela Hunt

Based on the Screenplay by
Andrew Hyatt

BETHANYHOUSE
a division of Baker Publishing Group
Minneapolis, Minnesota

Published by Bethany House Publishers
11400 Hampshire Avenue South
Bloomington, Minnesota 55438
www.bethanyhouse.com

Bethany House Publishers is a division of
Baker Publishing Group, Grand Rapids, Michigan

Printed in the United States of America

ISBN 978-0-7642-3254-1 (trade paper)

Library of Congress Cataloging-in-Publication Control Number: 2017964333

This is a work of historical reconstruction; the appearances of certain historical figures are therefore inevitable. All other characters, however, are products of the author's imagination, and any resemblance to actual persons, living or dead, is coincidental.

Author is represented by Browne & Miller Literary Associates.

18   19   20   21   22   23   24   7   6   5   4   3   2   1

Introduction to Luke's first book:

Now many have undertaken to organize an account of the events fulfilled among us, just as they were handed down to us from the start by the eyewitnesses and reporters of the word. Therefore it seemed best to me also, because I have carefully investigated everything from the beginning, to write for you an orderly record, most excellent Theophilus, so you may know for sure the truth of the words you have been taught.

Luke 1:1–4

Introduction to Luke's second book:

I wrote the first volume, Theophilus, about all that *Yeshua* began to do and teach—up to the day He was taken up, after He had given orders by the *Ruach ha-Kodesh* to the emissaries He had chosen. To them He showed Himself to be alive after His suffering through many convincing proofs, appearing to them for forty days and speaking about the kingdom of God.

Acts 1:1–3

CHAPTER
ONE

The Seventh Day of Junius

The hooded man darted into a niche in the dark alley, his heart pounding against his sternum. His ears, tuned to catch the slightest sound, warned him of approaching footsteps—*heavy* footsteps, accented by the metallic scrape of sword hilts against iron buckles.

The Greek pressed his spine into the recess in the aged wall, willing its shadows to cloak him. He could not be caught in this part of the city without a valid reason for venturing near Nero's prison. Not even his medical bag would suffice as an explanation, since the only residences in this part of Rome were the former palaces of Augustus, Tiberius, and Caligula.

He drew back, the wall biting into his shoulder blades, as two members of the Praetorian Guard moved through a nearby puddle of torchlight and continued on their way. "I still say it's a nasty business," one Praetorian remarked. "I have seen men die in all sorts of ways, but that has to be one of the worst."

The other man replied, but the crunch of gravel beneath their sandals obscured the rest of their conversation.

When they had turned the corner, the Greek physician held his small bag next to his chest and changed his destination to a place that would be infinitely safer.

— ᨏᨏ —

In the heart of Rome, directly across from a monument to Julius Caesar and the famous Roman Forum, another man sat in a cavern hewn out of stone. A single candle pushed at the darkness, scattering its light over a tattered blanket, an empty bowl, an overturned stone cup. The man's toes, riding above misshapen and callused feet, shone weakly in the gloom.

Paul, called Sha'ul by his people the Jews, closed his eyes at the all-too-familiar sight. Day after day, hour after hour, he leaned against the wall of his windowless prison and stared at his toes, which had long since ceased to fascinate him. Sometimes, especially if the guards did not remember to lower the daily allowance of water and food, those wizened appendages took on the appearance of men he had known: Demas, who loved the world more than Christ; Crescens, Titus, Alexander the coppersmith, Governor Felix.

He closed his eyes, slamming the door on the images of those who had deserted him. He would rather envision beloved friends: Timothy, so young and full of righteous zeal. Priscilla and Aquila, fellow tentmakers with whom he had shared laughter and many a meal. Barnabas, his constant encourager. Aya, his sister; Avniel, his nephew. And Luke. Beloved Luke.

Keeping his eyes closed, Paul crossed his arms and smiled as the iron bracelets clanked. As far as he knew, his friends were alive . . . and still free.

Thank you, Yeshua. May God be praised.

— ᨏᨏ —

Making his way past the Temple of Jupiter, Luke felt the tension in his shoulders ease. The Tiber River lay just ahead, and beyond it stood the Roman market where people did business at all hours. During the day, merchants of trade goods occupied the dilapidated booths, while vendors of another sort plied their wares after sunset. A hooded figure would not appear out of place in the crowded market, though a well-known Christian would be at risk anywhere in the city—

He flinched when a bony hand grabbed his shoulder and forcibly swung him around. "Hello, there." A thin-faced man gave him a wide, disturbing smile. "What's your pleasure?" He stepped closer, his breath stinking of infection and rotting teeth. "Boys or girls?"

Luke shrugged off the man's hand and staggered away, his heart twisting at the reminder that evil lurked around every corner in this city. Rome was reported to be the greatest city in the world, but Nero's Rome had begun to smell of decay, a rot that came from within.

That realization never failed to trouble his spirit. Influenced by the world's greatest thinkers, artists, scholars, rulers, and military men, Rome had been home to some of civilization's most noble men, and home as well to the most dishonorable of people. In Nero's Rome, on any street corner a man could find beauty and perversity, generosity and stinginess, abundance and scarcity.

In the area where he walked, the walls of the buildings functioned as signboards on which public opinion was clearly—and often rudely—expressed. He read as he walked:

Alcmaeon, Orestes, and Nero are brothers.
Why? Because all of them murdered their mothers.

Count the numerical values of the letters in Nero's name,
And in "murdered his own mother"
You will find their sum is the same.

The Palace is spreading and swallowing Rome!
Let us all flee to Veii and make it our home.
Yet the Palace is growing so wickedly fast
That it threatens to gobble up Veii at last.

His friends would undoubtedly share the news about what was currently happening in Rome, but these buildings frequently offered better reporting because they did not attempt to soften the truth.

Still, he had not come back to report on Rome. He had come to see his friends . . . if he could find them.

He walked on, heading to the appointed spot—a statue of Nero near the Tiber—and kept his back to the river so that no one could creep up on him unobserved. The moon had barely risen, but the sliver of silver cast a white beam over the trash heaped along the river's edge. Though he would wait for as long as necessary, he hoped his escort would soon appear.

A flash of light caught his eye. To his left, on the walkway atop the Servian Wall, a Praetorian passed by with a torch in his hand. Two other guards and a prisoner followed him, and the moonlight revealed bloody stripes on the prisoner's back. What was this?

The Praetorians stopped, and one of the guards shoved the prisoner down. Faint cries reached Luke's ear, and he turned away, not needing to look in order to know what was taking place. Crucifixion had been a common form of execution even before Yeshua's death, and the sight was not unusual in the city of seven hills.

Luke's stomach roiled as the man released an agonized cry. Who was this condemned prisoner, and what had he done? A thief would have his hand chopped off; for treason or murder a Roman citizen might lose his head. But crucifixion was reserved for non-Romans who had committed truly heinous crimes.

Almost against his will, his gaze drifted back to the wall. The prisoner had been nailed to a post, his arms bent and fastened above his head, his feet nailed to the base. The two Praetorians who had positioned him moved back while the third lifted a bucket and sloshed some sort of dark liquid over the man's body. The man began to shriek, and the frantic note in the sound evoked an unnatural silence. Even the insects by the river stopped churring as the torchbearer stepped forward and touched the flame to the base of the support. The hungry flames rose up quickly to lick the wood and race over the prisoner as his frenzied cry became a plea for release at any cost. . . .

Then the man fell silent. The flames settled back to consume what remained, and the insects resumed their night music.

Horror snaked down Luke's spine and coiled in his gut. What sort of new torture was this? Luke looked to the right and saw more prisoners approaching under guard. Was Nero so demented that he considered human torches an economical way to light the city? The serpentine Servian Wall was long, encircling the old city and enclosing many important palaces and temples.

"Grace be unto you."

Startled, Luke turned and stared into the eyes of another hooded man, one whose cloak had opened enough to reveal a sword of the Praetorian Guard. But this man, he knew, was a brother in Christ.

"And also to you," Luke replied, his voice trembling.

A smile flashed within the hood. "Come. I will take you to your friends. But walk several steps behind me. For both our sakes, we should not be seen together."

Luke swallowed hard when the hooded man turned and entered a patch of darkness. Not daring to take his eyes from the broad-shouldered figure, Luke followed.

—ᴍ—

"Prisoner!"

Paul clung to the soft darkness as closely as he could, burying his head in his folded arms. He did not want to wake, did not want to lie in the dark breathing fetid air when he could experience a small measure of freedom in his dreams.

A revolting liquid assaulted his face, cruelly waking him. He sat up, sputtering and wheezing, as laughter floated down from above.

"There." A burly guard grinned down at Paul. "Rouse yourself when we call your name."

"My name—" Paul spat, desperately ridding his mouth of the taste of foul water—"is not *prisoner*."

"It is now." Grinning like a well-fed house cat, the guard walked away, leaving Paul wide awake and choking on his own stench.

He wrapped his arms around his bent knees and lowered his head. He was no stranger to prisons, but this one was the vilest, probably in the entire civilized world. Located in the heart of Rome, the centuries-old prison was comprised of two chambers of hewn stone. The ground floor consisted of one large space, occupied by the Praetorians who guarded this place and the prefect, whenever he chanced to visit. Beneath the ground floor lay the second chamber, a dungeon accessible only by way of a round opening in the stone floor of the first space.

At the moment, Paul was the only prisoner in the pit, although thousands of others had left behind tattered clothing, worn-out sandals, gnawed rodent bones, and layers of sweat, blood, and human waste.

Paul had lost count of the days he'd spent underground. His time here began following the trial, held two years after the great fire destroyed more than half the city. From his exalted golden throne, Nero listened to testimony and wept elephant tears as false witnesses spoke of seeing Paul and his followers dance before the leaping flames.

The verdict, which came from the emperor's own lips, was swift and nonnegotiable: "Paul of Tarsus, I find you guilty of arson, conspiracy, treason, and murder. You will be sentenced to die upon a date I shall set at my leisure. Until then, you shall contemplate your crimes in my prison. That is all."

A squadron from the Praetorian Guard led Paul in chains from the Forum to the prison, which was but a stone's throw away. They marched him across the ground floor and led him to the opening in the stone. "You'll like it down there," one of the guards said, his mouth curving in a predatory smile as he picked up a thick, knotted rope. "Your comrade Peter was held here before we crucified him."

When another Praetorian nudged his back with his foot, Paul sat and held the rope. He managed the descent with some difficulty, then dropped onto the filthy floor below. With a sinking heart, he had watched the rope ascend until it disappeared from sight.

How long ago had he made that descent? At least seven hundred thirty days. And although the guards occasionally pulled him up to meet with the prefect, those occasions were rare.

Dreams were Paul's only escape. Even his memories could not

compare, for many of them were as horrific as his reality. But in dreams he could walk beneath a wide sky, inhale the fragrance of sea air and fine leather, and hear the haunting cry of a hawk in flight. Sometimes he dreamed of leaning against the rough bark of a tree and closing his eyes, relishing the music of a shepherd or the snoring of friends around a makeshift campfire.

The worst thing about his prison, he often thought, was the desperate, deprived condition of his senses. In the depths of the prison, his eyes saw little but shadows, his nose inhaled nothing but stench, and his tongue tasted only thin gruel and his own rotting teeth. His hands, which had grown soft without the joy of honest labor, often swelled in the humid space, and his skin was so covered in grime that he could barely feel the texture of the stone that surrounded him.

In his dreams, Paul found release—so long as the Praetorians allowed him to sleep. Unfortunately, some of them thought it great sport to wake him in cruel and unusual ways.

Yet the guards' cruelty and the horrendous conditions in which Paul found himself were not the worst aspects of Nero's prison. More torturous by far was the knowledge that he, an apostle who had traveled hundreds of miles and spoken to thousands of people, had apparently been set on a shelf. Cast aside like an old man—which he was—and forgotten.

His own words came back on a tide of memory. *"Every competitor exercises self-control in all respects. They do it to receive a perishable crown, but we do it to receive an imperishable one.*

"So I run in this way—not aimlessly. So I box in this way—not beating the air. Rather, I punish my body and bring it into submission, so that after I have preached to others, I myself will not be disqualified."

Despair pooled in his heart. He had become what he feared—

an old, weak, broken man without an audience or a purpose. He had run the race to win, but . . .

"Please," he whispered, shutting his eyes against the sight of his awful surroundings, "one thing I ask, Yeshua—help me finish well."

—✦—

The hooded Praetorian led Luke through winding streets bordered by tall wooden buildings that appeared to be in danger of toppling with the slightest breeze. The structures in this part of the crowded city bore little resemblance to the marble-columned palaces and public buildings where he had walked earlier. The ground-floor apartments in this area were dedicated to trade and occupied by butchers, ironsmiths, woodworkers, dentists, and sculptors of household gods, while the workers and their families inhabited the upper floors.

Through open shutters Luke glimpsed life in all its many forms—people sleeping, arguing, feeding their children, plucking chickens, kneeling before their idols. Sputtering oil lamps and torches lit these buildings, reminding Luke once again that a single wayward spark could threaten the two million people who lived in the crowded city.

His escort paused at a busy intersection, and Luke made his way to the guard's side. "Do we part here?"

Without looking at Luke, the Praetorian shook his head, then turned and walked down the Way of Triumph, the paved street over which Julius Caesar, Augusta, and Cleopatra had once ridden. Finally the guard headed toward a group of pleasant-looking villas on a hillside. Luke followed the man up a set of stairs, then through a narrow space lit by a single torch. Luke could see nothing but cascading vines and a trickling fountain, but then his escort lifted a tapestry and exposed a rough wooden door. Taking an iron key from his pocket, he fitted it into the lock and pushed on the door. He gestured for Luke to enter.

Was this the place? Or was he stepping into a trap?

He studied the Praetorian's eyes—they were wide and as guileless as a child's. Trusting the man was not a spy, Luke drew a deep breath and ducked beneath the small doorway.

He found himself inside a courtyard garden. An air of faded gentility marked the large fountain, the remnants of a formal garden, and an intricately worked iron gate, but the space was cluttered with hammocks, small tents, and iron pots set over smoldering fires. Around those fires, on cots and sleeping mats, he saw dozens of men, women, and children, all of them eyeing him with suspicion, speaking in whispers, and instinctively huddling together.

And their faces! The eyes that rose to meet Luke's were haunted and wary, as though they could not trust even a man as harmless as he.

Lord, how could you have allowed the sort of evil that has driven your children into hiding like this?

"Luke!"

A woman's voice, resonant with joy, snapped through the collective anxiety like a whip. Luke spun around and saw Priscilla standing on the torchlit balcony, her lovely face alight with relief and happiness. "Stay there, I'll come down."

She moved down the stairs with the grace of a woman half her age and drew him into a tender embrace. "Praise God! We were beginning to worry about you."

Luke smiled. "I had to wait longer than I anticipated, but here I am. I never would have found you if your friend hadn't found me."

Priscilla turned to the Praetorian who had served as Luke's escort. "Thank you, Eubulus. Once again you have served us well."

Two red patches appeared on the man's cheeks. "It was nothing."

"It was a gift," Priscilla said, correcting him. "We know what risks you take every time you help us."

Luke watched in silent appreciation as the imposing soldier walked into the courtyard, stopping to speak to a man and woman near one of the fires.

"Priscilla," Luke said, turning back to her, "I didn't expect to find that you had so many guests. If my presence is an imposition—"

"You are always welcome in our home." She sighed. "We didn't expect to have so many guests. Many of these families lost their homes in the fire. Others have fled the threat of spying neighbors. Still others are known to be Christians, so they dare not be seen on the streets any longer. Since they have no place else to go, and we have room . . ."

"It's good you are here."

She inclined her head toward the villa. "Come, Luke. Aquila is inside—he will be thrilled to see you."

They went up the stairs and into the house. Priscilla took Luke's bag and cloak. The man near the fire turned at the sound of footsteps, and his face brightened when he saw Luke. "Brother, you are a delight to these weary eyes."

Luke stepped forward to meet his friend's embrace. "I'm glad to see you. Thank you for making the necessary arrangements. I wasn't sure I would be allowed back into the city."

"What did you say when they questioned you?"

"I said I was a physician."

"Did they ask you to offer incense to Vesta?"

Luke grimaced. "They did not."

"They must have been in a hurry. Or God distracted them." Aquila gestured to a bench by the fire, inviting Luke to sit. "We do not take many chances these days. These are dangerous times."

Luke sat, then pulled a bag of coins from his tunic. "Your letters broke the Philippian community's heart. We took up a collection for you." He placed the bag in Aquila's hand. "It's not as much as we had hoped."

Aquila smiled. "We are grateful for every coin. Supplies and food are running low, but still, the Lord provides. And now He has provided through the Philippians." He turned to a young boy who sat near the fire. "Tarquin? Will you take this bag to Herodion and Rufus? Ask them to put it wherever it is most urgently needed."

The boy, who appeared to be eleven or twelve, grinned before he took the bag and sped into the courtyard.

Luke watched him go. "He seems young to be entrusted with such a responsibility."

Aquila chuckled. "He is loyal. A Roman boy. The community took him in after his parents died in the great fire. Thousands perished during that time." He pointed to a young man standing beside the courtyard gate. "His cousin, Cassius. He came to us after he heard what the community had done for Tarquin. He was baptized a few days later."

Luke rose and moved onto the balcony, where he studied the faces of those milling around in the courtyard garden. "A good thing you have a large house."

Aquila grinned. "The house is not so large, but the garden has room for many. It is just what the Lord knew we needed."

"Everyone here can be trusted?"

Aquila's smile broadened. "We trust God. Come, sit, you must be starving. Tell me how the church at Philippi is doing."

"They are doing well. And thank you—I am hungry."

"Then come to the table, brother. Priscilla has done an amazing job of feeding so many. And after you eat, if you don't mind, we have some who are sick. If you could—"

"I can." Luke reached for his bag. "My belly can wait."

"None are so sick that they cannot wait until after you eat something." Aquila squeezed Luke's shoulder. "Let us take care of you for once. Later we will have plenty of time for you to do what you do best."

Reluctantly, Luke let himself be led to the table.

—◊—

Luke was not surprised by the illnesses he discovered among the refugees. A few women exhibited festering burns—always a problem when people and their cooking fires were crowded together—and a few children were suffering the effects of malnutrition. Several people presented wounds for him to examine—cuts, as well as infected insect and rat bites. Two babies had fevers, so Luke instructed their mothers to give them lots of water and bathe them, if possible.

He treated the afflictions he could, gave advice to those who needed to adjust their daily habits, and comforted those who were sick with worry. "Did Christ not tell us to be anxious for nothing?" he reminded them. "We are to cast our cares on Him."

When he had finished examining all who were ill, he looked up and saw Priscilla waiting at the edge of the courtyard. "Come," she said, smiling serenely. "The hour is late and we have more food."

He followed her into the house, into a lamp-lit room where a table had been laid with bowls of figs, a slab of cheese, and bread. Some sort of stew simmered in an iron pot, and the delicious aroma awakened his appetite.

"I knew that simple meal of bread and cheese wouldn't be enough," she said, gesturing for him to sit. "Not for a man who probably hasn't eaten all day."

"The food smells wonderful." He slid onto a bench. "Thank you."

Priscilla and Aquila sat across from him. After giving thanks to God, the three of them began to eat.

"I know I have only just returned," Luke said, breaking off a piece of the fresh bread, "but things appear to be worse than they have ever been. Rome has long been a place of debauchery and bloodshed, but darkness hangs over this city now—a darkness that was not present when I was last in Rome."

Aquila sipped his wine, eyeing Luke over the brim of his cup. "Nero's cruelty has worsened. He now holds regular games at the Circus Maximus. He still loves chariot races, but on days when the horses are resting, his games feature men, women, and children being torn apart by wild beasts."

"The crowd screams for more after each exhibition," Priscilla added, shivering. "It is horrible."

Luke shook his head. "Evil has overtaken his soul."

"Perhaps," Aquila said. "But Nero says those exhibitions are intended to remind the Roman people that followers of Christ burned more than half the city to the ground."

Luke blinked. "Does he really expect them to believe that?"

"He would like them to believe anything," Aquila answered, "rather than know the truth."

"And that truth is—?"

"The fires were his deliberate act," Priscilla said.

Luke glanced from wife to husband. "Truly?"

Aquila nodded. "One of Nero's grand plans—one he actually presented to the Senate—involved tearing down a third of the city so that he could build an elaborate series of palaces he called Neropolis. The Senate rejected his proposal, and not long afterward, fire broke out among the shops lining the Circus Maximus."

"Fires break out in Rome every day," Luke interjected. "And the wooden buildings are deathtraps."

"Agreed," Aquila said. "And many of the slums *did* burn. But the stone homes of the senators also burned—homes in the part of the city Nero wanted to destroy."

"Gangs—organized thugs—prevented people from fighting the fires," Priscilla added. "They threatened to torture anyone who stopped the flames."

"The Praetorians are supposed to fight fires when necessary," Aquila said. "Instead they remained billeted in the Castra Praetoria while the city burned."

"I have heard," Luke said, watching Priscilla ladle stew into a bowl, "that Nero played his fiddle while the fire raged."

"I heard that rumor, too," Aquila replied. "But it's not completely true. He was in Antium when the fire began. Convenient for him, really. No one could blame him for the blaze if he was away from the city."

"But he came back," Priscilla said. "When the fires neared his home. The fires could not be prevented from consuming his palace, yet Nero was able to open the Campus Martius and Agrippa's public buildings to house the impoverished people. He distributed useful supplies from Ostia and other cities, and lowered the price of corn to three sesterces per peck. He did these things to gain the public's favor—and the ploy worked, but only until the rumors spread."

"What rumors?" Luke asked.

Aquila snorted. "They say that on one of the nights Rome burned, Nero stood on a household stage and sang about the fall of Troy, likening the fire to that catastrophe."

"Everyone blames him anyway," Priscilla said, passing the stew to Luke. "Because even before the fire, he behaved as though the run-down condition of old buildings and narrow streets offended him. He lit fire to the city so brazenly that a number of former consuls caught his associates with oakum and pine brands on their properties but did not arrest them. He also desired the property of several grain storehouses, so he demolished the walls with siege machines and set fire to the inside, though the outer walls were made of stone. That fire spread and burned for six days and seven nights, prompting many in the area to take refuge around monuments or in the tombs. Many destroyed homes were owned by well-known generals who had decorated their walls with spoils from their victories. Temples burned, even those that were consecrated during the wars against Carthage and Gaul. Nero observed the fire from the tower of Maecenas and said he was 'engrossed in the beauty of the flames.' Then he donned the clothing of an actor and sang 'The Fall of Illium.'"

Aquila's mouth pursed and rolled like he wanted to spit. "Nero said he would pay for the removal of corpses and debris, but he forbade anyone from combing through the remains of his own estate, as he wished to gather the spoils for himself. Then he initiated a fund for the relief of damages from the fire and forced the people to contribute, until the private citizens had almost no money left."

"But he got what he wanted," Priscilla added, her features hardening in a look of disapproval. "Now no one can stop his grand plan for rebuilding Rome. He has already begun his *Domus Aurea*, the grand palace. I hear it will have a park, a lake, and several palaces—"

"The lake and park are to appease the people," Aquila interjected, "while the palaces are to reflect Nero's glory."

"When people think of him in years to come"—Priscilla shook her head—"I do not think they will remember his palaces. They will remember his cruelty."

"I saw an example of that cruelty tonight," Luke said, setting his jaw. "The Praetorians crucified a prisoner on top of the Servian Wall, then set the man afire. It looked like they were preparing to execute others."

"It happens every night." Priscilla's lower lip quivered. "And those prisoners were not criminals—they were Christians. Nero proclaimed that since Christians started the fires, they will serve as torches on the Wall."

"Why doesn't anyone stop him?" Luke asked. "The Praetorians have removed emperors before. They engineered the assassination of Caligula, didn't they?"

Aquila let out a sigh. "The Praetorians have not removed Nero because many of them trust the emperor and his lies. Rumors have been spread throughout the city, and those who do not understand people of the Way have no trouble believing such stories."

Curious, Luke asked, "What kind of stories?"

Aquila tugged on his beard. "Some say, brother, that an ancient Egyptian prophecy—supposedly well known to Christians— foretold the fall of 'the evil city' on the day Sirius rises. Sirius rose on the nineteenth, the day the great fire began. Those who

23

cling to this falsehood have no trouble believing that Christians fanned the flames of the fire, hoping for the complete destruction of Rome."

Luke's thoughts spun in bewilderment. "Since when have Christians *or* Jews placed any faith in ancient Egyptian prophecies?"

Grinning, Aquila tipped his finger toward Luke. "Exactly. Yet those who do not know us insist that Christians are not to be trusted. They cheer Nero on and applaud his plans for rebuilding Rome. Each time a Christian dies on the Wall or at the Circus, they yell for more."

Luke pressed his hand over his lips and stared at the stew in his bowl. "I . . . I seem to have lost my appetite."

"I am sorry," Aquila said. "I should not have burdened you with so much news all at once. You have been away—"

"No, I needed to know what has happened, because now I understand why Nero ruled against Paul at his trial." Luke pressed his hand to his chest. "Now I see why so many have crowded your courtyard. How much longer can you hide so many?"

Aquila looked at his wife. "We don't know. We are at a crossroad and yet we see no sign of this darkness being lifted. We don't know whether we should continue here or attempt to lead the community out of Rome."

"Where is Linus?" Luke tilted his head, remembering the gentle Roman who was a leader of the church in Rome. "Surely this is a decision for him to make."

Aquila lowered his gaze. "We lost contact with him weeks ago. I believe he's gone into hiding with the rest of the larger community. Their location, or even if they are still in the city . . . we simply don't know."

Luke rested his elbows on the table and propped his chin in his hand. He had always considered problems from a logical perspective, and surely this problem could be methodically considered and resolved. "With the threat of such great persecution, why stay in Rome?"

Priscilla gave him a rueful smile. "We are the only light left in the city. If we go, the poor and needy will suffer even worse than they do now."

Aquila lifted his hand. "But in remaining here, we risk everyone's lives. We have families with women and children. If we are discovered, the emperor's Praetorians will take everyone prisoner."

Luke sighed. "I understand. It is not an easy decision."

Priscilla leaned toward him. "Luke, when you speak with Paul, perhaps . . ."

"Yes." Luke nodded slowly. "He will shed light on this. I will ask Paul for his counsel—he will know what to do."

"We would be grateful for his insight on the matter." Aquila pushed the bowl of figs toward Luke. "And you, my friend, should eat more. You are too thin."

Priscilla smiled in agreement. "I know you are used to hardship, but when food is available, you should take advantage. Especially when it is offered with love."

Luke felt his reserve thaw. He had become so accustomed to being cautious and on guard; perhaps Priscilla was right. He needed to put his wariness aside and rejoice in the blessings around him.

"Thank you," he said, taking a fig from the bowl. "Thank you for reminding me that for everything, there is a season. A time to fast, and a time to eat."

CHAPTER
TWO

The Eighth Day of Junius

"Hey! Prisoner!"

Paul opened his eyes, then slowly unfolded his stiff limbs and pushed himself into a standing position. Dread and anticipation mingled as he stepped into the single circle of light that streamed from the stone chamber above.

He tipped his head back and squinted into the beam. "You want me?"

"Who else? You're wanted outside!"

Outside? Paul's thoughts tumbled over each other. Who would want to see him up there? He was a condemned prisoner, and no one, not even his best friends, wanted anything more to do with him . . .

A rope fell through the opening, a knotted cord that served as his only connection to the land of the living.

He put his foot into the large loop at the end and gripped the rope with trembling hands. Strong arms hauled him upward, pulling him from the depths of Nero's dungeon.

Blinking in the bright light above ground, Paul could not see the one who grabbed his arms and drew him onto the stone floor. When his watering eyes adjusted to the brightness of the space, he saw four men who appeared to be with the Praetorian Guard. One guard held a door open.

Paul shuffled on shaky legs toward the doorway. The upper chamber had been painfully bright, but the unfiltered sunlight was ten times worse. He raised his hands to cover his blinded eyes. The guards had no patience for his weakness. They pushed him forward, prodding with bony fingers and fists until he stumbled and fell onto a paved path.

A strong voice issued a command: "Get him on his feet."

As brawny arms lifted him upright, Paul struggled to find his balance. When he was able to stand on his own, he opened his eyes and saw two different Praetorians standing before him. Like the men who guarded him, they did not wear armor, yet these two wore finer tunics than those worn by the guards. The man staring at him with a narrowed gaze must be a man of some authority.

"So you are Paul of Tarsus," the stranger said, disdain dripping from every syllable. "The man responsible for reducing half of Rome to ashes."

Paul blinked. Could this fellow actually believe the rumors?

The officer snorted, then looked at his companion. "I expected more from this one. At least a prisoner who could stand erect."

Paul bit his lip and waited. He had nothing to prove to this man, and nothing to defend. He had already been judged and sentenced to die.

The man thumped his chest. "I am Prefect Mauritius Gallis, new commander of the cohort responsible for the emperor's prison and his palaces. You are now my responsibility."

"What—?" Paul blinked rapidly, struggling to look up at the light. "What happened to Prefect Calvinus Silvio? Did he retire?"

"He died."

Paul remained quiet as the second man handed Mauritius a parchment. The prefect held it, his eyes narrowing in a speculative gaze, then handed the parchment back. "Read it aloud, Severus."

Severus cleared his throat. "'His greatness, god-made-manifest Nero Caesar, has hereby proclaimed Paul of Tarsus a corrupter and deceiver, and declares that same man guilty of the crimes of treason, conspiracy, arson, and murder. For this crime he is sentenced to die by beheading at sunrise on the morning of the summer solstice, at the conclusion of the festival of Vestalia.'"

Paul lowered his head. At last, an ending to his story. To his suffering. And the summer solstice, the twenty-first day of Junius, was not many days away. How many? Paul couldn't remember.

"While you await your execution," Mauritius went on, "you will remain in prison. In the darkness. In a dungeon once described as 'able to craze any man's senses.'"

Paul kept his head down, his mouth twisting, as a sense of anticlimax washed over him. He had burned brightly in his many years, as fiery in his maturity as he had been in his youth, so how could he meet death like this? He had hoped to end his days in front of a listening crowd or at the hands of gladiators in the arena. He wanted to die as he had lived.

But to sit alone in the darkness and wait for days, then meet his executioner at dawn before anyone in the city awoke? That sort of death . . . was not what he had expected. Or wanted.

"Where?" he asked, lifting his head. "Where will I die?"

Mauritius's brows rose. "Here, of course. On this very spot, if you wish."

Paul hung his head again. This was not where he wished to die. If he had to face the executioner, let it be in front of those who would bear witness, who would see how a Christian faced death, with courage and hope and confidence—

Or would he die with a whimper? He could not say. He knew how he *wanted* to die, but the days of sitting in darkness had taken their toll on him.

And for a long time he had known how his story would end. When he was last in Caesarea, the prophet Agabus had taken Paul's belt, tied his own hands and feet, and proclaimed, "The *Ruach ha-Kodesh* says this: 'In this way shall the Jewish people in Jerusalem bind the man who owns this belt and deliver him into the hands of the Gentiles.'"

May the Lord's will be done.

"Have you anything to say?" Mauritius again, an insistent note in his voice. "Speak now, man, while you can."

Paul smiled at the thought of death. When his life was over, he would be . . . grateful.

"Insolent even now, eh?" Severus grunted a command to the other Praetorians: "Another twenty lashes for the old man."

"Wait." The prefect put out a restraining hand. "Isn't this man a Roman citizen?"

"He's a condemned prisoner who will lose his head in thirteen days," Severus replied. "So what does it matter?"

The prefect lowered his arm and walked away.

Rather than wait to be pushed to his knees, Paul sank to the ground on his own.

—⁓⁓⁓—

Drifting in the hazy world between sleep and wakefulness, Paul stands on a windblown road and watches an approaching crowd. They walk quickly in the bright sunlight—men, women, and children, most of them wearing simple tunics and unadorned robes. They do not watch the uneven road or look to the side in appreciation of the scenery. Instead, their faces follow him as a flower follows the sun. No matter if he moves to the right or left, forward or back, they watch him with unwelcoming, cold, piercing eyes, and Paul cannot understand why they stare at him so intently.

Do they want him to say something? *Do* something? Has he wronged them somehow?

He looks away, his gaze drifting off to safer territory. Perhaps he is only imagining their interest. The desert light is playing tricks on his eyes, or his ego is only assuming that they seek his face. He takes a few steps, head down, and counts to ten before he looks up again. He is certain they will have lost interest and begun to converse among themselves, but when he looks their way again, they have stopped moving. They stand motionless in the road, blocking his way, the light in their eyes flickering like heat lightning.

Paul swallows, feeling as though some large, cold object has insinuated itself beneath his breastbone. Now he hears sounds from the crowd—voices buzzing like a hive that has been turned upside down. These people are angry and they are waiting for him.

Mercifully, the sound of male voices pulled Paul from sleep. The guards had changed shifts and did not even look his way as they talked and laughed together in the room above his head.

He rolled over and grimaced when the tattered fabric of his tunic pulled at the crusty welts on his back. Twenty lashes had never taken so long to inflict.

"Yeshua," he whispered, closing his eyes to block the torchlight coming through the opening above, "is there nothing more for me?"

———∽———

As the shadows of early evening stretched themselves along the streets of Rome, Luke and Aquila stood outside the newly rebuilt Roman Forum, only a short distance away from the prison located at the base of Capitoline Hill. The building, Aquila explained, was used solely as a place of detention and execution, hence its limited size.

"They say," Aquila said, leaning against a column as he gazed toward the stately steps of the Forum, "a man could find a good deal of silver if he was willing to dig beneath the new building. A great many important men perished in the Forum because the flames spread so quickly. The fire took everything but their bones and the coins in their pockets."

Shuddering, Luke shifted his attention to the prison across the street. Several Praetorians stood at the entrance, but Eubulus had told them about a side door that opened only from the inside.

"They will change guards any moment now," Aquila said, straightening. "So here's this." He pulled a folded parchment from his robe and gave it to Luke. "These papers say you are visiting the prisoner on behalf of Arctos Peleus, a senator."

Luke lifted a brow. "Who is Arctos Peleus?"

"A former client. We made a tent for him once." Aquila gave Luke a wavering smile. "He is a follower of the Way, though for obvious reasons he keeps quiet about his devotion to Christ. We would rather not involve him, but he has given permission for you to use his name if necessary. He knows how important it is that you see Paul."

"Senator Peleus is a brave man."

"He is a true servant of Christ."

Luke slipped the documents into his tunic as a group of camouflaging vines moved and the prison's side door swung open.

Two Praetorians stepped out and left the door ajar. They talked for a moment, then one walked away. The bigger man spat on the ground, took the torch from the wall, and dropped it in a nearby bucket of water before going back inside.

"That's the signal," Aquila said. "Rap twice and Eubulus will open the door for you."

Luke gripped his bag. "I will see you tomorrow, if the Lord wills."

"The peace of the Lord be with you, brother."

"And with you."

The men clasped shoulders, then Luke slipped out of the alley and hurried across the street to the prison door. He rapped twice. The door opened, allowing Luke to slip inside.

He found himself face-to-face with a brawny Praetorian. The man acknowledged Luke with a brief nod and then led him through a short hallway that opened into a wide, unusual chamber. The room, carved out of stone, was a vaulted trapezoid, its sides varying in length. A desk sat in the center, and benches lined the walls.

The space appeared to be used for interrogations and procedures. So where was the prison?

"Here." Eubulus's face flushed as he pointed to a hole carved into the stone floor. "The man you seek is down there."

Luke stopped dead, staring downward, his heart surely beating loud enough for the guard to hear. "Down there? But how do I . . . ?"

The Praetorian bent and picked up a heavy rope. "Put your foot in the loop and I'll lower you." He stared at the floor as if ashamed to meet Luke's gaze.

The man held out the rope, and Luke studied the loop at the end. This Eubulus was supposed to be a believer in Christ, but how sure was Aquila of the man's faith? He could drop the rope while Luke dangled in midair, or he could leave Luke in the lower chamber and summon one of his superiors.

But what choice did Luke have? Aquila trusted this Praetorian, and Luke trusted Aquila. And Paul needed them both.

Luke walked to the edge of the opening.

"Wait." Eubulus gestured to Luke's cloak. "I'd leave that up here, if I were you. Wouldn't want you to ruin it."

Luke frowned, then undid the clasp at his neck and set the cloak on a bench. Dressed only in his tunic and sandals, he picked up his bag and sat on the floor, allowing his legs to dangle in the empty space. Finally, he picked up the rope.

Eubulus glanced uneasily toward the front entrance. "Going to take all night?"

Sighing, Luke placed his foot into the loop and grasped the rope with his free hand while holding his bag with the other. "Are you ready?"

The Praetorian smiled, revealing a gap where his front teeth should have been. "I've been waiting for you."

"All right—but don't drop me. My bones are not as young as they once were."

Eubulus chuckled. "I'll pull you up before the night watch ends."

An instant later, Luke found himself descending into darkness.

—⁓⁓—

Luke released the rope when his foot touched solid rock. Wary of stepping out of the light, he gingerly slid his foot from the loop and watched as the guard pulled it up. What if this were some sort of trap to catch and imprison Christians? What if Paul wasn't even *in* this dungeon?

He glanced around the space, but his eyes, unaccustomed to the heavy darkness, revealed nothing. He lowered his bag to the floor and stood motionless, blinking into the blackness, waiting for his vision to improve. His eyes, too, were not as strong as they had once been and seemed to take longer to adjust.

The torch in the upper chamber allowed only a narrow stream of light into the dungeon. The light did little to repel the gloom, but after a moment it was enough for Luke to make out objects on the floor— an overturned bucket, a bowl, a pile of rags.

But the worst thing about the lower chamber was the stench, an overpowering combination of odors: the sweet, wet smell of rats, the reek of vomit, the earthy odors of sweat, urine, and blood.

He pinched his nose and tried to breathe through his mouth. As a physician, he frequently inhaled the smells of illness, cancers, and decay, but this was the scent of hell itself.

He startled when he heard the clank of chains. He had nearly convinced himself that the Lord had removed Paul from this horrible place, but when he turned, the pile of rags moved and a bald head reflected the light from overhead. The head lifted, and beneath a pair of brows Luke spied the shine of two eyes. A voice, rusty with disuse, broke the silence: "Am I dreaming or are you my friend Luke?"

He would know that voice anywhere. "Paul?" He stepped toward his friend and sank to the stone floor, ignoring the filth around him. "You are not dreaming. I am here."

The man on the floor wrapped thin arms around him, then shuddered in a sigh. "Praise God."

Luke bit his lip, alarmed by the skeletal feel of the man he embraced. "Can you sit up?"

"I think so." A grin flashed through a scraggly beard. "I hope so."

Luke steadied his friend's shoulders until Paul sat upright. As he pressed his hand to Paul's back, Luke's fingers encountered the stickiness of coagulating blood. "You have fresh wounds."

Paul shrugged.

Moving with extreme care, Luke peeled a filthy robe from his friend's back, then turned Paul toward the meager light to inspect the new wounds atop a dense web of scars. "Well," he said, knowing Paul would not accept pity, "I've seen you look worse."

"Only twenty lashes this time," Paul said, dry humor in his voice. "I suppose I was not worth the full complement."

Feeling more confident now that he had a job to do, Luke pulled a jar of salve from his bag and applied it to the apostle's wounds. "This may sting a bit, but the result will be worth the pain."

"A good thought," Paul said, forcing the words through clenched teeth. "You should write that down."

"I didn't come to write—I came to see you. To take care of your body, so it can adequately house your soul."

Paul grunted. "Truth be told, I wouldn't mind if it set my soul free."

"Not yet, friend. Not yet. Now." Luke sat back on his haunches. "How are your eyes?"

A wry smile flashed in the thicket of his beard. "You know the good thing about having poor eyesight? Down here, there's nothing to see." He laughed. "The messenger of Satan that has troubled me for all these years has little power over me in this pit." He turned and squinted at Luke, then smiled. "Truthfully, I did not expect to see your face again—at least not in this life."

Luke set his mouth in a grim smile. "Nor I yours."

"I don't know who you had to bribe to get into this place—" Paul groaned when Luke touched an especially nasty welt— "but surely the money could have been put to better use for our brothers and sisters."

"Perhaps," Luke said. "But I didn't hear a single note of disagreement when the idea was proposed. Even the Corinthians donated generously, if you can believe it. And while the money did help with my travel expenses, I am here tonight because of two brothers—Eubulus, your guard, and a senator called Arctos Peleus. If I am stopped and questioned outside the prison, I am to show a signed document from the senator."

Paul narrowed his eyes. "Does this man realize how dangerous that would be? Even the Senate is anti-Christian these days. They dare not cross Nero—at least not openly."

"The senator knows." Luke smiled as he scooped more salve out of the jar. "I would like to meet him and thank him for taking such a risk."

Paul snorted softly. "I am grateful. But considering who he is, this will certainly not be the last risk he takes." He released a long sigh. "I have become an old man inside these walls, Luke. Every bone is wracked with pain. My eyesight has grown even weaker."

Luke wiped his hands and put the salve away. "Come toward the light so I can take a better look at you."

Luke shifted to make room for his friend. Once Paul stepped into the dim circle of light, Luke studied Paul more carefully.

The apostle to the Gentiles had never been a tall man, but he seemed to have grown shorter since Luke had last seen him. His face, now sharply angled and bony, had gone as pale as goat's milk, stripped of the tan that came from years of walking in the sun. A layer of dark grime mottled his skin, and pain had carved merciless lines into his visage.

Yet Luke noticed more than physical changes. Paul, the determined, defiant apostle, now wore a tired face marked by anxiety and grief.

"I am a worn-out old man," Paul whispered, slowly lifting his head to meet Luke's gaze. "My eyes may not bother me overmuch down here, but there are other things. Thoughts. Memories. Dreams."

Luke clicked his tongue against his teeth. "I am glad I can offer you a few comforts. I have brought you a new tunic and cloak. A jar of water to wash your face. By the time I leave here, you will be a *clean* old man."

He took a cloth from his bag, then uncorked the jar and poured water onto the cloth. Then he lifted Paul's face to the light with one hand and wiped gently with the other. "I'm glad to see you have kept busy while I was away," he said, keeping his voice light. "Getting yourself arrested again, challenging Nero, and apparently finding the time to burn down half of Rome. Well done, old man."

Paul's eyes glinted with humor.

Luke's smile faded. "I heard about your trial. I know you stood before Nero alone."

Paul shook his head. "Demas deserted me and went to Thessalonica, and Crescens back to Galatia. Only Onesiphorus endeavored to visit me during the trial, and his company did bring me a great deal of cheer."

Luke froze, the wet cloth inches from Paul's face. "You know I would have been at your side if—"

Paul squeezed Luke's arm. "You are here now . . . and I am grateful."

As Paul clung to his arm, Luke helped the bent man step out of his rags and into the new tunic. When Paul had washed as best he could, Luke took a pair of scissors from his bag and attempted to trim the wild beard. When he had finished, he sat back on his haunches, looked over his handiwork, and sighed. "There. You'd turn heads if you walked down the Appian Way."

Paul wagged a finger at him. "You should not tell such lies to a friend. I do not need a looking brass to know I am not worth a second look."

He walked back to the wall on shaky legs and sank stiffly to the floor, bracing himself against the stone.

Luke watched, his heart squeezing so tight that he thought he could not draw breath to speak. Once, not so many years before, Paul had been a firebrand, the first one to rise in the morning and the last to seek his bed at night. For the sake of the gospel he had labored tirelessly, talked until his voice gave out, walked until his feet bled, risked his life in perils from both men and nature. Now he was but a shadow of the man Luke had known so well.

Paul must have guessed at Luke's thoughts. "I have traveled all over the world for our Lord, willing to die for His sake at any moment," he said. "But I did not expect the end to come like this. I do not remember ever feeling this lonely since . . . since my trials in Tarsus."

"There you go, complaining again." Luke forced a note of teasing into his voice, then thought better of it. This was a time for sincerity, for complete honesty. "I trust Christ will not abandon you," he added. "Even in this horrible hole."

Paul nodded. "He is here. He is all I have. But He does not reveal His purpose for me in this place. And I can't—I struggle to accept that I am meant to waste away until the end."

"Perhaps this is a final trial. A test of your faith."

"Perhaps." Paul looked away. "If so, it will be a short test. My execution date has been set. I will die at sunrise on the twenty-first day of Junius, morning of the summer solstice. Thirteen days from now."

Luke stared, momentarily speechless in his surprise.

Paul did not give him time to react. "Tell me some good news," he said. "Give me something to hold on to during the time I have left."

Luke could think of nothing but the staggering news he'd just heard, but then he remembered. "There is good news from Crete and Ephesus. Titus and Timothy have silenced the false teachers and straightened out the believers' doctrine."

A smile gathered up the wrinkles of Paul's ancient mouth. "Good. And what news have you of this city?"

"Rome?" Luke blew out a breath. "Nero's city is stained with the blood of our brothers and sisters. Aquila and Priscilla are facing a difficult decision—they must decide whether to stay or flee persecution. They wanted me to ask you for wisdom."

Paul lifted his head. "What does Linus advise? He is the leader of the community here."

"They've lost all contact with him. He's taken many of the community into hiding."

"He is still alive?"

"We pray he is."

Luke let the silence stretch, then stepped into the darkness and sat next to Paul. "There is much for us to discuss, but the community with Aquila and Priscilla needs answers now. What would you advise them to do?"

Paul's chest heaved as he sighed. "What wisdom can I give, Luke? I would have gone right; Christ sent me left. I would have gone left; Christ pushed me right. I have many regrets and have made many mistakes, but everything I have done, I have done for Christ. He has used even my bumbling for His glory."

Leaning forward, Luke rested an arm on his bent knee and considered the apostle's reply. He would share Paul's response with Priscilla and Aquila, although he had a feeling Paul's answer was not exactly what they wanted to hear.

—⁓—

"You know," Luke said, after an interval of companionable silence, "there is a man in Rome—a former slave, in fact—who teaches that an orator cannot be effective unless he has a pleasing physical appearance."

Paul lifted a brow, tipped his head back, and laughed—the first laughter that had passed his lips in weeks. "Then I," he said, when he could breathe again, "must be a complete failure, for I am physically unimpressive."

Luke shook his head, politely waving the matter aside, but Paul would not let it go. "Tell me what this man says. Has he written it out?"

"Probably. I heard him speaking outside the Forum."

"Then please tell me what he said. I have had so little entertainment down here."

Luke sighed. "All right. His name is Epictetus, and his argument is this. Suppose a consumptive comes forward, thin and pale, to testify to a certain matter. Epictetus says his argument will not carry the same weight as a man who testified in good health, with a pleasing appearance. 'One must show,' Epictetus says, 'that by the state of his body, he is a good and excellent man. But a Cynic who excites pity is regarded as a beggar, and everyone takes offense at him.'"

Paul chuckled. "I hope you didn't mention this Epictetus to comfort me. If what he says is true, I should never speak in public again."

"What he says is *not* true," Luke insisted, "but as a physician, I found his argument interesting. If a man is sick, certainly he should do his best to seek healing. If he cannot follow that simple wisdom, perhaps he is not worth listening to."

"Thank you, my dear physician." Paul stretched out on his back, pillowing his head on his hands. "I haven't felt such merriment in weeks."

"Humph," Luke answered, and Paul smiled, grateful for the companionship.

But as he closed his eyes, pretending to nap, the spark of humor that had lightened his heart faded. He had never been a typically handsome man—he was a head shorter than most, with crooked legs and a hooked nose. His beard had always been sparse, and after shaving his head in Cenchrea in order to satisfy a vow, the hair never fully returned to cover his head.

He had been jesting when he said he should never speak in public again. But now, in the darkness of his prison, he realized that barring a miracle, he *would* never speak in public again. He would never again stand before a crowd or a household or a synagogue to share the news about Yeshua the Christ. Not because he didn't have the body of an excellent orator, but because he would never leave this prison.

An odd and unexpected twinge of disappointment made him wince.

After meeting the Messiah, all he wanted to do was spread the word about how wrong he'd been. Since coming to Rome, all he wanted to do was finish well. Finish the long and difficult race, cross the line with his chest thrust out and his face flushed with exertion.

But how could he do that in this pit? How could he finish his long run with this ruined shell of a body in a place where he saw and influenced no one?

How, Yeshua? He listened for an answer, but all he heard was Luke's strong and steady breathing.

—⟋⟍⟍⟍—

Luke and Paul talked through the night—through the darkness that enveloped them after the torch burned out in the chamber above, then through the gray light of dawn when the first rays of a new day streamed through the opening above the dungeon. Luke noticed that Paul's eyes closed in weariness when Eubulus's gruff voice broke the silence: "Physician! Time for you to go."

Luke was about to say farewell, but the apostle had fallen asleep. Grateful that his friend was able to rest in such a horrible place, Luke rose from the sticky floor and caught the rope that spilled through the opening. "I'm ready."

The guard hauled Luke up with surprising ease, then helped him free his sandaled foot from the loop. "All done?" Eubulus asked.

Luke shook his head. "Not nearly. If the Lord wills, I will be back tonight."

As the Praetorian gave him an incredulous look, Luke pulled on his cloak and moved toward the sunlight, grateful to begin a new day.

THREE

The Ninth Day of Junius

"Unless the Lord intervenes," Luke told Aquila and Priscilla over breakfast, "we will lose Paul at sunrise on the summer solstice. Nero has set the date."

"So soon?" Priscilla's face rippled with anguish, and Aquila's went blank with shock.

"Is—is—" Aquila stammered—"is there nothing we can do?"

Luke sighed. "Not unless you have power over the emperor."

"We can pray," Priscilla said. "Paul would want us to pray, and we will do that." She shifted her gaze to Luke. "How should we pray? What are his greatest needs?"

"He is physically shattered," Luke said, "but the cantankerous old soul remains full of conviction. His faith is strong."

Priscilla passed a bowl of grapes to her guest. "That is welcome news. I have been praying the solitude of that dreadful place would not crush him."

"He is definitely not crushed," Luke said. "But he does seem to struggle with the knowledge that his work is coming to an end. He has been serving Christ for so long . . . he does not know how to stop."

"For more than thirty years, preaching is all he's known." Aquila looked at his wife. "And tent making. Remember how he used to work alongside us in Corinth? We'd spread out a camel-hair panel and see who could first attach an entire row of loops. Priscilla and I would sew like mad, our fingers flying, but Paul would stop and talk about Yeshua to anyone who gathered around to watch our little race. In the end, Priscilla usually won, though no one cared because they were so fascinated by what Paul had to say."

"He won many hearts that way," Priscilla said, giving Luke a calm smile. "Including ours. That's how Aquila and I knew it was God's will that we leave Rome and move to Corinth."

"In the beginning I thought we left because Claudius had ordered all Jews to depart," Aquila said. "Yet God was behind the emperor's decree. If he had not forced the Jews out of Rome, we might never have met our brother and teacher Paul."

"Speaking of leaving"—Priscilla sought Luke's eyes—"did Paul offer any wisdom on the matter of what we should do?"

Luke drew a breath. "He would urge you to discern for yourselves where Christ is calling you next."

"No specific instructions?" Aquila asked. "No clear answer?"

Luke shook his head. "He only offered the example of his own life. 'I would have gone left,' he said, 'but Christ pushed me right.'"

Aquila and Priscilla glanced at each other, and Priscilla squeezed her husband's hand. "I suppose we were hoping for an easy answer," Priscilla said, "but as in all important decisions, it appears we must pray, wait upon the Lord, and listen for His direction for ourselves."

She had scarcely finished speaking when a clamor at the courtyard gate drew their attention. Aquila rose immediately and strode quickly down the stairs, Priscilla following close behind him. Luke hurried to the balcony railing, wanting to be ready in case they needed his help.

A knot of people had surrounded a figure at the entrance; a moment later the people separated enough for Luke to see a woman, her eyes red-rimmed and wild, her body slumped over, and her tunic bloody and torn.

Priscilla had gone pale at the sight. "Octavia! What has happened?"

"I found her," a man answered, his own tunic spotted with blood. "She was wandering the streets like this."

The distressed woman collapsed onto a bench as Priscilla rushed to her side. Obeying his instincts, Luke ran down the stairs and knelt in front of the woman as he searched for injuries. "Tell me—where are you hurt?"

Wide-eyed, the woman looked frantically around the gathering before settling on Priscilla's face. "Oh," she said, her voice a mere whimper, "Priscilla . . . please help them."

"Octavia," Priscilla said with a firm tone, "you must tell us what happened and where you are hurt."

Octavia covered her eyes and moaned. "My baby . . . my little boy. They broke down the door. We should have come here. I told my husband we should have come here—"

"You are bleeding," Priscilla said.

Octavia shook her head. "No. It's my baby's blood. They pulled him out of my arms and sliced my boy open, then handed him back to me. My husband tried to stop them, but they ran him through with a sword. Then they laughed as they left, and I couldn't stop my baby's bleeding. So much blood, everywhere. Everywhere . . ."

Octavia's anguished words dissolved into sobbing. Priscilla

sat on the bench and wrapped her arms tightly around the woman. She looked up at Luke and locked eyes with him. *So much pain,* her expression seemed to say. *All at the hands of the Romans.*

Luke turned his attention back to the distraught woman, lest Priscilla see the growing frustration that had to be evident on his face. Why was God allowing His children to suffer like this? He looked around and saw other mothers holding tight to their youngsters, fathers standing close to their wives, their shoulders taking on the heavy weight of responsibility. This poor woman was a bloody, living reminder of Rome's persecution, and the worried people in this courtyard would not sleep tonight.

"Priscilla." Luke gentled his voice. "We should take Octavia inside and get her cleaned up. We should keep her out of sight until she has calmed down. Perhaps one of the other women can help?"

Priscilla turned to the young man who had brought Octavia through the gate. "Caleb, can you bring us a basin of water and a fresh cloth? And please have your sister meet me in the house right away."

Caleb hurried off while Luke lifted Octavia and carried her up the stairs.

—⚊⚊—

Luke knelt behind Paul, a bowl of ground herbs in his hand. Working as gently as possible, with two fingers he deftly spread the ointment into the wounds on the apostle's back.

"I wish you could have been there," he said, squinting to see in the dim light. "They were all watching that poor woman. She was covered in the blood of her husband and baby, both of whom had just been slaughtered by the Praetorians. Everyone in the courtyard stood in shock, their faces twisted with fear. They are terrified, Paul. They have faced much tribulation, but they have never witnessed anything like this."

Paul lifted his head from his bent knees. "Christ promised us difficult times. He said we would be handed over to those who would persecute us for His sake."

Luke lowered the ointment and moved to sit in front of Paul, then studied the bent old man. Though years of trials had disfigured Paul's body, and struggles and deprivations had placed their stamps on his face, his eyes still shone with faith and power and steadfastness. "You know you will die in twelve days, but still you are confident of the truth and mercy of Christ and His promise of eternal life."

The corners of Paul's mouth lifted. "I know the One in whom I have believed . . . and I remain assured that departing this life will lead to joy and peace everlasting."

"You are strong in the faith, but I do not see that same conviction in the others staying at Aquila's home. Those men, women, and children—they are not as mature. Many of them are spiritual babies yet."

Paul's mouth moved just enough to bristle the silver whiskers on his cheek. "I cannot fix their faith."

"No, but you can inspire it. Look at how your letters have inspired people in other communities."

Paul lifted a brow. "You want me to write another letter? These fingers"—he raised his gnarled hands—"can barely hold a pen."

Luke stood and held up Paul's tunic. "Enough complaining. You need to rise up and move. Walking will get your blood flowing, which will help your wounds heal."

"Where are we walking?" Paul asked, groaning as he pushed

himself off the floor. "Shall we go down to the river? Or perhaps we should visit our friends Aquila and Priscilla."

"Would that we could." Luke helped Paul to his feet, then draped a robe around his bare shoulders. "Remember when we were sailing around Crete and ran into that storm? I'd never seen such a violent squall."

"You'd never seen a great many things." Paul took two shuffling steps, stopped, and looked longingly at the circle of light cast on the floor. "Can't we discuss that journey over there?"

"There's no room to walk over there," Luke replied. He took Paul's arm and urged him forward. "As I recall, I was standing on the deck, hanging on to a rope while the crew tried to pass ropes under the ship to hold it together. I didn't think those winds and the rain would ever let up, but you seemed to pay the storm no mind. And then after a full day of howling wind and raging waves, you stood and said an angel of God had appeared to you, so no one should worry. None of the two hundred seventy-six men aboard the ship would die."

"They were all carrying on so," Paul muttered. "Pretending to drop anchors from the bow while they conspired to leave the ship."

"Nonetheless, you convinced them to stay aboard. When you thanked God for the bread and began to eat as if nothing was wrong, I'm sure many of them thought you were mad. After fourteen days of being driven across the Adriatic, maybe they could be forgiven their doubts."

Paul grunted.

"But those men listened to you. When we drew near the shore and some of them were ready to jump overboard to escape being dashed against the rocks, you warned them that unless they stayed with the ship, they would not be saved. Again they listened. Why?" He paused and studied Paul's face. "Because their strength had failed in the midst of that terrible storm, but yours did not. They witnessed your unshakable faith in the face of death. They saw that you did not doubt but instead were immovable. All two hundred seventy-six of those sailors lived because you demonstrated for them an unwavering trust in Christ's promises."

Paul bowed his head. "Are we finished? Can we sit for a while?"

"Not yet." Luke urged Paul forward. "Let's walk a little farther. Keep the blood flowing."

After they had taken a few more steps, Luke adopted a friendlier tone. "The Way is growing, Paul. The communities are filled with men, women, and children who have never met you. They will *never* meet you. They will need a written account of your journeys and the apostles' acts after Christ's ascension."

"Hummmph."

Paul's response was not exactly enthusiastic, but Luke pressed on. "You know I wrote my first book for Theophilus—I wanted him to understand with certainty the important things he had been taught. Well, Theophilus also needs to know how the Holy Spirit worked through the other apostles among the Jews, and through you among the Gentiles."

Paul halted. "You risk people looking to me instead of Christ."

Luke shook his head. "It is your strong assurance of the Messiah's teachings that opens the door to belief in the Lord Jesus. I myself never met Him in the flesh, but the day I heard you preaching in Troas, I saw Christ in *you*. You are a looking brass; you reflect the Savior."

"You give me too much credit, my friend."

"I believed in Christ that day," Luke continued, "and I left my family, my friends, and my patients behind because I saw the same unshakable faith the soldiers and sailors saw on that sinking ship."

As if burdened by Luke's praise, Paul pressed his hands together and bowed his head. Luke stilled his tongue, allowing the old man a minute to think and pray. He knew he was asking a lot of a condemned prisoner, but if the matter were not important, he would not have brought it up.

"It must not be my story alone," Paul said, keeping his head lowered. "You would have to interview many others. And the book would not be complete without Peter's account, so how will you interview him?"

"I spoke with Peter several times." Luke smiled. "Before his crucifixion."

They stood in a quiet so thick, the only sound was the soft whistle of Paul's breathing. Then the older man resolutely lifted his head. "You could write it *here*?"

"I am sure I could. I would smuggle in the tools necessary for the task."

"You could write it in the time we have remaining?" Paul asked.

Luke nodded. "I believe I could get the information I need in twelve days. I will take notes when I visit. Later, I will go back and transcribe them. From my notes I'll write the book. Priscilla and Aquila have literate friends—they can make copies."

Paul tugged at his beard for a moment. "Rome has changed since the last time we were together. If you were caught trespassing here, you could be condemned to die. You are not a Roman citizen, so you would not be granted a trial."

"I am already a conspirator and trespasser, and one of my closest friends has been condemned to die." Luke crossed his arms. "I would not be afraid to join him."

Paul drew a deep breath, then clapped Luke on the shoulder. "So be it. You are a fine writer, my friend. If the Lord gives us strength, let us write another book."

—⟪⟫—

Paul sat on one side of the circle of light and studied his friend's countenance. Tonight Luke had brought nothing with him save his medical supplies, but the physician had a quick mind and a good memory. So if they spoke of things that might prove helpful to followers of the Way, Luke would remember.

"I pray for the new believers every day," Paul said, bending one leg as he struggled to get comfortable. "Not all of them will be faithful until death."

Luke lifted a brow. "Surely if they are taught—"

"We cannot forget Christ's parable of the sower," Paul interrupted. "A farmer went out to spread some seed. As he was scattering it, some seeds fell by the road, and the birds came and ate them up. Other seeds fell on rocky ground, where they didn't have much soil. They sprang up immediately because the soil wasn't deep. But when the sun came up, they were scorched; and because they had no roots, they withered away. Other seeds fell among the thorns, and the thorns choked them out. But others fell on good soil and produced fruit. They yielded a crop—some a hundredfold, some sixty, some thirty."

He leaned forward to search Luke's eyes. "Consider the people of Rome. Many Romans have heard the good news, but they discarded the truth of the gospel as soon as they heard it. Others received the good news and marveled at it, but when faced with a new challenge, they preferred to return to their old lives."

"None of those people are at Aquila's house," Luke said. "Those in Aquila's group have risked their lives for Christ.

They have surrendered their homes and left friends and relatives behind."

"Still," Paul said, holding up a finger, "there are some in Aquila's group who will be like the seeds that fell among the thorns. They *look* like good seeds, they may *talk* like good seeds, but when the world entices them, they will fall away."

Luke narrowed his eyes. "How do you know this story? Did you speak to one of the twelve?"

With a shiver of vivid recollection, Paul looked up. "I did not receive this knowledge from any human, nor was I taught it. It came through a revelation of Yeshua the Messiah."

Luke closed his eyes and nodded, and Paul could see that his friend was committing the words to memory. As a youth, Luke had received a classical Greek education where he had been taught to turn words into images, which were more easily remembered. Many times Paul had remarked on Luke's excellent memory, but Luke had simply shrugged and said he was using his "memory palace"—a mental trick that had always served him well.

"Yes, we will write this book," Paul continued, girding himself with resolve, "for those who will persevere until the end. They are the ones who will bear fruit."

—⁓—

Wiping sweat from his brow, Mauritius Gallis, one of two prefects of the Praetorian Guard, strode through the crowds along the Aurelian Way and cursed every step he took. He should not be living so far from the heart of the city. Just before the great fire, he and his wife, Irenica, had taken possession of a lovely villa on Palatine Hill, his reward for twenty years of faithful service. But on that hot night in July, they had fled the raging flames with their only daughter, Caelia. Along with dozens of other noble citizens, they now found themselves living in substandard and inordinately expensive temporary housing.

But what could he do about it? Nero had taken over Palatine Hill for his construction project, and the Domus Aurea, or Golden House, had been under construction ever since.

Just that morning he had heard about a particular dining chamber in Nero's new pleasure palace. An ingenious mechanism, cranked by slaves, made the domed ceiling revolve like the heavens. While the painted ceiling turned, another apparatus sprayed perfume and dropped rose petals onto the diners below.

How was that novelty supposed to make up for Mauritius's losses? His wife had lost her home, and Mauritius had lost his happy wife.

Irenica had not been at all happy in the new house, but when had she ever been truly content? She had been unhappy when Mauritius joined the Praetorians and had to live with his cohort in the Castra Praetoria, where the guardians of Rome were housed. She had not been happy when he was promoted to tribune, earning the right to live with his wife. She had not even been happy when he informed her that he had become one of the two prefects of the Praetorian Guard—the highest rank a Praetorian could achieve.

He could recall only two occasions when she had been perfectly happy—at the birth of their daughter, and the day he carried her across the threshold of the house on Palatine Hill.

His brow furrowed at the thought of ten-year-old Caelia. Last night she had not seemed herself. She usually greeted him with great enthusiasm, a flower in her hand or a drawing she had sketched, but last night he had been greeted with an odd silence. After a quick search he found Caelia in her room, her handmaid by her side. She was napping, but her eyelids rose at his touch and she managed a sleepy smile.

"Father," she murmured, not lifting her head. "I hope you had a good day."

Troubled, he looked at the slave. "How long has she been asleep?"

The slave bowed her head. "All afternoon, *Dominus*."

"Has she a fever?"

The slave shook her head. "I don't know."

Biting back a curse, Mauritius had pressed his hand to his daughter's forehead. Caelia's skin felt slightly warm but not hot, so surely she was fine. All children suffered from slight illnesses, he reminded himself. The morrow would find her refreshed and in good health.

With hope in his heart, he entered his house and stopped before the doorman. As the old slave took his cloak, Mauritius glanced into the atrium. "Have you seen Caelia this afternoon?"

The old man shook his head.

"And *Domina*?"

The slave pointed into the house. "Inside."

Mauritius glanced into the empty atrium, then strode to his daughter's room. The handmaid was gone, but Irenica sat in the bedside chair. Caelia lay on her bed. The rosy blush that usually graced her cheek had vanished.

"Caelia?" he asked, hoping she would open her eyes. She did not.

Irenica stood. "She has not eaten anything all day," she said, coming forward to grip Mauritius's arm. "I have sent for a physician, but he has not arrived."

"This will prove to be nothing," Mauritius said, even as his heart told him otherwise.

"This is *not* nothing," Irenica insisted, a note of alarm entering her voice. "She does not move. I have been by her side ever since she did not rise this morning. I have talked to her, pled with her, begged her to open her eyes and eat something . . ."

Mauritius glanced at his daughter's motionless form, then gripped his wife's shoulder. "You should eat something. Step outside and get some fresh air."

"But what if she wakes and calls for me? She grows worse."

"The gods would not allow that. This morning I burned a sacrifice of incense at the *lararium*. I said my prayers, so the gods will hear and heal her."

"And if they do not?"

"I have done my duty—I made a sacrifice."

"Is that *all* you can do?" she snapped.

Mauritius caught her hand, which she jerked out of his grip before turning and walking out of the room.

Mauritius sighed and knelt by his daughter's bedside. "You must get better now, Caelia," he said, speaking with quiet, desperate firmness. "I have done what the *paterfamilias* should do." He took her hand and rubbed it, willing health and motion back into the overheated flesh.

She did not stir.

———⁓———

"Tell me," Paul said, his eyes lighting up. "What news have you heard of Barnabas? I miss my old friend."

Luke grimaced. "I wish I *had* news. In truth, I have not heard much about him."

Paul groaned in disappointment. "I hope he is well. I think of him . . . often." A small smile played at the corner of his lined mouth. "He was always such an encourager, especially to me."

"Tell me more about him." Luke leaned forward, propping his chin on his hand. "I have not had the opportunity to spend much time with the man."

A faint smile touched Paul's mouth with ruefulness. "Three years after I saw the Lord, I went to Jerusalem to meet the other believers. But none of the others would see me—they ran whenever they heard I was in the area. Barnabas wasn't afraid, however. Instead, he sought me out, listened to the story of my encounter with Christ, and then he took me to see the other disciples." Paul chuckled. "For once, I didn't have to say anything. Barnabas remembered every word. He told the others about how I had seen the Lord on the road to Damascus. He told them about my going to the desert and how I had been speaking boldly about Yeshua in the synagogues. Because the words came from Barnabas, the other brothers listened."

"He was part of the crowd at Pentecost, yes?"

Paul nodded. "He was a righteous man even before he heard the gospel message. When he realized the Temple funds would no longer support orphans and widows who had become believers in Yeshua, he sold some property and gave the money to the deacons so they could distribute it among the poor."

Luke frowned. "Didn't he save your scrawny neck once?"

Paul laughed. "You don't need to remind me. It is true— I was arguing with the Hellenes in the synagogue, and they began plotting to kill me. So the brothers sent me home, back to Tarsus. But I took the gospel with me and never stopped talking about Yeshua."

Luke nodded as he looked around the dungeon, taking in the filth, the dirty rope, the overturned bucket in the corner. How could Paul laugh in a place like this? God might have already performed a miracle by keeping Paul sane and coherent after so much time in this pit.

"Barnabas found me again—in Tarsus." Paul looked up from beneath craggy brows. "I didn't expect him, yet I thanked God he came."

"Was that the first time you labored together?"

"Yes, the brothers in Jerusalem sent him to Antioch to check on the growing community there. So we reunited, and Barnabas stayed to work with us. One night while we were serving the Lord, the Ruach ha-Kodesh said, 'Set apart for me Barnabas and Sha'ul for the work to which I have called them.' So the brothers prayed and laid hands on us, and then the community sent us out. Led by the Ruach ha-Kodesh, we went down to Seleucia, and from there we sailed to Cyprus. When we arrived at Salamis, we preached in the synagogues. John Mark, Barnabas's young cousin, was with us."

Frowning, Luke pressed a finger to his lips. "It's clear you love and respect Barnabas, but still you had a falling out. Otherwise I would never have become your traveling companion."

Paul lifted a brow at him, and even though he was only a shadow of what he once had been, Luke saw raw power in his reproachful expression. He and Paul had never had a serious disagreement, and Luke couldn't help feeling grateful.

"We had two disagreements," Paul said, iron in his voice now. "The first was over young John Mark. The young man abandoned us on our missionary journey, leaving us short-handed. When we made arrangements to revisit the churches we had founded on our first trip, Barnabas wanted to bring John Mark with us. I disagreed—I did not want quitters on our team." Paul gave Luke a brief, distracted glance. "I was sure the lad would quit again, but Barnabas thought John

Mark should be given a chance to redeem himself. So Barnabas and I parted ways."

"A shame," Luke said, keeping his voice low. "The young man *did* redeem himself."

"He did," Paul admitted. "Perhaps I should have been more merciful. And yet God brought good out of my stubbornness. By traveling in two different directions, Barnabas and I doubled our ministry."

"You said you disagreed with Barnabas twice," Luke said. "Were you wrong the second time, as well?"

"Definitely not." Paul paused to take a breath, then continued on. "We were in Antioch, where Barnabas and I had experienced complete freedom in our worship and fellowship with the Gentile believers. We were truly one in the Spirit—we prayed, worshiped, and ate together. All went well until a group of Jewish Christians from Jerusalem came to visit. That group, born under the Law, came to me and said there should be no table fellowship between Jews and Gentiles. That pressure was enough to make Peter leave the Gentiles' table and eat only with the Jews—as if circumcision somehow made them holier than other believers."

"I doubt that's what he was thinking."

"Perhaps not, but that's how it appeared to the Gentile brothers." Paul turned, seeming to study Luke's face. "You're Greek—surely your culture understands the significance of table fellowship. It is reserved for those who are your closest friends and companions. That's why the rabbis could not accept Yeshua—He ate with drunkards and sinners."

"He loved them." Luke said the words aloud, more for his benefit than Paul's. For some reason the thought had never occurred to him: Christ ate with sinners to show His love for them.

The realization made Peter's action all the more shameful. By refusing to eat with Gentile believers, he must have appeared to despise them.

"Even Barnabas." Paul peered into the darkness, as if he could see the past in its depths. "Even he was carried away with their hypocrisy. I had to oppose Peter publicly, for he was clearly in the wrong. Barnabas realized it, of course, because he understood that a person is set right not by deeds based on Torah but through putting one's trust in Messiah Yeshua. If righteousness comes through Torah, then Messiah died for no reason! I died to the Law so that I could live for God."

"It must have been difficult," Luke said, thinking aloud. "So many times you apostles spoke for a holy, perfect God, but you are imperfect. Mere humans. Yet you were striving to be the hands, feet, and voice of Christ himself."

A half smile crossed Paul's face. "'Who will rescue me from this body of death?'" He chuckled. "Do you remember that from my letter to the Roman community?"

Luke nodded. "I remember Tertius writing that as you dictated."

"I was thinking of the Roman punishment—surely one of the worst ever devised. The man sentenced to death is chained hand, foot, and torso to a corpse, and he must drag it around wherever he goes. Eventually, the decaying body infects the living one, and the healthy man is overcome and dies." A grimace flitted across Paul's features. "I was trying to explain how the fleshly nature remains part of us even as we struggle to live and walk by the Spirit. To listen to Him, to obey Him. But sometimes we listen to the flesh, and that road leads to death."

"What happened . . . after?" Luke asked. "After you corrected Peter and Barnabas."

Paul's smile faded. "'Whoever avoids correction despises himself, but whoever heeds reproof acquires understanding.'" His shoulders relaxed as he shifted his position. "They listened, and they learned."

"I'm confused." Luke held out his hands. "You derided the Jews for following the Law against eating with Gentiles, but later, when the Jews in Jerusalem told you to take a vow, you purified yourself and shaved your head."

Paul blew out a breath. "The community at Jerusalem welcomed me, but they also warned me that other Jews had heard I was teaching our people to forsake Moses, not to circumcise their children, and not to follow any of the customs. They suggested that I take a vow with four other men simply to demonstrate that I had not abandoned the teachings of Moses. So I did."

Luke stared. "But hadn't you died to the Law? Isn't that what you said just a moment ago?"

With a sigh, Paul closed his eyes. "I don't blame you for being confused. For though I am free from all men, I have made myself a slave to all so that I might win over more of them. To the Jewish people I identified as a Jew so that I might win over the Jewish people. To those under Torah I became like one under Torah—though not being under Torah myself—so that I might win over those under Torah. To those outside Torah—though not being outside God's Torah but in Messiah's Torah myself—so that I might win over those outside Torah." He opened one eye. "Does that make sense?"

Luke nodded slowly. "I think so."

"Good." Paul smiled. "Because I don't think I could say all that again."

CHAPTER
FOUR

The Tenth Day of Junius

"You must be exhausted." Priscilla stepped aside as Luke entered the house and dropped his bag onto the table. "How fares our friend?"

"Paul is doing well," Luke said. He attempted to smile, but the last few days had drained him.

"Have some water and something to break your fast." Priscilla hurried to dip water from a jug. "Then you can go upstairs and sleep."

Luke took the cup she offered. He accepted a loaf and was about to climb the stairs when he heard a commotion at the gate. He looked at Priscilla, but she was already heading down to the courtyard.

Luke took a bite of the bread and moved to the balcony railing, curious about who would visit so early in the morning. He saw a man and woman standing at the entrance to the courtyard. The man had his arm around the woman and was earnestly speaking to Priscilla.

Priscilla glanced up at the balcony, took the young man's

hand in hers, and nodded. She pointed them to a shelter under a terebinth tree, then strode up the stairs.

"Friends of yours?" Luke asked as she hurried by.

She shook her head. "Runaway slaves. They are believers, and their master has threatened to beat them if they don't renounce Christ. I will have to discuss this with Aquila."

She went into their bedchamber while Luke thoughtfully chewed his breakfast.

The city of Rome was home to more slaves than citizens, a fact that made the free men anxious. Any slave foolish enough to kill his master would bring a death sentence on all slaves in the household, so few slaves attempted to rebel. But runaways were common, with slave hunters frequently hired to find and return an owner's property.

He studied the couple in the courtyard. The man found water for the woman and was offering her a drink. Clearly they were a couple, though slaves could not legally marry. When the woman accepted the dipper, she lifted her arm, exposing a slight bulge at her belly.

Luke lifted a brow. Pregnant, most likely. No wonder they had run away. But while he understood their reasons, he could not say what Aquila should do. Harboring fugitive slaves was against Roman law, and Aquila would be severely punished if these two were found at his villa. On the other hand, being a Christian had become illegal, too, so what would it matter if he hid this couple?

He ran his hand through his hair, his concentration evaporating in a wave of fatigue. He would be more helpful to everyone after he'd had a few hours' sleep.

—⟋⟍—

After a morning nap, Luke came downstairs, intending to ask about the runaway slaves.

Priscilla must have read the question on his face. "Moria and Carmine," she said, clearing a space on the bench at the table. She glanced at her husband. "Aquila says we might have to send them back."

"You know the Roman law," Aquila said. "But more than that, you know what Paul told Philemon."

Priscilla shook her head. "This case is different. Philemon was a Christian, so he welcomed Onesimus back as a beloved brother, not as a slave. He would have freed him immediately."

"Did he?" Aquila looked at Luke. "Will you ask Paul? What should we do with this couple—send them back to their master or keep them with us? Or perhaps you have an opinion of your own?"

Luke searched his thoughts and realized he had no ready answer. "I will ask Paul tonight."

———※———

Priscilla and Aquila had greeted with enthusiasm Luke's plan to write another book, yet Luke's heart sank as he looked over the implements they had gathered for his use. Aquila had procured a set of fine brass pens, three stoppered bottles of ink, and several heavy rolls of papyrus. If, heaven forbid, Luke lost his grip on one of those rolls, the spindle might unfurl many feet of papyrus across the prison's filthy floor, rendering it unusable.

He walked to the table where his hosts had happily displayed their contributions for the cause. "I am grateful for all you have done," he said, giving the pair what he hoped was an appreciative smile, "but since I must slip in and out of the prison unobserved, it seems best that I carry very little in my bag."

Disappointment colored Aquila's face. "Is it . . . too much?"

"Perhaps." Luke picked up one of the pens. "If I carried just one pen and one jar of ink, and sheets of papyrus instead of an entire roll—"

Priscilla pulled several cut sheets of papyrus from a woven basket. "I tried to consider every possibility," she said, handing them to Luke. "I know these are quite large, but I'm sure Paul has a lot to say."

Luke blew out a breath. "Remember how I must descend into Paul's cell. I have to hold on to a rope while Eubulus lowers me. My hands are occupied."

Priscilla did not hesitate. "Then you need a leather bag over your shoulder, like the saddlebags worn by a donkey or mule." She nodded. "I will arrange everything, so do not worry. Tonight when you visit Paul, you will have all that you need."

Luke caught Aquila's eye as Priscilla rushed away. "She is a wonder."

"Indeed she is," Aquila said, his eyes crinkling at the corners as he watched his wife descend the stairs. "I don't know what I would do without her."

"I was reared to be a Jew in all things," Paul began, his gaze drifting toward some interior field of vision Luke could only imagine. "Circumcised on the eighth day, born into the nation of Israel and the tribe of Benjamin, a Hebrew of Hebrews. In regard to the Torah, a Pharisee; as for zeal, persecuting Messiah's community; as for Torah righteousness, found blameless."

Luke nodded, urging Paul to continue. Though he already knew about Paul's background, he also understood his friend's

penchant for thoroughness. This would be Paul's last opportunity to tell his story, and he wanted to convey it completely.

Luke dipped his pen in the inkwell and held it above the papyrus he had spread on his knee. "Go on."

Lying on his back, looking up at the column of dim light,
Paul smiled. "I was born in Tarsus, where I attended a primary
school taught by a righteous scribe. There I learned my letters
backward and forward. There I studied Torah. When I was old
enough I attended secondary school, where a rabbi taught us the
oral Torah, the traditions of our fathers." His eyes crinkled as
he lifted his head to look at Luke. "I explain this because I know
you Greeks did not have the same experiences in childhood."

"I am almost jealous," Luke replied, scratching notes on the
papyrus. "While you were studying the Word of God, I was
learning to read and to wrestle. My *paidagōgos* placed a great
deal of emphasis on physical strength."

"Yes, the stern slave that attends all well-bred Greek boys
when they start school. I once tried to explain the Law as a
paidagōgos, but my countrymen could not understand. They
thought of the paidagōgos as the *teacher*, not a temporary
nursemaid they should outgrow." Paul shook his head. "At least
I can rejoice that some of them realized the truth."

Paul closed his eyes, and Luke waited, not sure if his friend
was thinking or sleeping. Finally, he asked, "And after secondary
school?"

"Ah." Paul sighed. "My family moved to Jerusalem. I was
happy about the move, while my sister hated leaving her friends.
After we settled, my father apprenticed me to a tentmaker. His
real purpose in moving the family to Jerusalem, though, was to
allow me to study under the Sanhedrin. Even as a youth I was
zealous for the Law and the traditions. My zeal attracted the

attention of Gamaliel, one of the most esteemed rabbis, and he chose me to join his students. So when I was not learning how to construct tents, I was studying Torah." A frown furrowed his brow. "Gamaliel emphasized the oral traditions over the Law. He said the oral traditions made the Torah Law easier to understand and safeguarded the Law."

Luke lifted his pen. "You've lost me. Not having grown up with a religious education . . ."

Paul cast him a sympathetic glance. "The Torah says, 'Remember *Yom Shabbat*, to keep it holy. You are to work six days, and do all your work, but the seventh day is a Shabbat to Adonai your God. In it you shall not do any work—not you, nor your son, your daughter, your male servant, your female servant, your cattle, nor the outsider that is within your gates.'"

"Yes, I have read that in the Torah."

"Well, we Pharisees, who value the Law above all things, were not content with those words. What, exactly, was considered *work*? Could you walk around your house, or was that a violation of the Sabbath? Of course you had to move about in your home, so we defined how many steps you could take outside your home. If a man could take twenty steps before reaching his neighbor's house, his movement would be limited to twenty steps on Shabbat. But what if he started walking and accidentally lost count? So we should not take more than ten steps. That way, if a man lost count and actually took thirteen, he would not transgress the Law, which allowed him twenty."

A rueful smile crossed Paul's face. "We took the words of God's guidance in the Torah and fashioned them into cages in which we felt secure. For years we worried about tithing grains of salt and whether or not we could lie with our wives on Shabbat. So when Yeshua healed a man with a withered hand on the seventh day, the Pharisees immediately began to plot Christ's murder."

Luke paused in his writing. "It sounds . . . illogical when you put the matter into perspective."

Paul chuffed. "They could not see the irony right in front of their eyes. They condemned Yeshua for healing on the Sabbath, but they saw nothing wrong with plotting his death on the same day."

Paul stared into the darkness, an indefinable spark in his eyes. "One year I was at the Temple during the Passover feast. I was about twenty, filled with righteous zeal and self-importance, as I had been one of Gamaliel's students for several years. Pilgrims filled the Temple courtyard, and I hated having to walk among them. I found myself resenting my own people because they disturbed my studies and created havoc in our ordinary routine.

"I was walking to one of the inner chambers when I noticed something unusual—an unbearded youth on the Temple steps. Ordinarily I would not have looked twice at a lad in such rough clothing. Clearly, he was one of those who had traveled from some obscure village to attend the festival. But this boy stood in the center of a group of priests and rabbis; they were conversing with him, and he answered their questions without hesitation. I could not hear his words, but I could tell he spoke with a confidence unusual for a grown man, let alone a youth. The priests listened, staring at each other as if they could not believe what they were hearing.

"While I watched, a man and woman pushed their way through the crowd, and from the worried looks on their faces, I realized they must be the youth's parents. The father spoke firmly to the boy, and yet the lad did not flinch at the rebuke. He simply gestured to the building around him and smiled.

The mother embraced the youth, wiped tears from her cheeks, and placed her hands on his shoulders. The priests did not try to stop them. Instead, they stood in silence as the boy and his parents left the Temple."

Paul shifted his attention to Luke's hand, which was busy writing down the words just uttered. "It was not until I read your first book, Luke, that I realized who the boy was. I had seen Yeshua as a child and did not realize whom I beheld that day . . . not that anyone else did, either. But He was confounding the experts and religious leaders with His knowledge even then."

Luke lowered his pen and smiled. "His mother told me the story herself. She and Joseph were terrified when they discovered Jesus wasn't with them on the journey back to Nazareth."

"Some of those priests might have been terrified, too," Paul said, a thoughtful look crossing his face. "If they had fully understood what they were witnessing, they would have behaved far differently when He confronted them later."

—◊◊◊—

Paul drank deeply of the water Luke gave him. The water from Aquila's house tasted clean and sweet, nothing like the liquid the guards occasionally lowered in a rough wooden bucket. That water tasted of slime and dead things, and if the light had been bright enough to see clearly, Paul was certain he would see insects swimming in it.

He leaned against the wall and folded his hands, quietly rejoicing in unexpected blessings—the company of a friend, a new purpose, pure water. Even knowing the date of his death was a blessing, for it would bring an end to his pain. To everything, there was a season . . .

Luke, who had been making notes on his manuscript, abruptly lifted his head. "Aquila wanted me to ask you about something else."

"Whatever it is," Paul said, "the Lord will guide him."

"He would still like your opinion. After all, there is wisdom in a multitude of counselors."

"Ah. Did he ask you about this matter?"

Luke sighed. "Yes. And I said I would ask you."

"I will not be with you much longer."

"All the more reason to ask while you are with us."

Paul nodded slowly. "What is his question?"

"Two slaves came to Aquila's gate. They ran away from their master's household because he threatened to beat them if they did not renounce Christ. And I suspect the woman is carrying a child. Should Aquila allow the couple to stay with the community, or should they be sent away?"

Paul closed his eyes. "Aquila may not agree with my answer."

"He would still want to hear it."

"Very well." Paul leaned toward Luke. "The Lord has assigned a path to each of us. A man who was circumcised when he believed should remain circumcised. A man who was uncircumcised should remain uncircumcised. A slave who was called to believe is the Lord's freedman, and the one who was called while free is Messiah's slave. We were all bought with a price, so we are all slaves to Yeshua. Each one should remain in whatever situation he was called, unless the Lord provides a legitimate escape."

Luke gave Paul an uncertain look. "So we should send this couple back."

"How can they please their master by running away?" Paul spread his hands in frustration. "A slave who runs has stolen his master's property. Slaves should obey their human masters with respect and reverence, with sincerity of heart, as they would obey the Messiah—not as people-pleasers but as slaves of Christ doing God's will. They should perform their duties with a right attitude, serving their masters as they would serve the Lord. Whether we are slave or free, whatever good we do we will receive back from the Lord."

"But their master wants them to renounce Christ!"

Paul closed his eyes and prayed for patience. "Their master worries because they have become Christians, and he stands to lose his property if they are seized by the Praetorians. If this couple freely returns to their master, if they say they will not renounce Christ but will serve their master with the same zeal they serve the Lord, he may take them back without punishment. But even if he *does* beat them, how can a beating harm their souls? He will not kill them, for they are valuable, and a beating only hurts for a little while."

"He would be beating a pregnant woman," Luke added.

"Only a fool will beat a pregnant woman if he fears she could lose her child, because the child will be his property, too." Paul paused, then let out a sigh. "We do not live in a perfect world, brother. We will face persecution and beatings, yet those things are nothing compared to the joy set before us. And who knows? Perhaps this couple's righteous example will lead their master to Christ. One thing is certain—if they run away, they will make Christ into a stumbling block for that man."

Luke tapped his pen against his knee. "I had not considered the state of the master's soul."

"Did Christ not die for the entire world?" Paul asked. "For the cruel master as well as for the innocent child? We cannot know what others will do, but we must be willing to lay down our lives for Christ just as He laid down His life for us."

He leaned against the stone wall and watched as tiny particles of dust rose heavenward in the single column of light. "I am a free man, yet I am anything but free. I have made myself a slave to all so that I might win some for Christ. That is all that matters, Luke."

—ɯ—

As Paul slept, covered by a blanket from Aquila's house, Luke squinted at his notes. Even though some of this material would have to be cut, all of Paul's stories were fascinating. Luke had never considered that Paul might have encountered Jesus at the Temple. The Temple's three pilgrimage festivals—Passover, Pentecost, and Tabernacles—drew Jews from across the world several times a year. How many times had Paul and the religious leaders worshiped at the Temple and not realized they were in the presence of the Son of God?

He blinked when the light brightened. A torch appeared in the opening overhead, held by the guard Eubulus. "Physician?"

Luke thrust his head into the light. "I am here."

"The prefect wants to see you."

"He knows I am here?"

Eubulus snorted. "The prefect knows everything, eventually."

The rope dropped.

Luke paused to take a deep breath and steady his quivering nerves. The prefect had learned of Luke's trespass. He had also probably learned that Eubulus played a part in the situation. Luke could present the document from Arctos Peleus in his defense, which meant the esteemed senator might find himself awakened tonight by the Praetorian Guard.

Luke folded his notes carefully and slipped them into the saddlebags Priscilla had given him. After hiding his inkwell and pen in the chamber's deepest shadows, he put the saddle-bags on his shoulder and stepped into the loop at the end of the rope.

Five minutes later, he stood before the broad desk in the upper chamber. The prefect and his second-in-command, a stout-looking man called Severus, stood behind the desk. Their eyes probed Luke as if they had never before seen a Greek. Eubulus stood beside Luke, silent and as tense as a bowstring.

Mauritius cleared his throat. "You know, usually people want to escape this prison, not break into it." He pointed to the leather bag hanging over Luke's shoulder. "Eubulus tells me you are Paul's physician."

"I am."

Mauritius transferred his attention to Eubulus. "You have friends with useful connections, Physician. Then again, I have always heard that Greeks make the best doctors, as they are clever."

Luke remained silent. Was he about to be arrested or congratulated?

The prefect crossed his arms. "The emperor has declared Christianity a forbidden cult, and Paul of Tarsus the chief offender. Yet you, a Greek Christian, boldly sneak into a Roman prison. *My* prison. Risking your life with the help of one of my guards."

Luke forced a smile. "As you've said, I have friends with useful connections."

Mauritius scowled. "I know this one beside you. Eubulus is a good man who has fought and bled for Rome. His judgment—admittedly more compassionate than most—is the only reason I have not arrested you."

Luke bowed. "I am most grateful—to Eubulus and to you.

And I assure you, sir, my visit here has been innocent. I came only to comfort my friend and see to his health."

A muscle clenched at the prefect's jaw. "Good news indeed. For you."

Luke bowed again. "If I may ask, sir . . . may I come again? Without having to trespass?"

The prefect studied Luke a moment. "You realize this prisoner is to die in eleven days."

"I do, yes."

"And if I discover that you are plotting an escape attempt, your life, as well as the life of the prisoner, will be forfeited."

"We are not plotting an escape."

Mauritius glanced left and right, then met Luke's gaze. "You may visit this sick prisoner, but only under cover of darkness. You may be recognized, and I will not have a known Christian boldly entering my prison in daylight."

"Understood," Luke answered with a bow.

The prefect turned to his second-in-command. "Escort the Greek to the street."

The Praetorian took Luke's arm in a rough grip, then pushed him out the prison door and into the dawning of a new day.

CHAPTER
FIVE

The Eleventh Day of Junius

Dawn seemed to come reluctantly, glowing halfheartedly through a cloudy sky.

Luke threaded his way through the shadowy streets of Rome, avoiding the crowded areas. His meeting with the prefect had reminded him that he *did* have many acquaintances in the city, and those friends had friends who might be happy to turn a Christian over to the emperor's guards.

He walked past the newly rebuilt Roman Forum, the House of Vestals, and the marble palace of Caligula, where slaves were busy sweeping the wide steps. He examined the area carefully before turning onto the well-traveled Way of Triumph, but he did not spot anyone he recognized. Even if he had, he could not avoid the road if he wanted to reach Aquila's villa.

Several donkey-drawn carts crowded the thoroughfare even at this early hour, their unshod hooves clomping over the stones in the street. The odors of manure and urine assaulted his nostrils, although the combination was a sweet perfume compared to the stench of Paul's dungeon.

Luke breathed deeply and walked on, moving quickly past the Temple of Apollo and the Palace of Augustus. No trace of blackened stones remained in this section of Rome, and he could almost pretend the great fire had never occurred. To escape prying eyes, he slipped between two donkey carts, both loaded with garbage from the street. The men who guided the donkeys walked with their heads down, looking for trash, so he did not think they would mind if he pretended to be involved in their business.

The rubbish collectors went several more yards before stopping. Luke looked up and felt his stomach clench when he saw a group of Praetorians striding toward the intersection ahead. A number of bound prisoners trudged behind them, followed by more Praetorians.

A cold panic gripped Luke and he froze.

"Make way there!" One of the Praetorians marched apart from the others, shoving aside anyone who encroached on the guard's path. "Out of the way. We are about the business of Rome!"

"Nasty business." The trash collector spoke in a low voice, but Luke could not help but overhear him.

He moved closer to the man. "What business are these men about?" he asked.

The rubbish collector spat on the road before answering. "They are taking these prisoners to the Circus."

Luke frowned. "They will die in the arena?"

The man shook his head. "Aye, but not before *lighting* the arena. These people say their God is the light of the world, so Nero has taken a fancy to the idea of human candles for his night games."

The second rubbish collector released a bitter laugh. "I wouldn't mind these Roman candles, but a body doesn't burn as long as a well-soaked torch."

Luke brought his hand to his mouth in an attempt to disguise the horror that had to be revealed on his face. His eyes were irresistibly drawn to the prisoners who shuffled behind the Praetorian Guard. Many of them walked with the stiff, painful gait of men who had been recently beaten, and some could walk only because another prisoner supported them. They were bloodied, caked with mud, and—

Terror lodged in his throat when he recognized a man he'd seen in Aquila's courtyard. What was his name? Caleb. He had been one of the first to help Octavia, and he had brought water and a clean towel to wash the blood from her face.

As the Praetorians turned into the entrance for the Circus Maximus, Caleb gave Luke a piercing look. Luke drew a breath and parted his lips to speak, but the man shook his head ever so slightly, sending a wordless message: *No. Do not risk your life by acknowledging me.* And then, despite the pain and fear he had to be experiencing, Caleb lifted his chin and smiled. "This is nothing," he cried, his voice shattering the quiet of the early morning, "when compared to the glory I will taste when I meet Jesus the Christ, who died to set men free!"

Luke stood amazed, his eyes filling with tears as he watched other men shout in victory while they marched toward the Circus where they would meet their deaths . . . and their Savior.

"Can't deny their courage," one of the trash collectors remarked. "Braver than many a gladiator, I'd warrant."

"You can't know that," his fellow collector argued, "until they're facing the blade or the fire."

"You *can* know," Luke said, daring to disagree. "When you have confidence in the One in whom you have believed."

—⁓—

Paul pressed his face against the softness of his new blanket. "Thank you, Yeshua," he whispered. "For earthly comforts and small blessings."

Shivering with chill and fatigue, he released his grip on his thoughts and let himself drift away. Amazing, how fitfully he slept when the days had lost their rhythm. With only a single opening for light, he often lost track of the hours and days. On cloudy days he existed in a seemingly endless dawn; when his guard forgot to light the torch, he lived in a nearly eternal night.

But Luke had brought sanity and order back to his world. Luke, who arrived just after sundown and remained until dawn. God bless Luke. He had proven to be a rope that tethered Paul to reality.

Paul felt himself drifting into a doze in which memories of his day blended with fragments of past memories. He saw himself talking to Luke and smiled as Luke again spilled ink on the papyrus sheets. Though writing inside a dark prison was not easy, Luke had proven himself capable. He would find a way to accomplish their task.

Luke was always methodical, precise, and thorough. The man enjoyed talking with people, gathering up the details of their stories as easily as a farmer's wife gathered eggs.

"Uncle Sha'ul?"

He blinked at the sound of a familiar voice and discovered that his surroundings had changed. He was in a different prison cell, one filled with light from a high window. The walls were made of stone blocks neatly fitted together. A door with iron bars stood between him and a corridor, where a boy stood. A beloved boy he recognized—Avniel, his nephew.

"Avniel?"

"Uncle Sha'ul, I have something important to tell you."

Paul blinked. Avniel was now a man fully grown, so this was surely a dream. Yet HaShem often revealed His will through dreams and visions . . .

Paul rose and went to the door. "Does your mother know you are here?"

"Never mind about that, Uncle—you are in danger!"

"I am where Christ wants me to be, Avniel. Now go home to your mother and—"

"They have taken an oath, Uncle. They are determined to kill you tomorrow."

Paul gripped the iron bars and lowered himself to the floor, then gestured for his nephew to do the same. When the boy sat across from him, Paul leaned closer. "Tell me everything."

Avniel nodded. "I was with friends from my study group. We were in one of the Temple chambers when a group of forty or so of the leaders came down the hallway. We knew we weren't supposed to be in that room, so we hid ourselves in the back. They never saw us."

Paul stared at his hands. "They held some sort of meeting?"

"Nothing official—the leaders were hiding, too. They whispered, but we heard enough to understand that they had all taken an oath not to eat or drink until they killed you. They said they were going to the ruling chief priests to announce their oath. They would urge the chief priests to go to the Roman commander tomorrow morning and say they wanted to interview you more thoroughly. But when the Roman brought you out of the Fortress, they would kill you before you could reach the Temple."

Paul smiled. Now everything made sense. "Avniel, can you tarry here a little longer?"

"Of course, Uncle."

"Good." Paul stood and called to the centurion outside. "Centurion! I have an urgent message for you!"

The centurion did not appear immediately, and when he did come around the corner, he gave Paul a look of pure skepticism. "What sort of urgent message could you possibly have?"

Paul reached through the bars and turned Avniel to face the soldier. "Take this young man to the commander, for he has the message. Trust me, the commander will want to hear it."

The centurion sighed, then looked over Avniel as if doubting that a boy so young could possibly have news of any importance. Finally, he pulled Avniel away from Paul and prodded him toward the exit. "That way. I'll take you to the commander."

After watching him go, Paul slid down the wall with a smile on his face. He knew how the situation would end. Avniel would relay his story to the commander, who could devise a plan for Paul's escape. The Temple leaders would not have access to him.

But their hatred for him was so great, they would break their rash blood vows and present their charges in a Roman court . . . and Paul would find himself in Rome, telling Nero and his officials of his transformation from persecutor to preacher.

He knew this because, the night before, Yeshua himself had stood beside Paul in his prison cell. "Take courage," Yeshua said in a low rumble that was both powerful and gentle. "For just as you have testified about me in Jerusalem, so you must also testify in Rome."

Paul dropped to his knees and gazed up at a figure that spoke of power, holiness, and ageless truth. "So be it," he had whispered, closing his eyes. "I am willing to go."

When he opened his eyes again, he was awake in his dungeon, accompanied only by the rustlings of rats.

"I remember everything, Yeshua," Paul said. He folded his hands across his chest. "And tomorrow I will share the story with Luke."

—⚹—

Aquila sat at his window, watching as the morning sun emblazoned the sky with streaks and slashes. The night had been a long one, and earlier, from the same window, he had studied the orange glow over the Circus Maximus. For several weeks, burning Christians had provided light for the emperor's night games, where gladiators fought to the death, wild animals devoured criminals, and drunken onlookers cheered.

He swallowed hard and wrapped his arms around himself. The horror of his brothers' and sisters' deaths still had the power to pebble his skin, but he had prayed that their sacrifice would bring a different kind of light to those who observed them. If they had gone to their deaths bravely, who could say how God might use them?

He heard a footfall on the threshold and turned to see Priscilla in the doorway. "I woke," she said, stepping into the room, "and you weren't beside me."

Aquila cleared the lump from his throat and gave her a smile. "I couldn't sleep."

Priscilla settled onto the bench at his side and squeezed his arm. "Luke made it back safely. He sleeps now."

Aquila nodded, relieved. Luke was able to take care of himself, but Aquila couldn't help but feel responsible for anyone staying beneath his roof.

"He was shaken when he came through the gate," Priscilla went on. "He saw Caleb among the prisoners on their way to the Circus."

Aquila lowered his head as fresh anguish seared his soul. Would he be praying for Caleb to die bravely tonight?

Priscilla rested her head on his shoulder. "My heart breaks for Rome and its people. We've loved this city for so long."

Aquila cleared his throat again. "Yet . . . yet lately I cannot think of it as anything other than what it has become. A reflection of Nero's madness."

"This time will pass. He cannot be emperor forever."

"But how many more will die before he does?"

Priscilla bit her lip but did not respond.

"This place," Aquila continued, "this decision weighs heavily on me. I have prayed, yet the Lord tells me nothing."

"He *will* give you an answer."

"But when, Priscilla? Every moment we wait is another opportunity for our group to be discovered. If we stay here, we put the lives of so many brothers and sisters in danger. All those living under our roof."

"Still, if we leave, how many others will suffer? The poor, the orphans—all those who rely upon our charity. Our love." She drew a breath. "Christ said He was sending us to dwell among the wolves."

"He also told us to be as wise as serpents."

"And as harmless as doves. And doves tend to stay in one place." She squeezed his arm again, then stood. "As Paul has said, we must each make our own decision."

Aquila blinked at her choice of words. *Each?* As individuals? They had been married for so many years that he no longer thought of himself as a separate person. He was Priscilla's husband and partner, one half of a team united in purpose, ministry, and love.

He turned, wanting to ask what she meant, but she had already left the room.

———ᵐᵐ———

Standing on the balcony of Aquila's villa, Luke watched the refugees in the courtyard below. They had been up since sunrise, cooking, constructing shelters, doing whatever they could to support each other. Would they stay here until the danger had passed? If so, they might be living in this crowded home for a long time.

He turned and saw Aquila approaching. "A blessed Lord's day to you," Aquila said. He pressed a cup of lemon water into Luke's hand. "You must be thirsty."

"Thank you." Luke drank, stood with Aquila, and watched the people below.

"How is Octavia?" Aquila asked.

"Holding up as best she can." Luke had checked on the woman as soon as he woke. He was worried that her mental state might have continued to deteriorate, but she was better this morning—grieving her losses but comforted by those around her.

He looked for the runaway slave couple, finally spotting them near the terebinth tree. Carmine was cooking something over the fire while Moria rested, one hand protectively sheltering her belly. Luke jerked his head toward the sprawling tree. "How are the newcomers?"

"They seem to be fine," Aquila said. He fixed his penetrating gaze on Luke. "Did you ask Paul about them?"

"I did."

"And what did he say?"

Luke took another sip of water, then sighed heavily. "He said they should return to their master and confess that they were wrong to run. They should submit to whatever punishment he wishes to mete out. Then they should work for him as they would work for Christ."

Aquila released a long, slow whistle. He leaned on the balcony railing and studied the couple below. "Christ never said following Him would be easy, did He?"

Luke managed a choking laugh. "Though His burden is light, it is all-encompassing. It demands everything of a man or woman."

"Just like a slave." Aquila smiled. "No wonder Paul keeps saying he is a slave of Christ. It is a fitting metaphor."

"It is reality." Luke set his cup on a nearby table. "I will speak to the couple, if you wish."

The words erased the worried line beneath Aquila's brow. "You will give them a choice, yes?"

"Of course." Luke looked out over the crowd, concern flickering in his eyes. "Do you think all of them counted the cost before coming here?"

Aquila crossed his arms. "Time will tell. Time reveals all." He gestured to the diverse group. "Do you think Paul and Barnabas imagined Christians in Rome when they set off to Antioch?"

Luke chuckled. "I'm not sure anyone did."

When Aquila turned, Luke followed his look and saw that Priscilla had just come through the courtyard gate. Smiling and serene, she was greeting her guests, distributing food from a basket, and instructing her servants to be sure everyone had warm clothing. Her voice carried over the noise of the refugees: "The nights can be chilly this time of year."

"She loves these people," Luke said.

Aquila tipped his face toward the sun. "They are like her children. Yet she also finds room in her heart for all those who are lost in Rome. That kind of love does not come so easily to me."

"I understand. It is difficult to love Romans when they trample on innocents and those we care about. It is even more difficult when we realize we are supposed to care about Romans." Luke peered toward the Circus Maximus, barely visible over the garden wall. "As I walked home, I saw prisoners destined to be burned on the Circus walls. One of them was a man from this group—yet I did nothing to help him."

Aquila shook his head. "There was nothing you could have done. His death will not be your fault."

"But he was one of us. Someone you may have led to Christ."

Aquila gripped the balcony railing. "Caleb was a true believer. Some of these people seek community. Others come here in search of shelter, food, and medicine, but they don't stay. I don't know their hearts, and I don't need to. God does."

"And that, my friend, is what troubles me at times. God knows my heart, and He knows I do not feel love for these Romans. Their evil makes no sense to me. The strength of their violence and hatred makes my skin crawl."

Aquila nodded in silent agreement. "Like sheep," he murmured, looking at Luke. "What will *you* tell them to do? Go or stay?"

Luke shook his head. "How can I give them an answer when Paul would not? I am only glad"—he patted Aquila's shoulder—"I am not their leader."

—✳—

Luke opened his saddlebags and pulled out the pages from his last visit to the prison. He spread them out on the table, groaning as he did so.

"What's wrong?" Priscilla asked, hurrying over.

Luke pointed to the papyrus sheets. "The notes I made last

night are a mess. Look." He pointed to a dark blob on the papyrus. "There I spilled the ink, and there—I'm not sure what happened. I must have lost my place. The conditions in that pit are deplorable. There's only a little light, so I spend most of my time writing in the dark. The room is horribly dirty, the floor sticky with filth. The place smells worse than anything you can imagine, and I think Paul has befriended the rats."

Priscilla's eyes went wide. "Rats?"

"At least he isn't eating them." Luke raked his hand through his hair as he studied the barely readable pages. "I intended to come back and put these notes in order, but I can hardly decipher them."

Aquila rose from his bench by the fire and picked up a few of the papyrus sheets from the table. "You need help," he said, "and here you have two helpers. Perhaps we can enlist some of the others, as well."

Luke looked at his host in dazed exasperation. "How can you help? I can't even read these notes and I am the writer."

"I'm sure it's not as bad as you think." Aquila sat at the table, took a clean sheet of papyrus, and picked up a pen. "Find the first page, look over your notes, then arrange the words in your head. Speak the words you want to write. Priscilla and I will be your scribes. Others will make copies of our pages."

Priscilla immediately sat by her husband and pulled another sheet of papyrus from the stack. She dipped a pen into the inkwell and held it above the page. "I'm ready."

Luke stared at his hosts, baffled. "I've never written this way. I've always taken a great deal of time to assemble my notes and sort through them—"

"We don't have the luxury of time," Priscilla interrupted. "Paul has only ten more days to live."

"You must trust the Spirit to guide you and give you the words," Aquila added. "Little by little, page by page, you will write this book."

Luke looked over the table and realized he had all the necessary pieces. He had his notes, jumbled though they were. And hadn't he been careful to store Paul's stories in his memory palace? If Jesus could feed five thousand men with five loaves and two fish, why couldn't the Holy Spirit help him translate his scribbled notes into a coherent book?

"All right." He took charge with renewed assurance. "This book will be called 'The Acts of the Emissaries of Yeshua the Messiah.'"

"I thought it was to be Paul's story," Priscilla said.

Luke held up a warning finger. "I cannot dictate *and* answer questions," he said, gently teasing her. "We have little time to spare, remember?"

"Sorry." She smiled. "I will not interrupt again."

"Good." Luke took a deep breath, then picked up his first page of notes. "I wrote the first volume, Theophilus, about all that Yeshua began to do and teach. . . ."

———

"Enter." Mauritius looked up as Severus led Eubulus into his office, then stood to the side, ready to carry out whatever order Mauritius issued.

The prison guard stood with his head lowered, his hands behind his back. Mauritius couldn't tell if the man's hands were bound, but he wasn't worried. These Christians had proven themselves to be a meek lot. Rarely did they object to their sentences, and even rarer was the Christian who responded to a judgment with physical violence.

"Eubulus." Mauritius held up a parchment and read the

indictment: "You have been charged with treason and dereliction of duty. I could add a charge of conspiracy because it is clear you planned your crime with others, but one death sentence should be enough. How do you plead?"

The big guard lifted his head, and the eyes that met Mauritius's were quiet and still. "I must plead guilty, sir. I did allow the physician Luke to visit Paul of Tarsus."

"Then despite your honorable record, you are judged guilty and must pay the penalty." Mauritius picked up a candle, dripped wax onto the papyrus, and pressed his signet ring to the wet wax. He handed the document to Severus.

Eubulus bowed and then started to turn, ready to follow the guard, when Mauritius lifted his hand. "Wait. Before you go, I need an answer to a question that troubles me."

Eubulus lifted a brow. "Sir?"

"Why?" More perplexed than he cared to admit, Mauritius studied the Praetorian before him. "You are a Roman, you are a *warrior*. What did these Christians do to you? Are you under a spell? A curse?"

Eubulus pressed his lips together, his thick eyebrows working like a pair of worms. "Nothing like that, sir."

"Then what happened? How did they bewitch you?"

"I heard their story—"

"What story?"

"About Jesus, the rabbi who was crucified in Jerusalem. And then I met a man, Peter, who saw Jesus alive three days later."

Mauritius felt his face heat in a surge of contempt. "And you believed this Peter?"

"I did. I was walking him to his own cross when he told me the story. And given that he was about to die for telling that story, I asked myself why he would lie."

"He lied because—" Mauritius searched for a reason and came up with nothing.

"He was not lying," Eubulus said. "I was part of the detail that crucified him outside the city. He asked only one thing at the end—that we hang him upside down, because he said he wasn't worthy to die like Jesus, the Son of God."

Mauritius looked away, his mood veering sharply to anger. Eubulus may not be aware that he'd been bewitched, but he certainly had. Only a fool would believe a story about a man rising from the dead after a Roman crucifixion, yet Eubulus was no fool.

"Then may your new religion bring you comfort, Eubulus." Mauritius motioned toward the door. "Enjoy your journey to the Underworld."

Eubulus walked without speaking as Severus and another Praetorian escorted him to a closed cart used for transporting prisoners. His wrists were bound with strong rope, and leg irons shackled his feet, forcing him to take small, mincing steps.

"The prefect has decided that you should be executed at the Castra Praetoria, in front of your fellow Praetorians," Severus said. "You will be given the honor of a military execution." His gaze shifted to Eubulus's face and thawed slightly. "I don't know what got into you, lad. You always seemed so sensible."

Eubulus shrugged. "Believing in a God who can defeat death seems sensible to me."

Severus shook his head as he opened a door at the back of the cart. "In you go. I'll see you again at the Fortress."

With difficulty, Eubulus managed the two steps that led into the wagon. He sat on the bench inside. Severus closed and barred the door, then thumped on the side of the conveyance.

Despite his resolve, Eubulus trembled as the wagon began to move. He had seen military executions, so he knew what to expect. His fellow Praetorians would be called out of the barracks. They would line the square courtyard. Mauritius or Severus would lead Eubulus into the center of the field. His crime would be announced, and he would be asked to kneel.

His palms went damp at the thought.

He would kneel before his fellow Praetorians, the finest of the emperor's soldiers, and his executioner would wait until Eubulus tugged at the neckline of his tunic, revealing bare skin just above his clavicle. The executioner would rest the tip of his sword against that bone. Then he would draw a deep breath and thrust the sword downward, severing the jugular and piercing the heart and lungs with one effort.

Eubulus would look out upon his friends and fellow soldiers, and then he would pitch forward, unable to bend around the shaft of steel slanting through his body. He would breathe his last while lying in the dust. But he would not die. Like Peter, his mortal body would grow still, but his eternal soul would awaken in another place, where Jesus, the One who conquered death, would greet him with a smile . . .

A shout distracted his thoughts. He heard the horse whinny and felt the cart stop. What was happening?

A moment later, the cart door opened. A man stood there, a man with powerful eyes and blindingly bright garments. "Come," he said, gesturing to Eubulus's hands and feet.

Eubulus took a quick breath of utter astonishment as the ropes fell from his wrists and the fetters from his ankles.

The stranger smiled. "Do not fear. The Lord has a plan for you."

Nodding, Eubulus jumped from the wagon to the road.

"Go at once to Aquila's house," the man said. "Tell them what has happened."

Eubulus thanked the man. Without looking around, he darted down a nearby alley and hurried away.

—∿—

Like anyone faced with a dreaded task, Luke put off speaking to the runaway slave couple until right before he had to leave for the prison. They seemed to feel comfortable among the community at Aquila's home. He had seen the woman, Moria, working with the other women, and Carmine had been quick to help the men fashion shelters and build cots.

He found them sitting together in a tent, sharing a loaf and a chunk of goat cheese. "May I speak with you?" he asked, bending to meet their gaze.

Both Moria and Carmine were quick to invite him to share their tent. "Would you like some cheese?" Moria held up their small portion. "There is enough for three."

"I have already eaten, but thank you." Luke crossed his legs and sat facing them. "Have you given any thought to what you will do in the next few weeks?" he asked. "Many in this community are talking about leaving Rome."

Carmine shot a quick glance at Moria, then shook his head. "In truth, sir, we have simply been grateful for a few hours' peace. We were hoping—praying—that a way would be made clear to us."

"That is good." The man's answer made Luke smile, dispelling the mingling of dread and anticipation he had felt at the thought of sharing Paul's advice. "Several of us have been praying about your future, as well."

"Oh?" Moria's eyes widened. "Can you tell us what is best to do?"

Luke tugged at his beard. "Following Christ is a decision each person must make on his own after much earnest prayer. Those of us who are leaders in the community will also pray and seek God's wisdom, which we will share. You should obey the leaders and submit to them, for they keep watch over your souls as ones who must give an account of their leadership."

A light flared in Carmine's eyes. "Have we left one master only to find we must obey others?"

Luke lifted his hand. "You have only one master now—Jesus the Christ. And as his servant, I asked Paul about your situation, and he has told us what you should do. If you truly intend to follow Christ, you will heed Paul's advice."

While Moria and Carmine listened, Luke gently laid out Paul's admonition. He did not know how they would receive the apostle's counsel—they could find it difficult and prefer to go their own way, or they could receive it with humility and obedience.

Often, Luke knew, following Christ meant doing the opposite of what the old nature wanted to do.

"Go back," Moria whispered, staring at the bulge at her belly. "Go back to our master."

"It is the right thing to do," Luke assured her. "Though I know it will be difficult."

Carmine stared at Moria with a look that said he was working hard to sort through a new set of perplexing choices. What would he do? Only he could decide.

Luke leaned forward, preparing to crawl out of the shelter. "Pray about your decision. Ask Christ to flood your hearts with His peace when you have made the right one. Then move forward with courage, knowing He will go with you."

As he slipped out of the tent and left the pair alone, he realized again the importance of the book he was writing. New believers like Moria and Carmine would need to read true stories to show them that Christ could be trusted. They would also need to read Paul's story, Stephen's, and Peter's to know that the early leaders had tested their faith and found it strong.

—〰—

Publius, the prefect in charge of the Exploratore, the emperor's personal bodyguard, lived in a rented villa with a grand view of the Circus Maximus. Hoping that his friend and equal might be able to shed some light on his problem, Mauritius sought his friend at home.

A slave let him in and led him to the atrium, where Publius was reclining on a couch while a slave girl served his dinner.

"Mauritius!" Publius called, grinning. "Will you join me?"

"I'll sit, but I'm not hungry."

"Come now." Publius raised a glass of wine and sniffed it in appreciation. "Nothing can be so bad that a fine wine can't improve it."

Mauritius grudgingly agreed to take a cup as he sank to a couch near Publius.

"What brings you to me on this fine night?" Publius asked. "Wandering the streets is not like you."

Mauritius ignored the question. "I wanted to ask you what we can do to ferret out any Christians in the ranks. Today I discovered that one of the guards at the jail is a Christian—he was letting a Greek physician visit a prisoner without permission."

"By Seth's big toe, that *is* an abomination." Publius grinned and popped a grape into his mouth. "So why did you come to me?"

"Because you have no scruples."

Publius pasted on a look of mock horror. "This Christian movement—it sprang from the Jews, right?"

Mauritius nodded. "It came out of Jerusalem."

"And the Jews are allowed to have only one god?"

"As I understand it, yes."

"So these Christians have only one god?"

Mauritius shrugged. "I don't know. I could always ask Paul of Tarsus."

"The man responsible for burning Rome?"

"He is nothing but Nero's scapegoat."

"How can you be sure?"

Mauritius stared into his cup and saw his own image reflected there. "You and I have arrested hundreds of men and seen every conceivable sort of debauchery. We've seen murders and conspiracies. We've pretended not to see lewdness and sorcery and wickedness. We Praetorians know a man capable of such things when we see him. This is not that man."

Publius shrugged. "It doesn't matter. We do know that Christians and Jews refuse to sacrifice to Roman gods, so there's your answer."

Mauritius frowned. "I'm not certain I—"

"Call a special assembly tomorrow morning. Set up an altar in the center of the courtyard. Summon each squad forward and tell them to sacrifice to Vesta, goddess of the hearth. The men will believe you are celebrating Vestalia, so they will think nothing of it." Publius grinned again. "Provide plenty of wine for the sacrifices, and they'll proclaim *you* a god afterward."

"Most of the men already sacrifice to Fortuna Restitutrix," Mauritius said. "Her altar is often used by the—"

"It does no good to have them sacrifice where you cannot observe them," Publius said. "*This* sacrifice must be public.

With your own eyes you will be able to see which men refuse to worship the gods of Rome . . . because they have given their allegiance to another."

After considering the idea, Mauritius decided to make it so.

———∽∽∽—

"By the way," Luke said, pulling papyrus sheets from the leather saddlebags, "the slave couple left Aquila's house tonight. They listened to us and decided to return to their master."

Paul nodded, grateful for the good report. "The Spirit will guide them, if they are willing to listen. They will do a great work in that household."

"If they survive it."

"They will."

Luke picked up his pen, dipped it in the ink, and looked at Paul. "Where should we begin tonight?"

"At the beginning," Paul murmured, lying on the floor. He crossed his arms on his chest and stared at the hole in the domed roof. The circle had become his sun, waxing and waning with the turning of the earth, bringing him light and warmth and life . . .

Just as Yeshua had.

"Where should we start?" Luke asked again.

"One minute," Paul said. "I am sorting through my thoughts." He felt less relaxed tonight, less able to concentrate. The atmosphere in the cell seemed heavier than on previous nights— probably because as soon as Luke descended into the pit, Paul told him that Eubulus had been sentenced to death.

Paul had been grieved by the news, too, though he did not take it as personally as Luke. Death was becoming more real to him with every passing day, and he was determined not to be afraid. "Death is like a figure that seems foreboding in the distance," he told Luke after sharing the news. "But as death draws closer, I am beginning to think it is nothing to be feared. By the time it arrives, I might even welcome it as one welcomes a friend."

Luke had shaken his head, not willing to entertain the metaphor, so Paul let the matter drop. Death was a reality Luke would have to face one day, but not yet. For now, they had a book to write.

"My life did not begin with hate," Paul said. "My parents loved HaShem and they loved me and my sister. They tried to provide everything for me, their only son—a love for the Law, a solid trade, a good family name. I was betrothed to Daphna at twenty, and we married as soon as she was mature enough to bear children. Both of our parents thought the match was a good one."

Luke's pen stopped scratching the papyrus. "You never told me you were married."

Paul shook his head. "Perhaps you shouldn't mention it in the book. I married because my parents wished it, and because it is the duty of every young man to take a wife and rear children in the knowledge of Adonai. As a young man, I noticed that all the men I admired—my teacher Gamaliel and practically all the members of the Sanhedrin—were married. Any good Pharisee would take a wife, so I did."

Luke leaned forward, his eyes gleaming with interest. "Did you love her?"

Paul felt a rueful smile twist his mouth. "I loved her as a Pharisee should—which is to say, I was intent on being her master and Lord. I did not strike her and I allowed her freedom in our home, but I was not particularly interested in anything she had to say. She was a woman, uneducated in religious matters, and overly concerned, I thought, with womanly things. If I had been married after I met Yeshua, I would have loved her better. I would have loved her as Christ loves her."

Paul stared into the light over his head, trying to remember what Daphna had looked like. "She was a little thing," he whispered, "and barely fourteen when we were wed. When I brought her home, I bade her sit while I explained all the things she should do in order to keep a proper religious home. She would have to be rigorous in her observance of Shabbat, the challah loaves would have to be baked the day before, and she would have to pray the proper prayer strictly before sunset on Shabbat. She would have to raise our daughters to be good wives. She would have to do this and that perfectly in order to please me."

"And did she?"

"What?"

"Did she please you?"

"Until she died." Paul pulled the admission from a well from which he seldom drew. The memories were too painful, even now, and too removed from the man he had become. "She died with my unborn child inside her," he said, his throat tightening. "And I felt I had killed her."

"Many women die in childbirth," Luke said, sympathy in his voice. "Especially women as young as your wife."

"I mourned her," Paul said, "and then I returned to my life of learning. Though some encouraged me to take another wife and have children, I was content to remain *agamos*, unmarried."

"Peter has a wife," Luke said, his thoughts clearly running in another direction. "And the believers at Jerusalem—the rest of the apostles are married, and James, and the Lord's brothers."

"That is HaShem's will for them." Paul rose up on his elbows.

"But not for me because I have devoted everything I am to spreading the news of the gospel. Apparently a wife is not for you, either."

Luke lowered his gaze. "I nearly married once. At Philippi I met a widow."

"Truly?" Paul turned to better see his friend's face. "You never mentioned her."

Luke shrugged. "She was a good woman and a great friend. I lived in Philippi for six years, shepherding the new church—"

"So why didn't you marry her?"

"Because I knew I wouldn't stay in Philippi. I sensed that the Lord had more work for us to do. Together."

Paul nodded in understanding. He and Luke had shared many joys as well as trials, and if anyone understood the bittersweet blessing of the unmarried life, Luke did.

"Now," Luke said, picking up his pen, "tell me about your relationship with Stephen."

Paul settled back on the floor and made himself as comfortable as his broken body would allow. "I knew Stephen from the Temple," he said, "so what eventually happened left me stunned and disbelieving. . . ."

—⁓—

Paul stopped speaking when he heard the familiar squeak. "There he is. Interrupting as usual."

"Who?" Luke looked around, his eyes wide.

"I call him Thaddeus," Paul said. "Jonah was given a vine to shade him from the sun, while I've been given a rat to keep me company."

"I'm here now," Luke said, glancing over his shoulder, "so Thaddeus can leave us in peace."

Paul pushed himself up, ready to resume his story. "I should continue now."

"Yes." Luke picked up a stack of papyrus sheets and settled them on his lap. "Tell me more about Stephen. You were both students under the Sanhedrin, correct?"

Paul nodded. "I was a few years older, but I remember when Stephen's group came to the Temple. Every year when the new boys entered, I always felt the sting of jealousy. When I first climbed the Temple steps with my father, I wanted to be the most eager, the best student of the lot. I did develop a reputation as being the brightest student in my group, but each year I studied the new lads with wary eyes. What if one of them loved the Law more than I did? What if one of the lads found greater favor in the eyes of Gamaliel?

"I would not have admitted it at the time, but now I see that I was proud. Proud of being a blameless student of the Law, proud of my devotion to HaShem. My father was proud of me, my teacher was proud, even my mother and sister expressed pride in my achievements. I memorized all six hundred and thirteen laws in the Torah, and like a fool I eagerly pocketed the praise of my parents and teachers.

"I had been a student of the Sanhedrin for about five years when I met Stephen. He was a first-year boy studying under a lesser rabbi, yet his eyes glowed with determination and an eagerness to please. He was always the first to respond to a question, and his answers, while not always what the rabbi expected, were original and thoughtful.

"The other rabbis praised Stephen to the skies. They congratulated his father when he arrived to walk Stephen home, and his mother strutted like a peacock when the family attended Temple services. I might have been able to ignore his success if

I hadn't overheard Nicodemus tell the high priest that Stephen was likely to be another Sha'ul. 'In fact,' he said, 'he might even surpass Sha'ul in honor and righteousness.'"

Luke's head rose abruptly. "Nicodemus?"

Paul chuckled. "I thought you might recognize the name. Yes, Nicodemus was a leader of the Pharisees, and a man of some importance among the priests and scribes. He was also extraordinarily cautious. He never made a statement unless he was certain of its truth, so when he predicted that Stephen might surpass my achievements—"

"You were hurt," Luke said.

Paul shook his head. "I was destroyed. I felt all my studying and striving had been for nothing. Therefore, I determined that not only would I be the best student, I would also strive to be the best example of a righteous Pharisee. I would live a blameless life. I would chastise others who searched for the easy path. I would follow the leaders closely and emulate their actions and attitudes.

"I did not want to harbor hate in my heart for a fellow Jew, but jealousy snaked into my soul and left its bitter poison. So years later, when Stephen began to speak of an itinerant teacher called Yeshua, I recognized my chance. He was following a liar, a false Messiah, and if he continued, in time Stephen would do or say something unforgivable. I had only to wait . . . and keep an eye on him. And that is exactly what I did."

—⁓—

"Rabbi Gamaliel!"

Sha'ul strode through the Temple courtyard, intent on reaching the man who stood with two Sanhedrin students. All three lifted their heads at the sound of Sha'ul's voice, but once they spotted him, they hurried off in another direction.

"Rabbi Gamaliel, is it true?" Breathless, Sha'ul planted his feet on the cobblestones and placed his hands on his hips. "Is it true you have let those blasphemers go with only a simple flogging?"

Gamaliel pressed his lips together. "Forty lashes minus one is no simple thing."

Sha'ul pointed to the steps that led from the Temple court-yard to the sanctuary. "That ignorant fisherman stood in this holy place and accused the high priest of killing the Messiah! Then he had the gall to add that God raised the false messiah from the dead! You should have ordered the fisherman and his companions to be crucified. If not that, you should have stoned them on the spot."

Gamaliel drew a deep breath and fixed his eyes on Sha'ul. In a calm voice, he asked, "What if their words turn out to be true? We would be accused of stoning or crucifying the servants of God."

"The servants of *God*? But Jesus of Nazareth was a glutton, a drunkard, and a friend of tax collectors and sinners. Those men preach that their so-called messiah was crucified, but you know the Law—any man hanged on a tree is cursed by God!"

"Sha'ul." Gamaliel gave him a smile that seemed forced. "Wisdom tells us one thing: if the plan or undertaking espoused by those men is of human origin, it will fail, but if it is from God, we will not be able to stop it. *No one* will be able to stop it."

"But—"

"The council has ruled on this," Gamaliel said, stepping away. "The matter is finished."

Sha'ul stiffened. "Rabbi, I have always respected you, but I am beginning to have doubts about your commitment to the Law."

The teacher stopped and cast Sha'ul a sharp look. "Do not

forget who has taught you everything you know. Hear me when I say the only wise action in this moment is to watch and wait."

Sha'ul pounded his chest. "My passion comes from my love of the Law given to us by the God of Israel. I am a true servant. If I act in any way, it will be because I love HaShem and His Law more than anything on earth."

Buoyed by confidence in his own zeal, Sha'ul stalked away.

———

"The last time I saw Stephen, he was lying on the ground, blood running from his head."

Paul swallowed hard to dislodge the lump in his throat. Even after all these years and the forgiveness of Christ, the thought of Stephen's death made Paul's blood run thick with guilt.

"I did not know it at the time, but the community of believers in Jerusalem had chosen seven faithful, Spirit-filled men to help the disciples serve those in need. They prayed and laid hands on these men, and one of them was Stephen."

Luke's pen stopped its scratching. "When did he become a believer in Christ?"

Paul blew out a breath. "I am not certain, but it might have been as early as the day of Pentecost. Or perhaps it was when Peter and John stood before the Sanhedrin and preached that *Yeshua ha-Mashiach ha-Natzrati*—Jesus the Messiah from Nazareth—had been raised from the dead to become the cornerstone of salvation. When the members of the great council realized that Peter and John had never studied at the Sanhedrin or been discipled by any of the leading rabbis, they were amazed that mere fishermen could speak with such authority. But what could they say when those fishermen had miraculously healed the man standing between them? Stephen could have been in the council chamber that afternoon. Perhaps that was the day he believed."

"Were you there, too?"

Paul shook his head. "I had gone to celebrate Shabbat with my sister and her family. But not long afterward I began to hear reports of Stephen and the miracles he performed in the name of Yeshua. Overflowing with love and power, he worked many wonders and signs among the people. Later, as I traveled from synagogue to synagogue, I heard troubling reports. Wherever Stephen appeared, Jews from the Temple—that is to say, those who had been educated by the rabbis, as I had been—were debating Stephen and losing those debates. Stephen spoke with authority, and he understood the Torah and the writings of the prophets. They could not find fault with his statements."

"What did Stephen argue?"

"He was not one to choose some obscure point of the Law and debate it. No, Stephen always presented the simple truth: that Yeshua was the Messiah and the Temple in Jerusalem was no longer the only place we could worship God. Such a message was dangerous, you see, because it threatened the authority of the priests and rabbis who ruled the people through the Temple."

"But surely Stephen didn't spend all his time debating. Hadn't the community chosen him to serve its members?"

"Yes." Paul's throat tightened in a spasm of guilt. "He actually spent very little time debating the religious leaders, because he was usually out in the street exhibiting charity to widows and orphans, preaching truth to the crippled and blind, and healing people in Yeshua's name. Meanwhile, I remained in the Temple, fasting, praying, and studying the Law lest I offend it in the smallest detail. When God looked down on us, He saw me being blameless and useless. Stephen, on the other hand, was ministering in His Son's name."

"Hmmm." Luke peered at his notes.

"You have a question?"

"I don't understand what instigated Stephen's trouble with the Temple leaders. I know you didn't like him, but he was busy doing good, so why—?"

"Because I wasn't the only one who didn't like him. Others were also jealous of his obvious gifts. Stephen did steer clear of trouble at the Temple, yet he visited the synagogues of Jerusalem and unintentionally stirred up trouble everywhere he went. I heard complaints from the synagogue of the freedmen, the synagogue of the Cyrenians, and the synagogue of the Alexandrians, who had always been known as superior thinkers. My home synagogue, the synagogue of Cilicia, was filled with learned men, and none of them could defeat Stephen with logic or words from the Torah."

"What did you do, then?" Luke asked. "You had been biding your time, waiting to see if the movement would die out . . ."

"I grew tired of waiting," Paul admitted. "Along with others from the various synagogues, I began to spread rumors saying I had heard Stephen speak blasphemies against Moses and HaShem. Then on an appointed day we incited the people of Jerusalem in the Temple courtyard until the incensed mob rushed Stephen, bound him, and led him to the Sanhedrin."

"Surely he spoke as he had earlier," Luke said. "Since he had addressed the Sanhedrin before."

"The mood had changed." Paul winced as he recalled what happened next. "And we who opposed him had made plans for his second appearance. We had false witnesses appear before the court, men who said, 'This man never stops speaking words against this holy Temple and the Torah. We have heard him say that this Yeshua will destroy this place and change the customs Moses handed down to us.'" Paul softened his voice. "I was in the council chamber that day, and I witnessed everything I am about to relate."

He waited, letting the silence stretch until Luke caught up.

"On that day, standing before the Sanhedrin, Stephen spoke a perfect account of the history of Israel. The scribes wrote down every word; the chief priests and rabbis sat spellbound, in awe of the power and authority in his language, his manner of speaking. He greeted the chief priests and rulers with respect. Then he began with Abraham and told our national history, moving through the years of Moses and the Tabernacle. He spoke of Solomon and the building of the Temple. And then he said, 'However, Elyon our God does not dwell in man-made houses.'"

Paul looked at Luke, who was driving his pen across the papyrus. "To men who had based their entire lives on the holiness of the Temple, those words were considered blasphemy."

Luke stopped and glanced up. "He insulted every member of the Sanhedrin, then."

"Yes, and they could not stand it. As they cried out in rage, Stephen kept talking. 'Oh, you stiff-necked people! You uncircumcised of heart and ears! You always resist the Ruach ha-Kodesh; just as your fathers did, you do as well. Which of the prophets did your fathers not persecute? They killed the ones who foretold the coming of the Righteous One. Now you have become His betrayers and murderers—you who received the Torah by direction of angels and did not keep it.'"

Luke's mouth twisted in a grim smile. "I imagine those comments were not well received."

"They were not. And Stephen's case was not helped when he looked up and his face began to shine with an unearthly light. 'Look,' he said, smiling up at something we could not see, 'I see the heavens opened and the Son of Man standing at the right hand of God!'

"That was the end. He had no sooner finished speaking when nearly every man in the chamber covered his ears and rushed at him. They might have torn him limb from limb on the spot, but someone remembered it would not be right to murder someone—even a blasphemer—on holy ground."

Luke held up a finger, silently imploring Paul to wait, so he did. Luke finished his notes, then looked over at Paul. "You said nearly every man in the room rushed at Stephen. Did you notice who remained seated?"

Paul grimaced in good humor. "Yes, I did. Only two remained in their chairs: Gamaliel and Nicodemus."

———❦———

Rising up on tiptoes in an effort to see above so many taller men, Sha'ul paced at the edge of the crowd that had risen up in the great chamber of the Sanhedrin. Then the object of his search appeared—like a piece of seaweed caught by a huge wave—Stephen was lifted by the crowd and taken out of the Temple. Screaming for justice and death to the blasphemer, the mob carried him past the Antonia Fortress and through the city gate.

The shouting quieted in the open land outside the city walls. The desert area had little to recommend it for beauty, but it did have stones.

The hostile horde dropped Stephen onto the sand. He struggled to his feet, wiped sweat from his brow, and regarded the widening circle of accusers. The mob remained silent, milling about him in that peculiar silence that occurred when a collective decision had been made but no individual was brave enough to act.

"Sha'ul!" Another Pharisee spotted Sha'ul at the edge of the crowd. "You are a renowned student of the Law. Do you agree that this man has committed blasphemy?"

Sha'ul looked around the circle, pleased to see that every eye had turned toward him. Including Stephen's. He stepped forward. "I do."

"Do you agree that this man deserves to die?"

Sha'ul intended to hold Stephen's gaze, but he could not. He expected to see defiance, temper, and arrogance in Stephen's eyes, but instead he saw . . . compassion. Even love. Paul turned his head. "I do."

The Pharisee strode forward, pulling his richly ornamented cloak from his shoulders. "Here. Hold this for me while we strike a blow for Adonai!"

Sha'ul took the cloak and draped it over his arm, then kept his arm extended in an open invitation for others. An instant later, others came toward him, burdening him with cloaks and mantles and hats and traveling bags until the items overflowed his arms and lay piled at his feet.

When the crowd around him cleared, Sha'ul realized the stoning had already begun. Stephen did not run, for he was surrounded, but neither did he cower or beg for mercy. Instead, he stood erect, his face lifted toward heaven, his arms outstretched, leaving his body vulnerable. As rocks struck his chest, limbs, knees, and head, he gazed at the sky, staring in what had to be a demonic delusion. After one particularly large stone struck his head, visibly chipping away a piece of skull, Stephen crumpled to his knees. "Lord Yeshua, receive my spirit!" he cried, slumping as another stone crushed his chest. Then, with what had to be his remaining breath, Stephen cried, "Lord, do not hold this sin against them."

Sha'ul watched in horrified fascination as Stephen exhaled and did not breathe again.

—⁓—

Luke, who had risen to stretch his legs, turned suddenly, his voice booming from the darkness. "Was Stephen the only Christian you knew personally?"

Paul took a moment to think. "He was the only Christian among my peers," he said, double-checking his memory. "But there was another. Nicodemus."

"I have talked to John," Luke said. "He told me about Nicodemus visiting Jesus in Jerusalem."

"Yes. Some have said that Nicodemus was embarrassed to be seen in the company of the Nazarene, but Nicodemus had never been shy about making inquiries. He went to see Yeshua at night because he could not reach Him during the day. Jerusalem was always crowded at festival time, and Yeshua was always surrounded with people. So Nicodemus made his inquiries, found out where Yeshua and His disciples were staying, and visited Him at that house."

"So he became a believer?"

"Not immediately," Paul answered. "Like many of the chief priests and religious rulers, Nicodemus was quite literal and exacting. When Yeshua told him that a man had to be born again, Nicodemus refused to accept the metaphor. He thought Yeshua was being foolish."

"What changed his mind?"

Paul shrugged. "He didn't change his mind, but he gave Yeshua the benefit of the doubt. He and several other Temple leaders had seen evidence of Christ's miracles, so they knew He had come from God. No mere man could have done the things He did. But Yeshua went on to explain the Scriptures, pointing out that the Torah was filled with metaphors—Moses lifting up the serpent in the desert, for instance. When the people looked at the serpent on the cross in faith, they were saved. In the same way, Yeshua told him, 'So the Son of Man must be lifted up so that whoever believes in Him may have eternal life.'"

"Nicodemus left Yeshua and pondered His words for many days. He began to see other signs and symbols in the Scriptures—how sin entered the world through Adam, and how salvation could redeem the world through a second Adam, Yeshua. When Christ stood trial and was crucified at Passover, Nicodemus realized that God had provided a sinless, perfect Passover lamb for the world—His Son, Yeshua the Messiah."

"So Nicodemus believed *then?*"

"Perhaps. By the time Christ died, however, Nicodemus was a true believer. He was with Joseph of Arimathea when he went to Pilate asking for Yeshua's body. Together they took the body of Yeshua down from the cross, wrapped it in linen with expensive myrrh and aloes, and placed Him in a new tomb."

"What did he do after Christ's resurrection?"

Paul closed his eyes, struggling to remember. "I believe he remained in the Sanhedrin, at least for a while. But while he was never the sort to broadcast his views, neither was he the kind of man to deny them. I lost track of him after I met the Lord, and I'm sure he has died by now. But one day soon"—he opened one eye and grinned at Luke—"I plan to ask him exactly what he did after leaving the Sanhedrin. I'm sure he has an interesting story to tell."

CHAPTER
SIX

The Twelfth Day of Junius

On his way to the prison, Mauritius stopped at the Temple of Jupiter to make a sacrifice. He stopped before the image of Jupiter and faced the lararium, where he placed an offering of wine, fruit, and three gold coins.

He began his prayers by invoking Janus, the god of beginnings, and Vesta, who governed the fire of the hearth through which Jupiter would receive his offerings. He pulled his toga over his head and prayed: "Father Jupiter, in offering this wine, fruit, and gold I pray good prayers, so that you may be propitious to me and my daughter, to my house and my household."

He picked up the vessel of wine and poured it on the hearth. "Father Jupiter, in offering to you the fruit and gold, virtuous prayers were well prayed, for the sake of this be honored by the wine offered in libation. Hear my prayer, Father, for the healing of my only daughter, Caelia."

When he had finished, he nodded to the priest, refolded his

toga around his shoulders, and set out for the stable and the Castra Praetoria.

—ᗰ—

The Castra Praetoria, barracks of the emperor's Praetorian Guard, stood in the northeastern part of the city, just beyond the inhabited district. Home to all ranks except the prefects and tribunes, the impressive square Fortress stood on one of the highest elevations in Rome, commanding both the city and the major roads leading east and northeast.

Tiberius had built the Fortress over forty years before. Since that time, men like Mauritius had gone there to train, rising through the ranks from tiro to sesquiplicarius to centurion, tribune, and finally prefect.

The Praetorians had no higher rank, nor did Mauritius want one, though he shared his authority with another prefect. The responsibility of reporting to a capricious, cruel emperor had already taken its toll on his family and his health. One day, perhaps, he would retire and live out the rest of his days in peace . . . so long as Nero didn't first burn down the city.

The knowledge that he had unknowingly allowed a Christian to serve at the prison troubled him immensely. Eubulus, the traitor, could have easily helped Paul of Tarsus escape, and what a fiasco that would have been. What if his "god" had told him to spirit the prisoner out of the city? Or murder Mauritius in cold blood? Who knew what a foreign god would do? Suetonius had described Christians as "a group of people of a new and evildoing superstition," and who understood people better than a Roman historian?

Last night he had sent a message to one of his tribunes, knowing that arranging a barracks-wide sacrifice would not be a hardship. Many of the men would welcome the break in routine, but those who were Christian . . . Mauritius smiled. He would find them easily.

He rode through the Fortress gates and looked around with approval, pleased by his tribune's good work. The center court-yard had been cleared of all training equipment, the sand raked. Two tables stood in the center of the courtyard—one supported a statue of Vesta, and the other had been converted into a larar-ium, complete with jug of wine and sacrificial cup. The men would know what to do; all Mauritius had to do was call the men forward, cohort by cohort.

He left the horse with a guard and went to his tribune's quar-ters. The man leapt to his feet and saluted.

Mauritius returned his salute and dropped into a chair. "Are we ready?"

"We were waiting on you, sir."

"Then summon the trumpeters and let us begin."

The tribune strode out of the room. Smiling, Mauritius slowly stood and sauntered to the edge of the courtyard where he stood next to a pillar and waited, one hand on the hilt of his sword.

At the first shrill blast of the cornu, the Praetorians sprinted out of their chambers and lined up in the courtyard. By the time the blasts stopped, nine cohorts of five hundred men stood in the courtyard, over eleven hundred men in front of each wall. The only men missing were several Exploratore and those on patrol.

Mauritius stepped forward and lifted his hand. "Men of the Castra Praetoria," he called, his voice rising to echo between the tall stone walls. "In honor of the approaching festival of Vestalia, today we will sacrifice to Vesta, goddess of the hearth, for Rome is the hearth of the empire. Each man shall take his turn, stepping forward to offer a sacrifice of wine, then returning to his place in line. All men shall remain until every guard has had an opportunity to make his sacrifice."

He locked his hands behind his back and studied the men in line. A thousand faces looked back at him—tanned faces, pale faces, thin faces, square faces, flushed faces. The faces were like masks. Almost anything could be going on behind those façades of rugged determination.

"Tribunes!" Mauritius commanded. "Lead the cohorts forward and begin!"

Mauritius stood in the morning heat, perspiration dripping from his hairline, as the slanting sun lighted the courtyard as brightly as a stage. One by one, the Praetorians advanced to the altar, murmured their prayers, sloshed wine into the cup and drank it. Then they returned to their lines, where Mauritius saw more than one man lift a brow and whisper something to his fellow Praetorian.

They were probably wondering if the gods had bewitched him. If they only knew the truth, for he feared a strange god had bewitched *them*.

There! His pulse quickened when he realized that one man—an evocatus he recognized—did not move forward with his cohort but remained in his spot as if rooted to the earth. And there! On the west side, two men did not go forward. And there! On the south side, directly opposite Mauritius, another man did not move.

One moment slid seamlessly into the next, and before he knew it two hours had passed. And in that two hours he had discovered at least a dozen men who had not been willing to sacrifice to a goddess of Rome.

When the last cohort had visited the altar, Mauritius walked forward, then turned, slowly surveying his men. "I never thought it would be necessary to strain flies out of the Praetorian Guard," he said, narrowing his gaze, "but that time has come. If you came forward to offer your sacrifice, remain standing. If you did not come forward, kneel!"

Over eleven hundred perplexed guards remained standing, but then, one by one, several men knelt, beginning with the evocatus Mauritius had recognized. What was his name? He had served as a centurion, later retiring to raise a family. When his family perished in the great fire, he had rejoined the Praetorian Guard at Mauritius's invitation.

Jove, that was his name. He shared his name with Jupiter, king of the gods and the chief deity of Roman state religion. If Jove had turned his back on the Roman gods, he should be doubly ashamed.

Mauritius lifted his chin and counted. Thirteen guards had knelt on one knee, and from the looks on their worried faces, he saw that they had realized his intention.

"You!" He pointed to Jove, half hoping the man would cite some unexpected reason for not coming forward. "Will you come forward now and sacrifice to Vesta?"

He waited in a silence that was the holding of a thousand breaths.

"No, sir." Jove lifted his chin and stared past Mauritius. "I cannot."

"Why not?"

Jove stared directly at the prefect. Mauritius expected to see a silent plea for mercy, but the eyes that met his were bright with confidence and soft with kindness. "Because, Prefect, I worship Jesus the Christ, the only true, living God."

Mauritius turned away in a rictus of repulsion. He strode down the line, asking the same question of each man who had knelt at his command. Others repeated Jove's refrain—they worshiped Christ and would not worship any other, not even under direct orders from their prefect.

"Praetorians!" Mauritius yelled, frustration evident in his voice. "If the man to your right is a Christ-worshiper, do your duty! Kill him!"

The silence that ensued was like the hush after a battle when the enemy lay dead and men paused to catch their breath. For an instant Mauritius wondered if his men would forget their training and question his command, but the instant soon passed. Swords flashed as they rose from scabbards, and men yelled as they gathered their strength and thrust their blades into the bodies of the traitors.

The executions were over in seconds. Thirteen Praetorians lay in the dust of the courtyard, their blood staining the sand as their companions stood nearby with troubled expressions on their faces.

Thirteen men—fourteen, counting Eubulus—not as many as he had feared.

Holding his hands tightly behind his back, Mauritius walked over to the spot where Jove lay, silent and still. He had turned his head as he fell, and his profile was clearly visible. Above the blood-drenched sand, Mauritius beheld the man's lined face and saw the suggestion of a smile on his lips.

What was it with these Christians? He had heard that Peter, another apostle, had died with a smile on his face.

Mauritius began walking away, unable to bear the sight a moment longer. "Do not question what you have done," he called. "Nero has decreed death to all Christians, and better that your Praetorian brothers die honorably here than to be burned alive in the Circus. That is all."

Confident that he had done his part to eradicate a dangerous religion, Mauritius turned to fetch his mount from the stable.

———～⋙～———

Severus was waiting when Mauritius arrived at the prison. The guard's brows were knitted with worry.

"Severus?" Mauritius walked to his desk and sat down. "Have you some troubling news for me?"

A muscle twitched at the Praetorian's jaw. "Unfortunate news, Prefect. Eubulus has escaped."

Mauritius stared in disbelief. "How . . . how is that possible?"

Severus shook his head. "I put him into the cart myself. I barred the door. The man wore iron fetters."

"So? Was the wagon ambushed?"

Severus rubbed his chin. "The two drivers tell different stories. One says they were halted and attacked by men on the street. The other . . ." He shook his head.

"What does the other driver say?"

"It's impossible. I've already detained the fellow for further questioning."

"But what did he *say*?"

Severus's gaze dropped like a stone. "He says they were suddenly surrounded by a bright light. The horses stopped and would not move until the light disappeared. When it did, the second man went back to check on the prisoner . . . and he was gone."

"A man in fetters couldn't have gone far."

"Um . . . the irons and chain remained in the cart. So did the ropes that had bound his hands. And the thing is, sir—the ropes were not cut."

Mauritius lowered his head to massage his temples. He

119

did not need this sort of trouble, especially with his daughter so ill. Why couldn't these Christians be more like ordinary criminals?

"Continue your interrogation of the second driver," he said, looking up at Severus. "The man is clearly lying, so he may have been involved in the ambush. Release the first driver. And when Eubulus is found, bring him to me immediately."

"Of course, Prefect."

"Now," Mauritius said, "any other news?"

Severus pulled a papyrus from his tunic. "Last night's report. Balbus took the night watch."

Mauritius took the paper and looked it over. "The Greek?"

"Came and went once again."

Mauritius stood and walked to the window, considering his options. He had given the physician liberty to visit the prisoner at night, but should that freedom be limited? "What do we know about this Paul of Tarsus?" he asked, spinning around to face the guard.

Severus lifted his chin. "Plenty of rumors have circulated about that one. Some say he is a magician, others that he is a god, and still others claim he is a madman."

Mauritius snorted. "Certainly madness of some sort surrounds the fellow. But why does this Greek continue to visit him in that disgusting pit? The Greek seems to be well educated, a man of culture. I know few men who would visit such a place, even if Isis herself were waiting for them there."

"Balbus says they are working together. Paul dictates to the Greek, who makes notes. They talk throughout the night."

"What does he dictate? Letters?"

"Balbus says they tell stories."

Mauritius frowned, then turned back to the open window.

What kind of stories did the man from Tarsus tell, and why was the Greek so interested in them?

He waved Severus away.

—∿∿∿—

"Luke." Aquila rapped on his door. "Are you rested? Because if you are, someone in the courtyard has a story you should hear."

"I'll be down directly," Luke called.

"Don't take too long."

Luke smoothed his damp hair with his fingers, then hurried out to meet his hosts. The long nights at the prison had wrecked his sleep patterns, so he snatched naps whenever he could. Fortunately, Aquila and Pricilla had reserved an upper room for his use.

He hurried down the balcony steps and found Aquila, Priscilla, and several others gathered around Eubulus.

"Friend," Luke said, grasping the man's arm. "It is good to see you. I was concerned when I heard that you were sentenced to die for your actions."

Eubulus looked away. "Yes, I was condemned to death," he said, keeping his eyes averted. "I was not surprised. A Praetorian who disobeys a commander—" he stopped and shrugged—"I knew what I was risking when I volunteered to help."

Luke gaped at the man. He knew Eubulus was taking a huge risk by smuggling him into the prison to see Paul, but the prefect had seemed so mild-mannered when he confronted them.

"Then how did you come to be here?" Luke asked.

In remarkably simple language, Eubulus described what had happened after he was put into the prison cart. "I should be dead now," he said, "but the man said the Lord had a plan for me. So here I am."

Luke felt the sting of tears in his eyes. "If Jesus has a plan," he said, smiling, "we will do our best to safeguard it. You will take off that Praetorian tunic and put on something else. You will remain inside these walls unless you absolutely must go elsewhere." He clasped the guard's arm again. "We owe you a tremendous debt, and we will do our best to support you. Until then, remember this—the servant of God cannot be killed unless God allows it."

The big man's eyes brightened, and he grinned as Aquila led the group in a prayer of thanksgiving for his deliverance.

—✺—

After the midday meal, Aquila went down into the garden and cleared his throat, trying to get the attention of all those gathered in his courtyard. The men, women, and children who had taken refuge in his house stopped what they were doing and gathered around.

He took in their faces, all those who waited to hear from him—they were no longer the faces of strangers, but friends. Luke, Tarquin, Cassius, Eubulus, Octavia, and so many more. For months they had worked, worshiped, and prayed together. They had become a true community, sharing all things. But now it seemed as though the world was determined to split them apart.

"We have been asked," Aquila began when everyone had quieted, "to build a community in this city, preach the gospel of Jesus Christ, love the people of Rome, and pray for its leaders. We have done all those things, everything the Lord would have us do, yet now it seems there is no clear answer about a way forward. Should we stay here when our lives are in danger at every moment? Or should we go, taking the gospel of Christ with us?"

Cassius, young Tarquin's cousin, lifted his head. "What does Paul say?"

Aquila looked at Luke, but Priscilla answered before he could speak. "This is something each man and woman must decide for themselves," she said. "Each of you must pray, and then do what you feel the Lord would have you do."

A flutter of alarm ran through the group. Aquila gave them a moment before lifting his hand again. "Some of you have families and children. It is not wrong for you to want to protect them by leading them out of Rome. Others, though, may feel called to stay."

"How can we go?" one man asked. "We risk our lives every time we slip through your gate. How could we all leave without drawing attention?"

Aquila nodded toward Eubulus. "We know the Lord has a plan for you, and no one knows the city better than a Praetorian. If you can think of a way we could safely move everyone out . . ."

Eubulus stood, hooking his thumbs over his empty sword belt. He rubbed his chin a moment, looked around at the group, and said, "An old aqueduct lies beneath the emperor's new palace. It has been half buried and forgotten, but it leads out of the city. An entrance to the tunnel lies beneath the property of a wealthy Roman family. They do not like the emperor's new palace and may be willing to turn a blind eye if we want to use the tunnel."

"Why would they want to help us?" Cassius asked.

Eubulus smiled. "They would never say so publicly, but they know Nero had their villa burned to the ground. They want the tyrant dead and Rome returned to the people." He drew a deep breath. "We may have their sympathy, but such an exodus will not be easy. We will have to make preparations, and we may have to travel in small groups, at least until we are deep into the countryside."

"Where would we go?" Octavia stood, fear evident on her face. "I have never lived outside Rome."

Aquila gave her a confident smile. "Each family may decide for themselves, but first we would go to Ephesus. The Ephesian community will shelter us until each family determines what's best for them."

"Is Ephesus safe?" Cassius asked.

"It is. Although the journey to Ephesus is a long one, Timothy lives there, the community of Christ is strong in that place, and the Greeks are far more tolerant of Christians than the Romans."

"Still." Another woman stood and looked at Octavia. "We were Romans before we were Christians. This is our home."

"Of course." Aquila pressed his hand against his chest. "I do not make this decision lightly, but I believe there is much good to be done outside of Rome—and we can do it."

He looked over the crowd as many nodded in agreement. He had made a good argument, and he might have instilled the confidence they would need to commence preparations—

A dissenting voice cut into his thoughts. "I believe," Priscilla said, coming to stand by Aquila's side, "we can do much good by staying here."

Aquila's heart twisted as he looked at his beloved wife. He could not be angry with her for expressing an opposing opinion. How could he be upset with the woman who had spent more than half her life at his side? She had every right to pray for wisdom, just as he did.

But if she stayed in Rome, she would eventually be discovered. And discovery, they both knew, meant certain death.

Priscilla gripped the rim of a stone fountain and looked at the people she loved as a mother and sister. "It is true we have never seen Rome darker," she continued, "but if we abandon it, will it not be cast into total darkness? How can we be lights on a hill if we desert the hilltop? How can we be the salt that preserves if we abandon the city to decay?"

More murmuring, more heads nodding.

"Who would have taken in Tarquin if we were not here? You have seen what happens to young orphans in this city. They starve to death on the streets or are forced into prostitution at the temples. What about the widows begging on street corners for coins to feed their children? Would you have them forced into slavery because we are not here to feed and clothe them?"

As the voices of assent grew louder, Cassius stepped forward. "We should not forget that Nero is the source of all this trouble," he said, his eyes narrowing. "The citizens of Rome are not responsible for the deaths in my family. Nero is. Aquila spoke of those who want to overthrow the emperor—are they not our allies? Think of the good that could be done once Rome is delivered from Nero's evil grip."

Aquila set his jaw as several voices agreed with Cassius. "There are no easy answers," Aquila added, raising his hand again for quiet. "And there is no right answer for all of us. You must trust God to lead you. But if some of us are going to leave the city, we need to leave soon. Every day brings new dangers. Every day"—he glanced at Eubulus—"another person from our community faces death."

"You should choose a date," Luke said, and Aquila's thoughts turned to the appointment Rome had set for Paul. "There is a time for prayer, and a time to act in faith."

Priscilla turned to him, and in her eyes Aquila saw a tide of fear. Talking about leaving was one thing; setting a departure date was something else altogether.

"I was thinking," Aquila said to Luke, "that we could leave at the summer solstice. We will leave Rome when Paul does."

Luke nodded slowly. "That . . . makes sense."

The courtyard swelled with silence as each person realized that their much-discussed plan had just become a reality. On the twenty-first day of Junius, a group from their community would leave Rome, probably forever.

Eubulus waved a hand to get the people's attention. "The most difficult part of moving our people out of the city will be getting word to the family who owns the land over the aqueducts. They will have to provide access to the tunnels so we can leave without being noticed. Someone will need to carry word to Palatine Hill. Nero knows this family, and he does not trust them. He has spies everywhere, so we will have to send a message with someone who would not arouse suspicion. Someone . . . unlikely."

His dark eyes searched the crowd. His gaze lingered over a group of women, and then a small voice broke the tense silence. "I'll go."

Aquila turned toward the source of the sound and spotted ten-year-old Tarquin with his hand uplifted. Smiling, he shook his head. "Thank you, son, but we could not send a child—"

"I can go," Tarquin insisted. "Who would think to question an orphan on the street? No one would look twice at me, and I want to help."

Luke tugged on his beard. "Do you know the area around Palatine Hill? It has been greatly changed in the last few months. We would not want you to wander into a dangerous area."

Tarquin's face lit with an impish smile. "I know the city as well as I know this courtyard. I could find my way without any trouble. And I'm fast and as slippery as an oiled fish. No one is going to catch me."

Priscilla looked at Aquila. "I cannot send a child. The risk is too great."

"I want to go." Tarquin grinned at Priscilla, and Aquila knew his wife could never resist that smile. "Please, dear lady. Let me do this to help everybody."

Priscilla glanced at Luke, then Eubulus.

"I can think of no one better," the Praetorian said.

Finally, she looked back at Aquila, and he nodded to her.

"All right," she said, returning Tarquin's smile. "But I will not stop praying until you have safely returned."

———✲———

As the meeting dispersed, Luke joined Aquila and Priscilla in a quiet corner of the house. Aquila wrote a letter on papyrus and sealed it with his signet ring.

"Can you discern a prevailing opinion?" Aquila asked. "I cannot tell."

"I believe most will go," Priscilla replied, "while some, I hope, will stay behind to continue the work here." She looked up as Tarquin came toward them, a broad smile lighting his face.

"Here is the letter." Aquila placed the sealed message in the boy's hand. "Show this to our friends on Palatine Hill. You will know the house—it has recently been repainted with a blue door."

Priscilla pulled him close. "You are a very brave boy, Tarquin. Be careful out there."

"I will," he promised. "I am fast—"

"And you are slippery." Luke smiled at the lad. "You will need to be. May the Lord guide your footsteps, my young friend."

The boy nodded, then slipped away through the courtyard gate.

"Now let us take stock." Aquila moved to the balcony and called to the Praetorian below. "Eubulus, I assume you will leave Rome."

The guard gave a nod. "I would not survive long if I remained here. Too many Praetorians know my face."

Priscilla looked at Luke. "And you, friend? What will you do?"

"I won't abandon Paul. I have promised to be with him until the end. But afterward . . . I may slip out of the city and join you on the road to Ephesus."

"Once we are gone," Aquila said, "we will not be able to help you navigate a safe exit. You'll be on your own."

"You have already done more than enough for me, so I would not ask you to wait on my account," Luke said. "Finishing this book and remaining with Paul might be the most important tasks I have ever undertaken. More important, I believe it is what Christ wants me to do."

"How is the book coming?" Priscilla asked. "Do you need our help today?"

"Yes." Luke nodded. "Though last night we spent some time working on what will be his last letter to Timothy. I wrote it for him as he dictated." He blinked back tears as the memory flooded over him. "In it he says his farewells."

Priscilla's hand went to her heart. "Is he so eager to—?"

"He is." Luke forced a smile. "Our brother is ready."

—∿∿—

"Tell me," Luke said, breaking a loaf of the delicious bread Priscilla had set on the table, "about how you first met Paul."

Aquila and Priscilla shared a smile, shook their heads, and

laughed. "Is this for your book?" Priscilla asked. "I'm not sure anyone would be interested in the story."

"Tell me anyway," Luke said. "I never know what the Spirit will nudge me to write."

Aquila lowered his cup of honey water and grinned. "We would never have met Paul if men didn't need to work in order to eat."

"You were all tentmakers, correct?" Luke said.

"Right," Aquila replied. "And we were much younger in those days."

"Sometimes I feel like we've always known him," Priscilla said, "because once you meet Paul—"

"No one ever forgets him," Aquila finished. "We were living in Corinth when we met him. We'd left Rome because of Claudius—"

"He made all the Jews leave," Priscilla inserted. "And no one knows exactly why."

"I have an idea why," Aquila said, swirling the water in his cup. "Romans crave homogeneity. They want to assimilate conquered territories and have everyone worship the same gods. While most cultures don't mind adding another god to their pantheon, we Jews worship one God only. And when we refused to worship the emperor or his gods, we became known as intractable. Uncooperative. *Un-Roman.*"

Priscilla shrugged. "In any case, we had to leave Rome. We hadn't been in Corinth long, and we were still trying to find new customers . . . and help."

"So you found Paul."

"Exactly!" Priscilla smiled. "We told friends we were looking for an experienced tentmaker, and one afternoon Paul came to our house. He said he had experience with tent making, and his next question was whether we were Pharisees or Sadducees."

"I said we were neither," Aquila said. "That we didn't have time to get into arguments at the synagogue. So Paul showed up the next afternoon with his tools, and we started working on a large tent for a wealthy family. But the entire time Paul was sewing, he was telling us about Yeshua. By the time we finished the tent, both Priscilla and I were believers."

"You know Paul." Priscilla passed a clay pot filled with stew and smiled with approval as Luke filled his bowl with the fragrant mixture. "Paul worked six days of the week with us, but on the Sabbath he would go to the synagogue and lead discussions."

"He tried to convince Jews and Greeks that the Messiah had come," Aquila said. "At first he tried to be subtle, knowing that most Jews didn't want to hear about Yeshua. But then he became impressed that the need was great and time was short, so his subtlety vanished. He started preaching that Jesus is indeed the Messiah."

"I'm sure you have heard," Priscilla added, "that his message did not go over well at the synagogue. One day Paul left the building, stood in the middle of the street, and shook out his tunic, shouting, 'Your blood be on your own heads! For my part, I am clean; from now on, I will go to the Goyim!'"

"So he went to the Gentiles," Aquila said, "and we went with him. When he sailed to Ephesus, we went with him. We made tents while Paul preached to the Gentiles, and as a result, many believed in Yeshua."

"He's so determined," Priscilla said, resting her chin on her hand. "You probably think he was hard to work with."

"I had wondered," Luke admitted, "whether he considered tent making a joy or a necessary evil."

"Paul does everything with joy," Priscilla said, smiling. "We used to have contests in the shop. Or we'd see who could sell a certain tent first."

Aquila nodded. "Paul is diligent, though with new believers he was as gentle as a nursemaid. He guided them patiently, taught them well, and consoled them when they wandered into false teaching. He did the same with us, because we certainly didn't understand everything."

"How could we?" Priscilla laughed. "We had lived in Rome, in Pontus, and several cities in between. We rarely visited the Temple, so to us HaShem was more a concept than a personal God. Paul made Him real. And then he introduced us to HaShem's Son." The glint of amusement left her eyes. "I still find it hard to believe that in a few days we'll be living in a world without Paul. I had hoped the Lord would allow him to live for many more years."

"His body is weak," Luke said. "If God granted him more years, he would no doubt spend them in physical misery."

"We must not be selfish." Aquila sighed. "We love Paul, and it will not be easy to let him go. Yet death will bring an end to his terrible suffering."

"But not to his testimony." Priscilla leaned forward and tapped Luke's arm. "The book you are writing, and Paul's letters to the churches, will allow his words to reach thousands of others."

"Who knows?" Luke smiled. "These books might be read for a hundred years."

Priscilla beamed at him. "Wouldn't that be amazing?"

"Indeed," Aquila said, lifting his glass. "Here's to a long life for Paul's written work—and yours, Luke. May it outlive you both and bring glory to Jesus Christ."

Luke lifted his cup, as well. "Amen."

—∽ᴍᴍ∾—

Mauritius sat at the foot of his daughter's bed, his hands folded and his eyes closed. According to the water clock, he had been praying to Jupiter and Bona Dea for the past hour, but he had seen no improvement in his daughter's condition. Caelia had not moved or opened her eyes, nor had the blush of life returned to her cheeks.

Why had the gods not heeded his prayers? Had they not seen his vigorous defense of their honor at the Castra Praetoria? He had killed thirteen good men for their sakes.

Because his daughter looked half dead, Mauritius was afraid to stop praying. What if he gave up and her soul fled the earth as he walked away?

He heard the swish of fabric and opened his eyes. The sound had not come from the bed, but from his wife, who had slipped through the doorway and now sat beside the sickbed. She, too, was watching Caelia, and the look of devastation and fear on her face was enough to twist Mauritius's heart.

"I was remembering," Irenica said in the voice she reserved for dreaded things, "when Caelia was a little girl. She used to sit at the window and watch the sparrows sing and fly around the garden. She would have stayed there all day if I had not urged her away."

Mauritius remained silent. How could he reply? He had not enjoyed the luxury of watching their daughter play; he had been too busy training the emperor's guards.

"Do you remember," Irenica went on, "our house on Palatine Hill? Remember the way the light slanted through the windows? The lovely trees and flowers in the garden? That garden was Caelia's favorite place on earth."

Again, Mauritius did not speak.

"I was a noblewoman in those days," Irenica said. "The wife of an important Praetorian. But now I am married to a man who burns innocents at the emperor's games."

Mauritius drew a strangled breath. "It is Nero's madness."

Irenica sniffed. "I don't blame Nero."

I blame you.

She did not speak the words, but he heard them nonetheless. She blamed him for every ill wind that had blown upon them, beginning with the fire that had consumed their stately home.

"It is not helpful that you tiptoe around as if the gods have already taken her," he snapped. "Have you not considered that you might be angering the gods by behaving as though they have no power to heal? Or perhaps they are angry because you spend more time in front of your looking brass than caring for your own child."

Irenica's spine stiffened. She stared for a long moment at the silent form of their daughter. Then she stood and turned to leave the room. She paused at his shoulder. "I have been faithfully sacrificing to the gods every day. My conscience is clean. I do not think I am the one the gods refuse to hear."

Mauritius closed his eyes as she walked away, then opened them again to stare at the motionless form of his beloved daughter.

—⟨∭⟩—

With her shopping basket on her arm, Priscilla walked briskly to the market, intent on purchasing vegetables and meat for the evening stew. With Eubulus's arrival she had another mouth to feed, and the Praetorian looked as if he could eat an entire cow at one sitting.

At least Moria and Carmine had gone back to their master.

She shook her head and chided herself for being too concerned with practical matters. She would happily feed a dozen more if they came to her home for safety or to hear about Jesus.

She purchased olive oil, dried fish, legumes, and figs. She had just leaned over to inspect a jar of saffron when she heard a voice she recognized—could it be Moria?

Priscilla lifted her head and saw Moria across the merchant's table. The slave was speaking to the merchant, but she appeared to be unharmed.

Priscilla waited until Moria had finished her conversation, and then she hurried around the table and took the young woman's arm. "Dear one, it is good to see you!"

Moria turned, her jaw dropping when she recognized Priscilla.

"Are you all right?" Priscilla asked, smiling. "And Carmine, is he well?"

Moria's eyes welled with hurt. She threw her arms around Priscilla and went quietly and thoroughly to pieces.

—⁂—

Priscilla tried to control her emotions on the walk home, but her chin kept wobbling and her eyes filled in spite of her resolve. She kept her head down and her steps quick, and within a quarter hour she had entered the gate of her own courtyard. After nodding to the men who kept watch there, she left her shopping basket with Octavia, gave her brief instructions about dinner, and ran up the stairs.

She found Aquila in their bedroom, working on Luke's notes. Thankfully, he was alone.

"Husband?"

He looked up, his smile twisting when he saw her face. "What happened?"

She forced the words out. "I saw Moria."

"And?"

Priscilla curled her hands into fists, fighting back the sobs that swelled in her chest. "We could not have been more wrong."

"Come." Aquila turned away from the table and held out his arms. "Tell me why we were wrong."

A whimper escaped Priscilla's lips as she went to her husband and sat on his lap, allowing herself to be comforted like a child. "I saw Moria," she began, "and she wept in my arms. She and Carmine *did* go back to their master, and he was grateful to see them. He said they had saved him a fortune in slave-hunter fees. Then he sent Moria to the slaves' quarters and he had Carmine taken away."

"Taken where?"

Priscilla gulped as hot tears slipped down her cheeks. "To the slave market. The dominus said he would sell Carmine so Moria would never be tempted to run again."

Aquila patted her shoulder, his expression tight with strain.

"I just—" she brought her hand to her mouth in an effort to stifle a sob—"I can't help feeling we were wrong to send them back. They could still be here with us, safe and united. They had been together so many years, and now their master has torn them apart!"

"It could have been worse, Priscilla. At least Carmine wasn't beaten. And while I regret that Moria's child will never know its father—"

"No." Priscilla put her hands on his shoulders. "We were wrong about that, too. We assumed the child was Carmine's."

Aquila lifted a brow. "The child wasn't his?"

"Carmine is Moria's brother," Priscilla explained, trembling. "Her unborn child was fathered by their master. He sends for his female slaves whenever he chooses and sells their children as slaves once they are old enough to be weaned. Think of it, husband—he treats them like brood mares."

Aquila's frowned deepened. "I am sorry to hear it."

"Moria wants to honor God," Priscilla went on, floundering in a maelstrom of emotion. "But how can she when her dominus treats her like a prostitute? Her brother used to comfort her, but now he is gone and she may never see him again. How is she supposed to serve her master willingly in that kind of situation?"

Aquila closed his eyes and pulled at his beard. Priscilla waited, her throat aching with regret, as he sorted through his thoughts.

"Dear wife," he said, his eyes gentle and contemplative as he smiled. "You should not listen to your heart."

"*What?*"

"I know this is not easy for you to hear. Someone with your sensitive and compassionate nature is always driven to react emotionally. But does the Scripture not tell us that the heart is deceitful above all things? We cannot trust the impulses of our hearts, but we must hold every situation up to the light of God's truth."

"But that man—their dominus—what he did to Carmine, what he does to his female slaves and their children. God cannot approve of that."

"Listen to yourself, dear one. You are angry with him, yet he is a man for whom Christ died. And yes, the master is a sinner—as we were before we met Christ."

She listened, unwillingly at first, but the harder she tried to ignore the truth, the more it persisted.

"So Paul was right," she finally concluded.

"Yes, but we will continue to pray for Moria and Carmine. And for their master."

Priscilla drew a shaky breath and leaned against Aquila's chest. "It is not always easy to know what to do."

"We have always known that in the world we will have trouble," Aquila said. "When we decided to follow Christ, we counted the cost and knew we would have no guarantee of earthly comfort. Christ didn't have it, and neither does Paul. Those who come after us will have trouble, too. If not Nero or a cruel master, then someone else who will try to break them. But still, we follow and do not turn back."

Priscilla drew a quivering breath. "I know. But still—my heart breaks for Moria. She is so young in the faith."

"We will pray for her to have strength and to find someone else to encourage her. And consider this—wherever Carmine goes, he will shine the light of Christ."

"I hope so." Priscilla tried to swallow the lump that lingered in her throat. "And I pray God will bring good out of Moria's situation."

Aquila's eyes searched her face. "What did you tell Moria when you saw her?"

"I told her—" Priscilla sniffed—"I told her about Esther. I explained that Esther wanted to be righteous before God, but she was taken into the pagan king's harem against her will. She had no control over her life either, yet God honored her desire to please Him. And Esther ended up saving the Jews from annihilation."

An approving smile blossomed out of Aquila's beard. "God has been good to me—He sent me a wise and beautiful woman."

"He has been good to me, too." Priscilla wiped her cheeks and somehow managed to smile. "He gave me a generous and slightly foolish man."

—⁓—

The tavern was touted as the best in Rome, but Mauritius saw little to recommend it apart from the large jugs of strong spirits behind the counter. Prostitutes worked the tables, leaving little to the imagination as they advertised their particular endowments, and gamblers tossed down markers and collected coins in the establishment's darkened corners. A couple of disheveled women with dirty hands served barely palatable food, but who cared about eating when men were as drunk as these?

Mauritius accepted a cup of ale from one of the serving women and looked across the table at Publius, who was struggling to hold his cup in one hand and a plump woman in the other.

"Mauritius!" Unable to slap his companion on the shoulder, Publius settled for winking in the general direction of Mauritius's form. "Your dark mood threatens to make this well-fed lass far more expensive than she needs to be. Here, let me order you a woman just like her. Elysius! Does this girl have a sister?"

"No, thank you." Mauritius scowled. "Not in the mood."

Publius leaned forward and blinked rapidly. "No, I can see you're not. Something wrong at the prison?"

Mauritius shook his head.

"You should not be troubled by the thirteen men who died this morning. You did the right thing."

"I am not upset about the executions."

"Something worse than *that*?" Publius pushed the woman off his lap. "Run along, sweetheart, and we'll play later. Go along now."

When the girl wandered away, Publius propped his arms on the table and leaned forward, offering Mauritius a close view of his discolored teeth. "Tell me—how is prison life? Have you finished rounding up all the Christians?"

Mauritius sighed and averted his eyes. "You know as well as I—Nero's command is nothing but a distraction, a black mark on Rome and the Praetorian Guard. Still, I try my best to carry out his orders."

"Your lot could be worse."

"How so?"

Publius shrugged. "You could be rotting facedown in a British river, slain by the sword of Boudicca herself. Dead at the hands of a woman, now that would be a *real* disgrace."

Mauritius stared, finding no humor in his friend's comment. He might as well be dead as far as his wife was concerned. She appeared to believe he was worthless as a husband and father, and impotent as a man of arms. "Twenty years of service to Rome, and what do I have to show for it?" he asked. "I risked my life to earn my citizenship and now I am forced to round up people who have done nothing wrong while Nero makes a mockery of everything Rome used to represent."

"The emperor is a lover, not a fighter. They say he is a master of the arts. That his voice raised in song has no equal."

"What man would dare say otherwise?" Mauritius shook his head. "I have heard him sing, and I would rather listen to cats screeching in an alley."

While Publius tipped his chair back and howled, Mauritius sipped his ale. "I was not trying to be funny." He lowered his cup. "You laugh, but Rome's enemies will pounce on Nero's weakness."

Publius lowered his chair, released a few last whoops, and blew out his breath. When he had himself under control, he picked up his mug. "He thinks himself a god, you know. But I see him every day, and I can tell you he is a libertine with a swollen paunch, weak limbs, a bloated face, blotchy skin, dull eyes, and curly yellow hair." Publius shivered. "My stomach tightens every time I meet the man."

"I am not fond of Christians," Mauritius said, "but why does Nero put them to death with such exquisite cruelty? Not only does he kill them in the most horrible ways imaginable, but he subjects them to mockery and derision." He lowered his gaze. "I could almost believe the emperor has been inspired by Morta. Only the goddess of death could take such malicious glee in killing those who oppose the gods of Rome."

Publius drank deeply from his mug, lowered it, and smacked his lips. "These are indeed troubled times, my friend. 'Tis a good thing the gods keep the day of our death a mystery so we can enjoy this life." His face went suddenly somber. "I'm sorry, I forgot. How fares your daughter today?"

Mauritius shook his head. "Worse. I pray to Bona Dea, but she does not reply."

"Perhaps that is because she is most concerned with women. Sacrifice instead to Carna or Meditrina."

"I have."

"Then to Febris or Asclepius, Felicitas or Fortuna. A hundred gods stand ready to do your bidding."

Mauritius lifted his hand. "Thank you, but I have called on all of them. I would pray to your big toe if I thought it could help." He wearily considered his situation. "Things are no better at the prison."

Publius's jaw dropped. "What would possibly give you trouble there?"

He drank again, then wiped his lips with the back of his hand. "As I mentioned, one of my guards was allowing an outsider to visit Paul of Tarsus at night. Eubulus was a good soldier, but I had to charge him with conspiracy and treason."

Publius shrugged. "As you should have. When does he die?"

"He should have died yesterday. But somehow—I have not yet found an explanation—he escaped the prison wagon, leaving his bonds and fetters behind. He has not been seen since."

Publius winced. "Something is wrong with that story. Sounds as though your drivers were drunk."

"Or simply negligent." Mauritius stared into his cup again and saw himself as tiny, frustrated, confused. "Publius, what do you know about these Christians?"

Publius leaned back in his chair. "I rarely find them in the establishments I frequent. I do know they have a strange affection for poor widows and ugly orphans."

"Do you believe them to be fools?"

"I think we are all fools, but if you want to see what the gods think of them, walk over to the Circus Maximus tonight. You will see they are barely fit to light the arena."

He laughed, and Mauritius glumly acknowledged his attempt at humor. "The man Eubulus allowed into the prison is a Greek physician. He comes every night to transcribe letters of some sort."

Publius's brow wrinkled, and something moved in his eyes. "Letters? Mauritius, your mind has gone to rubbish."

"Why would you say that?"

His friend lowered his voice. "If you were to seize these letters, find something, *anything*, that might relate to crimes committed by this Paul of Tarsus . . ."

Mauritius waved the thought away. "Nero doesn't need evidence. He's the emperor."

"Still." Publius drummed his fingers on the tabletop. "The threat of assassination hangs heavily in the air. Half the city believes Nero started those fires. What if you brought Nero something he could display as proof that this Christian actually did conspire to destroy Rome? You would be a hero in the emperor's eyes. You would be the most honored man in Rome."

Mauritius's thoughts spun as he stared at his friend.

"Think," Publius pressed, "of your daughter. How much better would the gods listen if the divine Nero made a sacrifice for her?" He slapped his thigh. "By all the gods, that's a brilliant idea. Girl! Over here! Bring me another drink!"

Ignoring his boisterous friend, Mauritius leaned back in his chair and sorted through his thoughts.

———m———

Mauritius walked home, his legs unsteady and his thoughts in a jumble. He had too much on his mind, that was the trouble. He had lost a treasonous Praetorian, he was overseeing an eccentric prisoner, his daughter was deathly ill, his wife discontented, and his emperor insane. Any one of those problems was enough to make a man long for retirement, but all of them together were enough to drive a man completely mad.

When his vision blurred—undoubtedly the effect of the cheap ale—he leaned against a wall to steady himself. He'd drunk too much, and it wouldn't do for the prefect of the Praetorian Guard to be seen staggering down a Roman street. Even in this unsavory part of town, Nero had spies who would sell their mothers for a silver coin.

He pulled himself upright and stepped carefully past a drunken man and woman who were rolling around in the gutter. He staggered past the doorway of a well-known brothel and glanced inside long enough to spot several Praetorians. For an instant he considered going inside—for an hour, at least, he could take his mind off his troubles—but the sound of shouting distracted him. The commotion could be anything from a violent argument to a merchant beating a thief, but as an officer of Rome, one of his duties was to maintain the peace.

He stumbled around a corner and came upon four Praetorians, all of them kicking at a pile of rags on the ground. He blinked, confused, and finally spotted a patch of dark hair among the rags.

"What is this?" he asked. When they did not respond, he reached for the dagger in his belt. "I am Mauritius Gallis, your prefect. *What is this?*"

The tallest guard peered at Mauritius's face, then threw his shoulders back. "Nothing to see here, Prefect. We are simply teaching this orphan a lesson."

Mauritius squinted in the darkness. "Is that *a boy* there?"

The guard shook his head. "He may look like a boy, Prefect, but we know he is a Christian spy."

"What?" Mauritius glared at the guard, his heart pounding. "How do you know he's a spy?"

"We caught him leaving Palatine Hill. So we asked ourselves— what's a beggarly orphan boy have to do with the patrician families near the Hill?"

"So we asked him," another guard said, avoiding Mauritius's eyes, "where he was going, and he wouldn't say."

"Wouldn't say much of anything," the first guard added. "So we gave him a beating."

"He did say his name." The second guard shrugged. "Not that it would mean anything to you, Prefect. Then he called on Jesus, though that one didn't offer any help at all."

Mauritius lifted a burning torch from the wall and held it over a shape that was clearly the body of a child. The dark fabric of his tunic was stained, the face bruised, and the eyes swollen shut. As Mauritius moved the torch over the area, puddles of blood shone black in the torchlight.

"Is he dead?" he asked, his thoughts suddenly veering toward his daughter. This child looked to be about the same age as Caelia . . .

"Probably." The first guard prodded the body with his foot. "I'd say he is."

Mauritius blinked, and suddenly it was not an unnamed orphan lying at his feet, it was Caelia. He saw her brown hair caked with sand and grit, her eyes swollen and bloody, her face marked with fist-sized bruises. He saw her thin arm bent at an impossible angle, her legs splayed on the paving stones, and her hands frozen in a paralysis of fear.

No. Not her. This was not her; it was a street urchin, not his child.

"What did he say?" Mauritius asked, his voice gruff.

The first guard frowned. "We told you, he wouldn't say anything—"

"His name, you fool. What was it?"

The first guard lifted a brow and looked at the others, and one of them finally answered, "Tarquin. He said his name was Tarquin."

Not Caelia. Not his child.

"You're right—the name means nothing." Mauritius turned his back on the body and looked at the first guard. "You know the rules. Get rid of the body at once. Rome's citizens are never pleased to see trash in the streets."

SEVEN

The Thirteenth Day of Junius

Though the rising sun had filled the villa with honey-thick sunshine, Luke sat at Aquila's table and struggled to accept the unwelcome truth. Daybreak had also brought a report from the street, and the news had filled Aquila's pleasant house with the dullness of despair. While some in the community might be able to move swiftly from sorrow to acceptance, Luke could not.

Grief welled up within him, black and cold. They might never have known what happened to Tarquin if Octavia had not seen the Praetorians tossing a child's body into the Tiber. While she was not certain of the dead child's identity, nonetheless she had hurried back to Aquila's to report her fears.

When Tarquin had not returned by midmorning, Luke knew they had no choice but to accept the bitter reality of what happened.

"What have we done?" Priscilla cried, pressing her face against Aquila's chest. "He was so young, and I sent him out—"

"I did too," Luke said and buried his face in his hands. "I should have gone myself."

"He wanted to go." Aquila's voice was hoarse with grief. "And he is not the first child to die. He will not be the last either, because there are many who believe in Yeshua. He called them, and they came happily to Him. They still do."

"'Let the little children come to me and do not hinder them,'" Priscilla quoted, the words dissolving into a whisper, "'for the kingdom of heaven belongs to such as these.'"

Luke turned away, unable to bear the reminder. Yes, he knew Christ loved the children, and yes, he knew Tarquin was with his Savior now. But Luke would never be able to think of the boy without visualizing the Roman brutality that had stolen his young life. As a doctor, he understood the fragility of a small body and how little violence was required to snuff the life out of it.

Roman barbarity and the Praetorian Guard had taken Tarquin. And in light of that realization, Luke struggled to find compassion for anything Roman.

—◊—

Paul found himself staring again at Stephen's bloody face. The lifeless eyes filled his field of vision and transformed, becoming the eyes of the little girl he had pulled from beneath a basket and handed over to the Temple guards. Their zeal, which he had encouraged, burned so brightly that one of the guards struck the child with the flat side of his sword, a blow that sent her mother into hysterics. Then the guards turned to her screaming father and silenced him with a well-placed thrust of the blade.

He had not been given permission to kill the blasphemers, but only to arrest them. However, none of the men with him would object to the act.

"Paul?" A voice called across the years and across the miles. "Paul, are you sleeping?"

Awareness hit him like a blow to the gut. His eyes flew open when he recognized the voice: Luke had come to see him. Again.

Like a welcome angel, Luke knelt next to him and gently touched his shoulder. "Are you all right? You cried out."

"Did I?" Paul exhaled a pent-up breath and allowed Luke to help him sit up. "The devil sneaks around in this darkness, taunting me day and night and on all sides. I feel crushed by the sins of my past."

He squeezed Luke's supportive hand, then released it and stared into the darkness. "I am haunted by images of children I persecuted and images of myself as a child. I see that well-intentioned young boy and long to warn him about the path he is about to take . . . But what is done is done. We cannot go back, can we?"

"No. We cannot go back," Luke agreed. "Still, has God not promised us to work all things for the good?"

Paul did not answer. "All these years I have been troubled by one particular vision. I see people, and I know they are people I persecuted. They are waiting for me. The devil, a torturous muse, whispers that they have found no peace, they have found no joy. They are waiting to confront me for my egregious sins against them."

Luke sat in front of Paul. "Do you recognize any of these people?"

Paul shook his head. "I persecuted so many, I cannot remember their names or faces. Yet I do remember one little girl and her parents. All three died before they could stand trial. Others in Jerusalem I took from their homes and handed over to the Sanhedrin. Some we killed in outlying villages. All of them followers of Christ, the true Messiah. All of them my brothers and sisters."

He lowered his head as a tear trickled down his cheek. "I did not expect to struggle like this at the end. I wish you could find me in a joyous mood, celebrating my imminent meeting with Christ, but . . . I am not yet done with this life. Some matters remain unresolved."

Luke seemed to hesitate before rising to his feet and standing next to Paul. "Come. You need to keep moving. It is not good for you to remain in one position for so long a time."

Sighing, Paul allowed Luke to help him up. He followed as Luke led him around the oppressive dungeon.

"Do you remember Philippi," Luke asked, "after you cast out the demonic spirit from the slave girl? Her owners had you brought before the magistrates."

Paul chuffed. "How could I forget?"

"Stretch your back a bit—elongating the muscle will help you remain flexible." Once Paul had followed Luke's instructions, the physician took his arm and guided him again. "I watched as the guards stripped you and Silas naked in front of the crowd. You were beaten and flogged to the point where I was concerned for your life. You were covered in blood from head to foot. I made it to your side but could do nothing to help as they dragged you both off to prison. You turned to me, though you did not cry out in pain, nor did you beg for mercy. You did not shout threats at those who had mistreated you. You simply said, 'God will make this good.'"

Luke stepped behind Paul, wrapped his arms around his shoulders, and lifted him until the sharp crack of a joint echoed in the domed chamber. "There."

Paul slumped forward as Luke released him, turning to behold his friend's face in the light.

"Trust your own words, my friend. God will make this good."

Paul rubbed his hands together. "Thank you. Now." He summoned up a smile. "Are we ready to work?"

"We are." Luke moved to his bag and pulled out fresh sheets of papyrus. "Where did we last stop?"

"We were in Ephesus," Paul reminded him, settling on the floor. "In the home of the tentmakers."

—⁂—

Sha'ul stood before the *kohen gadol*, or high priest, and several elders of the Temple. The high priest, brother-in-law to Caiaphas, before whom Yeshua had stood judgment, looked at Sha'ul with approval gleaming in his dark eyes.

"Sha'ul, you are to be commended for your swift justice toward this cult of the Nazarene. We have approved of your efforts and your vigilance toward guarding the Law."

Sha'ul bowed his head, glorying in the moment.

"However," the high priest continued, "we feel the time has come for us to let these things alone."

Sha'ul stiffened. "What has changed? Why would you withdraw your approval?"

Theophilus glanced at the other priests, then returned his attention to Sha'ul. "We have sided with your actions over Gamaliel's tolerance, but we are now certain the message has been disseminated. Most of the so-called Christians have fled Jerusalem. Those who remain no longer preach in public."

Sha'ul blinked in astonishment. "Are you all *blind*? They are working to promulgate their heresy right under your noses!"

One of the elders leaned forward. "Do not forget whom you are addressing, Sha'ul of Tarsus. Do not forget you are addressing the anointed high priest."

Sha'ul brushed the warning aside. For the past several years the high priest had not been appointed by HaShem, but by Rome, and he could not understand why he should honor a

Roman puppet. "I am a true descendant of Israel, circumcised on the eighth day, a representative of the tribe of Benjamin, a Hebrew of the Hebrews. If anyone doubts my love for the Law, let him speak now."

He paused and scanned the assembly. No one spoke a word.

"Hear me now, then, all of you. Damascus has become a refuge for followers of the Way. You all know the man Ananias, a devout observer of the Law, well respected by all the Jews living in Damascus. Or at least he used to be. I have heard reliable reports that he has since become a disciple of the Way."

The elders looked at each other, confusion clouding their faces.

"Damascus lies in the center of the caravan trade routes to Syria, Mesopotamia, Anatolia, Persia, and Arabia," Sha'ul continued. "You must understand that if this sect is allowed to flourish outside Jerusalem, their heresy will spread like wildfire. Imagine a day when Christ is more venerated than the holy Temple in Jerusalem!"

The high priest shifted in his seat, glancing uneasily at the elders around him. Then he glared at Sha'ul. "What would you have us do?"

Sha'ul bowed. "Write letters introducing me to the leaders in the synagogues of Damascus. Let them know that if I find any men or women belonging to the Way, I will bring them back to Jerusalem as prisoners. I will travel to Damascus with your letters, and together we can end this abominable cult that desecrates all that the children of Israel hold sacred. Send a clear message to these blasphemers—let them know they will be held accountable for speaking against the Holy God of Abraham and Israel!"

One by one, the elders began to nod in agreement.

—⟲⟳—

Invigorated by the urgency of his mission, Sha'ul traveled the road to Damascus with a stalking, purposeful intent in his gait. The barren landscape basked in morning sunshine that hinted of a sweltering day to come. But Sha'ul welcomed the heat. He even welcomed the pedestrians and donkey carts on the road—even the occasional camel that trotted by and scattered the pedestrians like flies.

Romans traveled the road, too, in chariots and on horseback, and yet Sha'ul paid them no mind. He had a singular, holy purpose: to take custody of the man called Ananias and make an example of him in Jerusalem. When Ananias stood trial before the Sanhedrin, he would undoubtedly be found guilty. Another member of the Way would be stoned outside the city gates, and others would think twice before listening to members of that dangerous cult.

The well-watered hills of Damascus had just come into view when Paul quickened his pace. He charged ahead, leaving his companions behind, but then a light from above flashed around him, a light so bright he could see nothing.

Falling to the ground, he lifted his head from the scree-covered road and heard a voice: "Sha'ul! Sha'ul! Why are you persecuting me?"

Sha'ul blinked, but his eyes refused to function. "Who are you, Lord?"

He had been expecting to hear the voice of Moses or Elijah or Enoch, so the answer left him speechless. "I am Yeshua, whom you are persecuting. Now get up and go into the city, and you will be told all that you have been appointed to do."

Sha'ul looked behind him, expecting to see his traveling companions, yet he saw nothing but white, a striking absence of color or darkness.

"What happened?" one of his servants asked. "Are you all right?"

Sha'ul reached out and found the man, then clung to his arm. "What do you see?"

"Nothing," the man answered. "We heard someone speaking to you, but saw nothing."

"Help me up," Sha'ul said. "And get me into the city."

For the next several hours, Sha'ul experienced a whirlwind of perplexing emotions. He knew what he had heard—the voice of Yeshua—and also what He had said, that Sha'ul had been persecuting Him.

The truth had stung like a wasp. He thought he was persecuting followers of a mere man, not the Lord. Not someone who could strike him blind and speak in a voice that rumbled like thunder and pierced the heart and soul of a man . . .

When his thoughts reluctantly shifted away from the supernatural, he realized his friends were leading him into the house of a man called Judah. Once inside, someone led him to a bed and bade him lie down.

"Here, a cold compress for your eyes." A woman—probably Judah's wife—laid a wet cloth across his eyelids. "Let me get you something to drink."

"Probably heatstroke," one of his servants said. "Keep him cool and he will be fine."

"Did you see anyone with him?" the woman asked.

"No," his servant answered. "But ever since he fell, he has been muttering that Yeshua is the Christ, the Messiah."

Had he been saying that? It had to be true, although he was not aware that he had been speaking.

For three days Sha'ul lay on a bed in a stranger's house and refused to eat, drink, or answer questions. His sensibilities were thoroughly rattled, and he fully expected to discover that he had either lost his senses or finally found them. He prayed silently as he waited, and God answered with a vision: Sha'ul saw Ananias come into his room and lay his hands on him, restoring his sight.

On the morning of his third day of blindness, Sha'ul got out of bed, changed out of his dusty tunic, and had his servant wash his hands and feet. Thus prepared, he sat at a table and waited.

At about the fourth hour, Judah and his wife stepped into the room. "Sha'ul," Judah said, "can you hear me?"

Sha'ul spoke for the first time in three days. "Has he come?"

"I have," an unfamiliar voice said.

"Ananias?"

"You know who I am?"

A cry of relief broke from Sha'ul's lips. "The Lord showed me a vision—I saw you coming to me."

Ananias received the news silently. The creak of a chair told Sha'ul that the man was sitting across from him. "They tell me you have lost your mind and gone mute and deaf. That you haven't eaten or had anything to drink for three days."

Sha'ul waited.

"I know who you are," Ananias continued. "Your actions against those who follow Christ have been well reported. I know you have come here on the authority of the ruling priests to arrest all those who call on the Lord's name. I also know about the harm you have done."

"I am a wretched man," Sha'ul admitted, drowning in waves of guilt. "I deserve death."

"Yes," Ananias responded. "We all do. And yet Christ has set us free."

Free? Free from what?

153

Your guilt.

The truth crashed into his consciousness like the surf crashing against a stony cliff. For three days Sha'ul could think of nothing but how wrong, how proud, and how arrogant he had been—seeking the approval of his peers and the Law instead of favor from God. But Yeshua offered freedom . . . the freedom that comes with forgiveness.

The hardness of Sha'ul's soul dissolved at the realization of Christ's mercy. Tears flowed from his eyes, rolling over his cheeks and dampening his beard.

Ananias moved closer, and Sha'ul felt work-worn hands touch his face and cover his eyes. "Brother Sha'ul, Yeshua—the One who appeared to you on the road by which you were traveling—has sent me so that you might regain your sight and be filled with the Ruach ha-Kodesh. Brother Sha'ul, receive your sight!"

Immediately, something like fish scales fell from Sha'ul's eyes. The world appeared again, bright and beautiful. Blinking in astonishment, he beheld the kind man before him. "Thank you." He clasped Ananias's hands in his own. "Thank you for coming to see me."

"I did not want to come," the old man said, shaking his head, "but the Lord said to me, 'Go, for Sha'ul is a choice instrument to carry my name before nations and kings and Bnei-Yisrael. For I will show him how much he must suffer for my name's sake.'"

The old man studied him with a curious intensity. "The God of our fathers handpicked you to know His will—to see the Righteous One and to hear an utterance from His mouth. For you will be a witness for Him to all people of what you have seen and heard. Now, why are you waiting? Get up and be immersed, wash away your sins, calling on His name."

Shock whipped Sha'ul's breath away. "I am ready," he said,

clutching Ananias's hand. "Tell me, is there something I should do to show my commitment? Some sign?"

Ananias took Sha'ul's arm and led him down to the Abana River, which watered the ancient city of Damascus. As Sha'ul's servant and his amazed traveling companions watched, Ananias baptized Sha'ul in the name of the Father, the Son, and the Holy Spirit.

Filled with a jubilation he could not contain, Sha'ul came out of the water and dried himself. Shaking off his former purpose as easily as he shook water from his hair, Sha'ul went in search of the nearest synagogue, where he stood to address the gathering and proclaim the Truth: "Yeshua is Ben-Elohim! He is the Son of God!"

—⁓—

Luke trudged over the narrow street, where blackened ruins rose at his right hand. The sleepless nights were bearing down on him with an irresistibly warm weight. Though his feet moved methodically, steadily, he was certain he could lean up against a wall and fall asleep . . .

A sudden sound snapped him back to alertness. As adrenaline spurted through his veins, he glanced around. What had made that noise?

Few people traveled in this part of the city, especially at this late hour, and thus far the route had proved safe. Nero had rebuilt the most important parts of the city—those near the Roman Forum and the palaces of Caligula and Tiberius. But out here, past the market and the Circus Maximus, blackened stones could still be found, along with the occasional human skull.

He spotted a knot of Praetorians in the road ahead, but if he abruptly turned aside, he might arouse their suspicion. Better to keep his head down and his guard up while he went on his way. If any of the Praetorians followed, he would double back and lead them to the market or some neglected spot near the Tiber. He might even follow the example of the Jews' King David and feign madness, anything to keep them from knowing who he was and where he was going—

"Halt there."

Luke's heart rose to his throat when one of the guards pulled away and turned to face him.

He stopped, planting his feet where he stood. "Sir?"

The guard came forward, his eyes narrowing in the moonlight. "What is your business in this part of the city?"

Luke closed his eyes to murmur a frantic prayer.

"What's that? What are you doing?"

Luke looked up. "I am a physician. I have a permit that allows me to visit a man in the prison who is ill. I have just left that place."

"Why does a physician see patients at night?"

"Because Prefect Mauritius Gallis commanded me to come after dark. He didn't want . . ."

Realizing too late that he might have said too much, Luke produced the senator's letter from his robe and held it before the guard's eyes. The man squinted, then jerked it from Luke's hand to examine it more closely.

Luke pressed his lips together. He had no wish to get Arctos Peleus in trouble, but neither did he desire to be imprisoned. He held his breath as the soldier looked over the document. Then one of the other Praetorians shouted, "Over there! Hurry!"

Three guards took off running down the road. The man with Luke thrust the document at Luke's chest, muttered "Get off the street," and took off after his companions.

When the Praetorians had disappeared into the darkness, Luke leaned against a crumbling pillar and bowed his head. *Thank you, Lord Jesus.* Once his racing pulse had quieted, he pulled himself upright and lengthened his stride, hurrying toward Aquila's home . . . and safety.

CHAPTER
EIGHT

The Fourteenth Day of Junius

An hour after returning to Aquila's, Luke sat at a broad table in the house, sorting through stacks of scribbled papyrus sheets. Aquila and Priscilla also sat at the table, pens in hand, ready to write as soon as Luke began stringing the words together.

Time was running short. Only seven days remained before Paul's execution, and Luke felt as though he had scarcely begun to write.

At the far end of the table, Octavia and Eubulus were reading what he had written thus far. Occasionally they murmured in appreciation, and more than once Luke looked up to see pleasure on their faces.

"This book will encourage many in the faith," Eubulus said, smiling at Luke.

Luke nodded. "I pray it will."

"I don't know how you keep going," Priscilla added. "You have not slept since returning from the prison. You must rest, Luke. Promise me you will sleep this afternoon—"

Luke was about to answer, but the sounds of commotion

caught his attention. He stood and moved to the balcony in time to see Cassius enter the courtyard with a burden in his arms—the precious body of young Tarquin.

Priscilla, who had risen along with Luke, pressed her hand over her mouth to stifle a cry.

"We found him!" Cassius shouted, waking those who were still sleeping in the makeshift tents. "They threw him away like trash."

Luke felt his gorge rise as Cassius climbed the balcony stairs. Aquila quickly gathered Luke's notes while Priscilla grabbed a blanket to wrap the body.

"Put him here." Priscilla spread the blanket on the table. "Do not worry, Cassius; we will give him a proper burial."

Aquila retreated, as did most of the men, but Octavia remained. The ritual of washing the dead traditionally fell to women, because according to the Law, whoever handled or touched a dead body would be unclean for seven days. Paul had tried to explain that such religious laws did not apply to Gentile believers, as most of the Romans were, but Jews found it difficult to disregard practices that had been part of their lives since childhood.

Using a wet cloth, Priscilla tenderly sponged mud from the boy's pale face and pushed wet hair from his forehead.

"This," Cassius fumed, "this is what trusting God gets you!"

The furious young man did not wait for a reply. Instead, he spun around and ran back down the stairs. Luke looked at Aquila, who met his gaze with a somber expression. Luke knew what the man was thinking. *We must leave soon.*

With a firm step, Aquila took his wife's arm. "Take care of the lad," he said, "while Luke and I go down to speak with the others."

—⟋⟍—

Paul (James Faulkner) has endured much for the sake of the gospel. Though haunted by his past sins, he clings to the truth that he is forgiven, not forgotten.

Old friends and partners in ministry, Luke (Jim Caviezel) and Paul (James Faulkner) are reunited when Luke ventures into Rome to bring solace to his trusted companion.

Writer and director Andrew Hyatt used Scripture as the primary reference to create the first theatrical feature film about the life of Paul the Apostle.

Emperor Nero has accused the Christians of burning down half of Rome and begun a rampage of persecution, prompting church leaders like Priscilla and Aquila (Joanne Whalley and John Lynch) to open their home to desperate believers.

Priscilla (Joanne Whalley) comforts a grieving Octavia (Alexandra Vino), whose family has been murdered by the Romans.

"All men are a slave to something."
—Paul (James Faulkner)

Saul of Tarsus (Yorgos Karamihos), persecutor of
Christians, is struck blind by a vision of the Lord Jesus
Christ on the road to Damascus.

A young Saul of Tarsus (Yorgos Karamihos) leads the charge in wiping out members of "the Way"—until his journey to Damascus is interrupted by a blinding light and a voice from heaven.

Paul, Apostle of Christ was filmed on-site in Malta—the very island where Paul was shipwrecked and bitten by a poisonous snake yet miraculously survived.

Luke (Jim Caviezel) shares Christ's message that "love is the only way" with Christians who await their imminent death in the Roman games.

"It will be a moment of pain, but only a moment. And then we shall be home in the presence of Christ forever." —Luke (Jim Caviezel)

Olivier Martinez (Mauritius) and Jim Caviezel (Luke) share plenty of on-screen time together, with Luke's visits to Paul in the Mamertine Prison.

Mauritius (Olivier Martinez), the ambitious Mamertine Prison prefect, struggles to understand how the weary, broken Paul (James Faulkner) can pose such a threat to Emperor Nero.

Luke (Jim Caviezel) joins Priscilla and Aquila (Joanne Whalley and John Lynch) on the bustling streets of first-century Rome.

Leaving the women to their unhappy task, Luke followed Aquila to the courtyard. Everyone was awake now, and many of the refugees appeared terrified. Women clung to their children, men stood with arms crossed and eyes defiant, and several of the children were crying. What had Cassius been thinking when he ignited such a scene?

"You saw my cousin's body!" Cassius said, pointing to the balcony where the women were preparing the boy for burial. "We must retaliate for this brutal act. Nero's guards killed Tarquin, and he was only a child!"

Aquila stepped forward to address the gathering. "Many of us are leaving the city in only seven days," he said calmly. "We must remain strong during the time we have left."

"So are we like diseased dogs?" Cassius asked. "We do nothing to defend ourselves while we are chased, hunted down, and killed?"

Priscilla went to the balcony railing and looked down on the impassioned young man. "We understand your anger, Cassius," she said, her voice ringing above the group. "Tarquin was like a son to us. We should never have sent him out. This is our fault."

"Why do you blame yourselves and not the ones who murdered him?" Cassius looked around the garden. "Who else have they taken? Your husbands, wives, brothers, sisters, children?" He pointed at Octavia. "That woman came to you covered in the blood of her baby. Would you tell her it was her fault?"

Aquila placed his hand on Cassius's shoulder. "And what would you do about it, brother?"

"We should do to the Romans what they have done to us." Cassius jerked out of Aquila's grasp. "We should murder them under cover of darkness. We should set fires and burn them in their homes while they sleep!"

Luke rubbed his finger across his lips, recognizing the irony. Cassius was advocating the same sort of savagery the Romans already blamed on Christians. The result had been *more* unrest, and no wonder. Violence always begat violence.

"Cassius," Aquila said, a sorrowful note in his voice, "you speak as if you have never heard the words of Christ."

"You never walked with Christ," Cassius said, "so how can you know He would not say these things in the face of an evil such as Nero?"

Arguments began to erupt as impassioned voices supported Cassius or Aquila. The noise grew louder until soon their neighbors might overhear—

"Quiet!" Luke waited, his hand lifted, until the noise faded to silence. "Be still. For your own sakes, keep quiet. None of us here have walked with Christ. But Paul has followed Him longer than any of us."

The silence deepened.

"I have watched Paul be beaten," Luke continued, "stoned, and flogged, and never once did he raise a finger against his oppressors. Not once." He waited for his words to sink in, then gentled his voice. "Let peace be with you, my friends, for though we live in the world, we do not wage war like the world. Paul would say that violence must be met with love."

Several heads dipped in agreement, and Luke sensed a clear shift in the mood of the group.

But not everyone had been convinced by his admonition. Cassius and his friends still wore their hatred on their faces for the entire world to see.

Luke sighed and turned away. He was carrying a good deal

of anger himself, but as an older and wiser man, he had learned to hide it well.

—∽ΩΩ∼—

Mauritius sat at the foot of his daughter's bed and glared at the Roman doctor. Across from the doctor, Irenica waited with her hands clasped, her face a mask of fear and distress.

"I'm sorry. She is not improving," the doctor said.

Mauritius gripped his knees. "Whatever the cost, I will pay it. If you have some medicine that will help, regardless of the price—"

The doctor shook his head. "It is not a matter of cost, Prefect. It is a matter of diagnosis. I have never seen anything like this illness."

Mauritius pressed further. "Please, we will do anything. She . . . she is our only child."

The doctor stroked his chin, then blew out a breath. "There is a certain balm from the East. It may be helpful, but it is not inexpensive."

"Procure it," Mauritius said. "I will be happy to pay."

"Very well." The doctor nodded and slipped out of the room, Irenica trailing in his wake.

Mauritius rested his chin on his hands and studied his daughter's sallow complexion. How long had she been ill? He closed his eyes and counted—six days. Occasionally, Irenica managed to get a little water down her throat, but Mauritius could not forget the dictum he frequently drilled into the minds of new recruits: a man could survive three minutes without air, three days without water, three weeks without food. Caelia was breathing, thanks be to the gods, yet she was not taking in much water, and she was not eating.

Soon her body would begin to relinquish its hold on life. Until then, he would sit and watch death bear down upon her with slow and solemn steadiness . . . all while knowing he could do nothing to stop it.

—⁂—

Luke settled on the floor next to Paul. His friend had been awake when Luke descended into the pit, and surely that meant his outlook was improving. On the other hand, if Paul was feeling more optimistic, Luke hated to be the bearer of bad news.

"How are my friends?" Paul asked, interest flickering in his eyes. "Are Aquila and Priscilla still planning to leave Rome?"

Luke drew a breath. "At the moment, things are a little . . . unsettled." He hesitated. "There was a young Roman boy in the community. Two nights ago he was killed by the Praetorians. He was much loved, and Priscilla adored him like a son."

Paul let out a sigh. "I am sorry to hear it."

Luke paused as his mind replayed the painful scene at Aquila's home when Cassius carried Tarquin's body into the garden. "Most of Aquila's people trust the Way, but Tarquin had a cousin who appears to be dividing the group. A growing number of young men want to retaliate. They seek revenge."

Paul propped his hand on his bent knee. "We cannot repay evil for evil. Evil can only be overcome with good."

"They are young in the faith and have not yet learned that truth. Considering all they have been through, can you fault their response?"

As the older man's penetrating gaze raked Luke's face, the physician knew his soul was being scrutinized, as well. "How did you answer them?" Paul finally asked.

Frustrated, Luke stood and began pacing in the gloom. "How

was I supposed to answer them? Render unto Nero what is Nero's? Yet you would have me say that love is the only way."

"After all you have witnessed, you still don't believe it?"

"Believe in what, *love*? I believe in love, yes, but this . . . this isn't like anything I've seen before. This is a world in the suffocating grip of evil. It is Nero's insane Circus. It is a passionate hatred. I hear the screams of people—*good* people, *believing* people—as they are tortured and murdered. Blood stains the streets of Rome, the blood of children. Widows and orphans starve to death. Babies born with the slightest defect are discarded or left for wild dogs to tear apart. *This* world doesn't know a thing about love."

"So we should give up on it? Think, Luke—did Christ give up on us? Our world could be cruel, too. We were sinners like these Romans, yet Christ loved us enough to die for us. He had all the power and authority of God at His command, but He forfeited His rights to become one of us, to suffer like us and show us the way. Violence was not His way. Love is His answer, for love is the only currency that will pay the heavy debt of sin."

"But this world spits in the face of love!" Luke shouted, then recoiled from the anger in his voice, which bounced around the walls of the domed chamber and seemed to grow louder with every echo.

He had never raised his voice in anger around Paul, but neither had he faced such perplexing questions before. Not until now.

He returned to Paul and sat across from him, his head lowered. "Forgive me."

Paul gave him a sympathetic smile. "The answer for the Roman people—for all people—is love. Because love suffers long. Love is kind. Love does not envy. Love does not dishonor. Love does not seek its own way. Love is not easily angered. Love does not delight in evil. Love rejoices in truth. Love protects, trusts, hopes, and endures all things."

Paul's words echoed in the cavernous space, too, drowning out the residual echo of Luke's shout and cocooning them in the peace and quietude of love.

"Love conquers all," Paul added. "Now do you understand?"

Luke nodded. "I think I do."

"You didn't write it down."

"I don't need to. You have already done so."

A wry smile played at the corner of Paul's mouth. "Forgive an old man his forgetfulness and trust me in this, Luke. I have followed a path that rejects love, and I have seen what that path does to the innocent. I have felt what it does to a person's heart, and I know it does not bring peace. Or joy."

"I am familiar with the path you have walked," Luke said. "And though you were misguided, you were not Nero."

"Was I so different?" Paul shook his head. "My righteousness was worthless because I offered it with pride, not love." He drew a deep breath. "Like the blind, we grope along walls, trying to feel our way forward. We look for light in darkness, for brightness while we step along in deep shadows. We look for justice from unjust men, for deliverance from those who cannot deliver us. We look for perfection in imperfect situations."

"And yet you believed you were acting out of a love for God," Luke said.

"Do not attempt to excuse my sin. Yes, I thought my intentions were pure, but my love was blind because I only knew about the Law. I was stubborn, set in my self-righteous determination." He focused on some vague point in the darkness, a look of unutterable distance in his eyes. "If water flows down a mountain, what besides a miracle can cause it to flow back up?"

Luke folded his arms around his knees. "Damascus was your miracle."

"Yes." Paul seemed to recollect himself as he smiled. "It was."

"But it was not so for others. The Jews did not welcome you into the city."

Paul nodded slowly. "They would have welcomed me if I had remained true to my purpose—if I had rounded up the believers and taken them back to Jerusalem to stand before the ruling *kohanim*. But I who had been the chief of sinners and the blindest of the blind could finally see that Yeshua is the Messiah. So they plotted to kill me."

"I'm sensing a theme here," Luke said, jotting a note on his papyrus. "A great number of people wanted you dead."

Paul snorted. "They had killed Yeshua and Stephen, so perhaps they were overconfident. What they didn't account for was God himself, who raised Yeshua from the dead and used Stephen's death to scatter the believers throughout Judea. Even if they had succeeded in silencing me, I knew God would use my death for good. But I also knew they *wouldn't* kill me—because God wasn't finished with me." The line of Paul's mouth clamped shut for a brief moment, and his gaunt throat bobbed as he swallowed. "Though He may be finished with me now."

Luke lifted his pen and held it before Paul's eyes. "Look. See this? See this pen?"

Paul looked up and nodded.

"God isn't finished with you, Paul. Not yet. I do not want to hear you say that again." He lowered the pen, dipped it in the ink, and peered up at his friend. "Tell me more about Damascus. How did you escape the plot?"

Paul gave a shrug of his shoulders. "They stationed spies at the city gates. Someone heard about the spies and reported it to Ananias, who then told me. He didn't know what to do, but Judah's wife—yes, I was still staying with them—said she had a large basket she used for sheep shearing. Since I've never been a very big man, the plan made sense."

"How so?"

Paul smiled weakly. "One night the believers wrapped me up and took me to the top of the city wall. While the spies watched the gates, they lowered me over the wall in Judah's wife's basket. I itched for a week afterward—all that wool—but I was able to get away from Damascus and journey to Jerusalem."

"That sounds like a good stopping point." Luke yawned. "I would stay longer, but I would be of no use to you." He gathered his materials and stood. "I must leave you now. I'll come again tomorrow night and will be well rested."

Paul lifted his hand in a mock salute. "Until then, brother. Sleep well."

"You too." Luke hesitated in the column of light, wishing he could take Paul with him. This horrible confinement hardly seemed fair. After all, if Paul was guilty of treason, then so was he.

But God had a sovereign plan for each of them, and Luke would not contest it.

———⚍———

Sha'ul stares at Stephen's bloodied face. The cloudy eyes seem to look right through him, and the lips, though motionless, appear eager to accuse him of betrayal, treachery, and murder.

The scene shifts. Sha'ul sees a younger version of himself at a wooden table, an open Torah scroll before him, his young wife grinding grain across the room. She hums a melody as Sha'ul runs his finger over the handwritten text, but his youthful face twists in horror when he realizes his finger is smearing the hand-written text with blood. Blood on his hands! Stephen's blood!

The scene evaporates, leaving him outside a small house in Jerusalem. He walks at the head of a contingent of Levites who serve as Temple guards. He steps aside as they pound on the home's wooden door while Sha'ul clenches a signed writ. He has been given permission by no less a body than the Great Sanhedrin to find and imprison any who claim to be part of the dangerous sect spreading blasphemy in Israel. Men, women, and children have fallen under the influence of the Way, and even though the false messiah is dead, his influence continues to grow.

"Open up!" one of the Temple guards cries. "In the name of the high priest!"

The guard's forceful kick slams the door open, but instead of encountering the man of the house, a woman and two children stand trembling in the doorway. One guard grabs the woman, another catches the boy, but the little girl ducks and runs away. Sha'ul whirls and follows her, finally finding the child beneath an overturned basket. He lifts the basket and jerks the girl to her feet, steeling his heart against the pleading expression in her brown eyes.

The scene changes again. This time Sha'ul stands on the well-traveled road to Damascus, a major trading center since the time of Abraham. A crowd is approaching. Without looking to the left or right, they stride forward in the blinding light—men, women, children. As before, their faces follow him no matter what he does, and their eyes remain filled with lethal calm.

Paul cannot escape their stares.

What do they want from him?

He looks away as a serpent of anxiety wraps around his chest and twists in his gut. He turns his back on the crowd and tries to think of other things—Jerusalem, his dead wife, the glory of the Temple. He shouts the names of God, evoking the power in the names—"*'El Elyon! 'El Ro'i! Yahweh-Rohi*, deliver me!" He turns, convinced he has managed to banish these somber specters, but when he looks down the road again, they remain in place. They stand perfectly still in the road, blocking his way, the light in their eyes reflecting the tide of fear in his own.

Paul swallows hard as the voices begin to buzz. Then he sees the little girl at the front of the group, her wide brown eyes focused on him. He stares back, guilt avalanching over him, as her eyes darken . . . and the scene shifts once more.

CHAPTER
NINE

The Fifteenth Day of Junius

Mauritius crossed the threshold of the Temple of Jupiter and approached the priest at the entrance. After paying the required number of sesterces, he went into the temple and knelt before the lararium. He lifted his toga to cover his head.

"Father Janus, in offering this incense to you I pray good prayers, so that you may be propitious to me and my child, to my house and to my household."

Next he poured wine into a shallow dish, the *patera*. "Father Jupiter, this cup of wine is given to you in honor of my family for the sacred feast. For the sake of this thing may you be honored by this feast offering."

He sat back on his heels and waited for the priest to bring out the sacrificial victim. As he waited, he looked around and realized he had not visited the temple in months. He had been too busy and life was too regular, blessedly uneventful. But desperate circumstances called for desperate measures, so for Caelia's sake he had promised Irenica that he would make a blood sacrifice to Jupiter.

She had been sick for seven days, and every day Irenica struggled to get water past their daughter's lips.

A moment later he heard the *clip clop* of hooves on marble. He turned and saw the priest leading a castrated bull. The animal had been washed and adorned with ribbons and strips of scarlet wool. The creature's horns were gilded, and his back was covered with a richly decorated blanket.

The priest stopped in the center of the room and bowed toward Mauritius. He stood on shaky legs, then picked up the bowl on the lararium. It was filled with *mola salsa*, roasted wheat flour mixed with salt.

Mauritius stepped over to the animal and sprinkled the creature's back with the mola salsa. When he had finished, he looked at the priest, who lifted a reproachful brow and nodded toward the wine on the lararium.

Mauritius winced in guilt. He had not made a blood sacrifice in so long that he had nearly forgotten the ritual. He went back to the lararium, picked up the patera, and poured wine on the animal's forehead. He then picked up the ceremonial knife and ran it lightly over the animal's back.

Mauritius moved back and folded his hands. What happened next would be crucial—the animal must show that it was a willing sacrifice by lowering its head. Any sign of panic or rebellion would be a bad omen, and Mauritius's prayers would not be answered.

The priest tugged downward on the rope at the animal's neck. The bovine lowered his head, greatly relieving Mauritius, and the priest was quick to draw a sharp blade across the animal's throat.

Blood spattered, and for an instant Mauritius wondered if the cut had been deep enough, but then the animal staggered and went down. Blood continued to flow, pooling around the great beast. Another priest entered to help complete the sacrifice.

Breathing in the metallic scent of blood, Mauritius pressed his lips together and prayed that the ritual would soon be over. The second priest helped the first turn the bovine onto its back. Another slice opened its belly. With the help of his assistant, the first priest examined the entrails: liver, lungs, peritoneum, and heart.

Mauritius shifted his weight, hoping the gods would not show their displeasure by fouling his sacrifice. But when the examination was done, the first priest looked at him and nodded.

Mauritius went back to the lararium and knelt. "Jupiter Dapalis, may you be honored by this feast offering, and may you remember my household and my sick daughter."

The bloodstained priest gestured toward the banquet hall, where Mauritius would be allowed to eat some of the sacrifice. Instead, he lifted his hand, thanked the priest, and walked out of the temple.

—◠◠◠—

Luke gazed upward, aware that the torchlight above was fading. The guard in the upper chamber must have fallen asleep.

He dipped his pen in a puddle of ink, then looked at Paul. "Everything in your life changed after Damascus, yet you went immediately into the desert and spent three years in Arabia. Of all places, why did you go there?"

Paul closed his eyes and smiled. "Peter and the others spent three years learning from Christ. I wanted to do the same thing. I had to learn how to pray, how to speak, and how to love."

"Were you out there looking for some sort of John the Baptist?"

Paul snorted softly. "In a way, perhaps. But I had the Holy

Spirit as my teacher. Out in the desert, Yeshua showed me how much I would suffer in His name. Just as John did. Just as Peter did."

"You were not discouraged during this time. Why?"

"How could I be discouraged? I was a slave to Christ, and since He wanted me to stay, I stayed. I needed to learn, and where better to do that than the desert where there are no distractions? HaShem trained Moses in the desert. David learned to trust HaShem while he dwelt in desert caves. While I was in the desert, Christ revealed himself to me. I had no contact with any of the disciples until after I returned to Jerusalem."

Luke lowered his pen and dared to broach a subject that had long intrigued him. "You once wrote of visiting the third heaven. What did you mean by that?"

"The first heaven is the sky," Paul said.

"And the second?"

"The second heaven is where the sun, moon, and stars dwell. The first and second heavens are visible. They are not part of the unseen world."

"The third heaven—is it not visible?"

Paul shook his head. "Yeshua came down to us from the third heaven," he answered, his voice so quiet that Luke strained to hear the words. "It is where God lives with the holy angels."

An anticipatory shiver rippled up Luke's spine. "So it is an actual place, then."

Paul nodded. "It is a real place above the earth, above the sky, above the heavens. It is the place where God rules over His creation and our lives. It is the home of departed saints. But it is not part of the visible world."

Luke blinked, then fumbled to find his pen in the darkness. He had to take complete notes of what he was hearing. "While you were there," he said, still fumbling, "did you travel in your body, or did only your soul visit that place?"

Paul gave him a sidelong glance. "I don't know. I only know I was caught up to the third heaven, but whether in the body or outside the body I don't know. God does, however. I was caught up to Paradise and heard words too sacred to tell, which a man is not permitted to utter."

"Paradise." Luke let the word hang in the silence for a moment. "Jesus spoke of Paradise. While He hung on the cross, He promised the thief next to Him that they would be together in Paradise that same day."

"The tree of life is there, in the midst of the angels." Paul's face had a look of deep concentration. Whatever he had seen, he was seeing it again. "It is a place of such beauty . . . words cannot begin to express its loveliness. When I returned to earth, my surroundings seemed"—his mouth twitched— "faded." He turned toward Luke, his eyes softening. "In six days I may visit that place again."

Luke frowned. "Do you doubt it? You, who have encouraged so many others, cannot be doubting the promises of Jesus now."

"I don't doubt Him," Paul whispered. "I doubt myself. Because I know nothing good exists in me, and I can boast only of my weakness. I have served Christ, but I have never forgotten how completely undeserving I am."

Luke lifted his small oil lamp and saw how his friend was exhausted. Moving quietly, he gathered up his notes. He had just picked up his bag when a shadow swallowed up the fading light from above.

"Prisoner!" a guard barked. "On your feet! The Greek, too!"

—⟨⟩—

Irritable and exhausted, Mauritius narrowed his gaze at the two dirty men before him. He had come to the prison after leaving the temple, thinking a few hours away from home might help clear his mind. But he had found the Greek with his prisoner again.

How many times did a physician need to visit a dying man?

He crossed his arms and stared at the two men. Paul of Tarsus looked to be in terrible condition, despite his physician's help. The Greek appeared exhausted and filthy, as well. And they both smelled of death and decay.

Mauritius studied the crooked outline of Paul's back. He gestured toward the bench in the room. "Would you like to sit?"

Paul shifted his weight. "I will stand."

"I noticed the shape of your spine," Mauritius said. "Yours is the posture of a man who has been repeatedly flogged. They say the spine bends and does not heal properly." He turned to the physician. "Am I correct?"

The Greek nodded stiffly.

Determined not to let his personal frustration affect his encounter with this prisoner, Mauritius made another effort to be pleasant. "I am sure you are aware of the responsibility I bear for the detainment of the prisoners here in this place."

Paul tilted his head. "I am well aware that to lose a prisoner means death for the man in charge."

Mauritius dipped his chin in a curt nod. "Then you understand my current concern."

The Greek looked confused, but Paul understood. "You think we are plotting an escape?"

"A man found guilty of arson and murder meets in secret with a Greek. Perhaps you are not only plotting an escape, but an uprising."

The Greek laughed. "An uprising? For what purpose?"

Mauritius was undeterred. With a smile, he said, "Vengeance. The followers of your cult are being beaten, raped, and killed. One might understand why you would seek vengeance upon those who carry out the emperor's orders."

The physician went silent, giving credence to Mauritius's words.

Paul of Tarsus lowered his head. "We are not planning an uprising. It is for the Lord's sake that we face death all day, that we are considered as sheep to be slaughtered."

"Even sheep will revolt if whipped hard enough."

A flash of fire lit the prisoner's eyes. "Prefect, do you think I have come to Rome against my will? That I am in this cell by accident? I am not."

Caught by surprise, Mauritius stared at the man. No one wanted to remain in that horrid dungeon. For some, execution was a welcome relief. Had Paul of Tarsus completely lost his senses?

No, surely not. The man seemed sharp enough when he spoke to his friend.

"I care very little about the circumstances that brought you here," Mauritius went on. "At the moment I am concerned with the documents being generated in my prison. You will turn these over to me at once. I will read them, and depending on what I find, I will determine what should be done about them." He looked at Severus, who stood yawning by the door. "Consider the Greek a threat until proven otherwise. Take the writings from his bag and leave them with me. Since he seems to enjoy visiting so much, lower him back into the cell with the preacher from Tarsus. When the sun rises, he will not leave but will remain with his friend."

Mauritius rose and thumped his desk. "I will speak to you further once I have had a chance to read what you've written."

CHAPTER
TEN

The Sixteenth Day of Junius

Aquila woke when his wife shook his shoulder. "Luke did not come home last night." Priscilla peered out the window and wrung her hands. "I went up to see if he wanted something to break his fast, but he wasn't there and his bed hadn't been slept in."

Wide awake now, Aquila sat up and ran his fingers through his hair. "He could have been detained."

She pressed a hand to her chest. "The Praetorians could be flogging him as we speak. Or he could be floating in the river like Tarquin—"

Aquila lifted his head at the sound of loud voices in the courtyard. Throwing on his tunic, he left his bed and ran to the balcony, where one look down revealed that the day had begun with another misadventure. Cassius and his young friends stood in the center of the garden, and one of them had a sword strapped to his side.

Aquila hurried down the stairs. "Have you lost your minds?" he called. "Keep your voices down!"

179

Cassius whirled to face him. "We have just gotten word—Luke has been imprisoned with Paul. He has been charged with conspiracy."

Fear blew down the back of Aquila's neck. "Conspiracy—of what sort?"

"Does it matter?" Cassius said. "Because he is a Christian, he could have been imprisoned for no reason at all. We must put a stop to this madness."

Aquila brought his hands to his temples as his head began to pound. Too much was happening, and all too quickly. He needed help, but most of these people were new Christians and too frightened to provide much assistance.

One of the older men spoke up. "Cassius speaks of revolt! He would risk our lives and the lives of those in my family. He dares to put us at risk before we have a chance to get safely out of Rome."

Cassius turned on him. "Coward! *This* is the moment to act."

"And do what?" The men turned when Octavia spoke, her hand at her throat. "What would you do, spill *more* blood on the streets of Rome? We have to wait only five more days, brothers and sisters. In five days most of us will be leaving the city."

"You are all cowards." Cassius stepped forward and met Aquila's gaze without flinching. "I have gathered brave men who are willing to storm the prison and free Luke and Paul."

"To what end, Cassius?" Aquila asked.

"We will have justice!" Cassius beat his fist in the empty air. "Think how foolish Nero will feel when he hears he has lost the man accused of burning Rome."

"But it won't happen like that," Octavia said, her voice rising above the rumbling of the men. "If you are caught, they will come here and take all of us. They will even take our children."

"Like they took Tarquin?" Cassius stepped onto a stone bench where he could command the gathering. "Listen to me! We can align ourselves with the powerful anti-Nero families to over-throw the emperor. We can bring peace to Rome when we rule."

Octavia shook her head. "Christ asked us to care for the world, not rule it. This world is not our home. The kingdom you are imagining will not be the kingdom of heaven. How could it be when it would be ruled by imperfect men?"

As the arguing grew louder, Aquila trudged upstairs to the balcony, gripped the railing, and called for silence. When the hubbub finally quieted, he took a deep breath and leaned toward them. "Listen closely, brothers and sisters. You may leave the city or you may stay, but if any of you take up arms, you have no place in this community. You should leave now."

"Oh!"

He glanced over his shoulder and saw Priscilla watching from the bedroom doorway, her face streaked with tears. "I have heard everything," she said, moving toward him. "And I understand your position. We cannot advocate violence, but what can we do about Luke?"

Aquila sighed heavily. "He is a foreigner. He has no rights in Rome."

"Perhaps all is not hopeless," Priscilla said. "I know some influential women. I will speak to them—perhaps one of them can ask her husband to help."

Aquila squeezed her arm. "Be careful. We have very little time, and we should do nothing that puts the others in danger. You know Luke would gladly forfeit his own life to get these people to safety."

She nodded and brushed wetness from her face. "I know. But I cannot help but worry. About Luke, Paul, and . . . Cassius."

"I worry about him, too." Aquila looked toward the garden again where he could see Cassius speaking with his friends. "I was greatly encouraged when Octavia stood firm in the middle of the argument. Though she has lost everything, she still spoke of the peace of Christ. Cassius, on the other hand . . . I'm not sure he has ever known it."

A tear trickled down Priscilla's cheek as she looked into the courtyard. Aquila reached out to wipe it away.

"I am sorry," she said, her voice breaking, "but I cannot stop thinking about Tarquin. That poor boy. We sent him out there, never dreaming the Praetorians would harm a child."

Aquila set his jaw. "I should have taken the letter myself."

"I could have gone."

"No." Aquila caught her hand. "We have lost so many, Priscilla. I cannot bear the thought of losing any more. Not when we are so close to leaving. I know you are torn, but you must realize we are not leaving the community. We are simply going to serve elsewhere." He forced a smile. "We'll be like Paul, spreading the good news of Christ no matter where we go."

When Priscilla turned to face him, he was startled by the depth of sadness on her face. "What is wrong, dear one?"

Fresh tears sprung to her eyes. "I pray you will be able to forgive me."

"For what?"

"Because . . . I hate to say it, but I think God may be calling us to walk different paths."

Aquila tipped his head back, as surprised as if she had slapped him.

—⟨∞⟩—

Leave Priscilla?

Aquila stumbled onto the street, desperate to be away from the house. The courtyard was too busy, the house too crowded for him to think clearly. People kept asking him to solve their problems, but none of them had considered that he might be dealing with a problem of his own.

Leave Rome without Priscilla?

Impossible. They were married, and what God had joined together, no man should break apart. They were one flesh, one heart, and, until recently, one mind.

So what had happened?

He thrust his hands behind his back and stalked down the street, his mind a hundred miles away from his surroundings. He had been ambivalent at first, uncertain of whether they should go or stay, but then Eubulus had been arrested and Caleb burned alive. How could he keep his community—most of them young believers—safe in such a city? How could he safeguard and nurture their faith when that faith was threatened with violence every day?

Even Christ had hoped to find a way out when He faced death on the cross. He had suffered through torturous hours in Gethsemane, but Aquila's people had been suffering for months . . .

He had to lead them to safety; he saw that clearly. The Spirit of God had given him a sense of certainty and determination. He was a shepherd, responsible for the sheep in his courtyard. He was also responsible for Priscilla.

If he did not love her so much, he could call her into the privacy of their bedchamber and inform her that she would have to go with him. By God's design, the man was the head of the home. Even the pagan Romans understood that much.

But Christ had opened Aquila's eyes to a new understanding.

Men and women were equal in Christ, and men were not to command their wives but to love them. To serve them, to sacrifice for them just as Christ sacrificed His life for His sheep.

"For this reason a man shall leave his father and mother and be joined to his wife, and the two shall be one flesh," Paul had explained. "This is a great mystery—but I am talking about Messiah and His community. In any case, let each of you love his own wife as himself, and let the wife respect her husband."

Would he be loving Priscilla as Christ intended if he forced her to obey his wish? Priscilla wouldn't think so. Paul wouldn't think so, either.

Aquila stopped on a street corner and studied a woman buying fruit at a market stand. She took great care in choosing the best for her family, just as he had to choose the best path for his community.

The answer was clear—they had to go. But if Priscilla felt God wanted her to stay, who was he to argue? Paul taught that wives should obey their husbands, but he also taught that in Christ there was neither Jew nor Greek, slave nor free, male nor female. They were all one in Christ Jesus.

But they were also one in marriage.

Aquila turned on the ball of his foot and went back the way he had come, moving forward with long, purposeful strides. He turned down the alley that led to his gate, then stepped inside and ran up the stairs. He found Priscilla in the kitchen, spun her around, and kissed her with the passion of a starving man.

"I know you," he said, finally releasing her. "I love you, and I know your heart aches for the Roman people. If you feel God is calling you to remain here, I will not force you to go with me. I will give you my permission and my blessing to remain, but God is calling me to get these people to safety. I will obey Him . . . though I cannot imagine living in a house if you are not in it."

Priscilla nodded, looking at her husband through tear-clotted lashes, then slid her arms around his neck and pulled him close.

—⁓—

Luke had struggled with the reversal of his days and nights since beginning his work with Paul. He found it hard to sleep in the daytime, and difficult to overcome his weariness when they talked at night.

But after spending nearly twenty-four hours in Paul's dingy cell, he realized his struggles were nothing compared to what his friend had endured. Time seemed to stand still in the underground dungeon, for the light from above rarely changed except to disappear completely on those occasions when the guard neglected to relight a torch.

"The natural tendency of the body is to sleep at night," he said, musing aloud as he tried to get comfortable on the stone floor. "But in this place the meager light is almost constant. This confuses the body, which doesn't know whether to wake or sleep, although the inclination tends toward drowsiness."

"The light is blue during the day, like now," Paul mumbled from where he lay with his head pillowed on his arms. "And golden at night. In time, you'll be able to tell the difference."

Luke glanced over at his friend. "You are awake?"

"How could I sleep with your babbling?" Paul sat up, pinched the bridge of his nose, and peered through the column of light. "Luke—it is you, right?"

"Of course it's me. Who else would keep you company down here?"

With a snort, Paul moved closer to the light.

"May I suggest something?" Luke asked.

Paul extended his hand. "Be my guest."

"If we sit back to back in the circle of light, it may be that the sun will provide some physical benefit. Something about sunlight seems to bring healing and comfort," Luke added, sliding into position. "I have found that invalids who are little exposed to sunlight soon grow pale and waste away."

"Perhaps that's why Yeshua said He is the light of the world."

"Good point, my friend." Luke felt Paul's spine press against his back. "Now, isn't this more comfortable than a stone wall?" He felt the older man give a slight nod of his head, followed by a sigh.

If Luke could provide some support for his friend, this un-expected detention would be worth it. Of course, being here without his papers would not help him finish his writing. Per-haps God did not intend for the book to be finished. Perhaps God had brought them together only to support each other during this troublesome time . . .

"I must admit," Paul said, "solitude has its virtues, but com-panionship is infinitely better."

"Indeed." Luke turned his head. "But I must say that I pre-ferred visiting you at that charming villa the governor rented the last time you were imprisoned in Rome. The Palatine area was much better situated."

Paul chuckled. "Do you ever miss traveling?"

"You cannot be serious," Luke replied. "Why would I miss clouds of dust, sand between my toes, and horrible sunburn? Oh, and there is nothing quite like the aroma of camel dung in the morning."

"Are you saying you wish we had never met?"

Luke gave a light snort. "You know, I had a great life before

I met you. I was an educated physician, reasonably wealthy, respected and sought after by women."

They both laughed.

"Yes," Luke said a moment later. "Sometimes I do miss it. The open road seeps into your blood, does it not?"

"I have always wanted to ask," Paul said, shifting his weight. "What made you become a physician in the first place?"

"I suppose I've always wanted to help people. But even more than that, I enjoy interviewing them." Luke shrugged. "That's what a physician does, you know. You talk with the patient, learn about his life, hear about his symptoms, and then try to ease his pain. Sometimes I think the most important thing a doctor does is listen."

Paul made a soft sound of agreement. "You are a good listener, and I have always been grateful for you. Your unwavering commitment kept me going on many of those cold, miserable nights in the wilderness. With you across the fire, it was easier to ignore my rumbling belly." He laughed again. "Not to mention the added benefit of those awful songs you used to sing in the middle of the night."

Luke grunted. "They were songs from my childhood. I've told you time and time again that singing helps me relax so I can go to sleep."

"The songs didn't bother me so much. Your singing, on the other hand—you sounded like Timothy's grandmother."

"I didn't know she was a singer, too."

"I'm not sure which was worse, Luke, your singing or Peter's snoring. I won't miss *that*."

"Like a herd of cattle tumbling down a mountain, wasn't it?"

They laughed at the memory, and then Paul's voice grew wistful. "Those days with you were truly wearisome, yet I do

187

miss them. The journeys we shared together. I praise God for putting you in my life, brother. I'm not sure where I would be without you."

"You would most certainly be dead," Luke said with a grin. "If the malaria had not killed you, the blood loss from the stoning would have. Patching you up has been my full-time vocation." He shook his head. "I thought you were finished on Malta. The look on your face when that viper jumped out of the brush—"

"I thought I was finished."

"Then you tossed the thing into the fire like it was nothing. No one could believe what they were seeing."

"I had to keep up appearances, even if I was about to keel over into the fire myself."

"And those islanders jumping up and down, screaming at each other when you didn't die from snakebite."

"I don't know if it was a miracle or if I ran into the stupidest snake on earth. Maybe he forgot to inject the venom when he bit me."

Paul laughed, and as the rich sound of his laughter bounced and echoed off the curved walls, Luke felt as though they had been joined by dozens of beloved friends. Nothing comforted like the sound of a friend's laughter.

Paul's elbow bit into Luke's ribs. "Are you going to write about that snake?"

"As soon as the Romans return my papers."

—∽∿∾—

Mauritius slid his cup of ale to the side, making room for the scribbled pages they had taken from the physician's bag. Publius had already gone through them, and Mauritius was eager to hear his report.

Publius smoothed out the last sheet of papyrus, then set it atop the stack. "I'm done."

"Anything incriminating?"

His friend shook his head. "It is all quite boring, really, and as messy as Zeus's toenails. But from what I can decipher, it's about a man who travels around giving lengthy speeches. The only exciting bit is about the stoning of a Jewish fellow."

Mauritius frowned. "As I told you. There's nothing about the fire."

"Unfortunate, isn't it?" Publius lifted a brow, clearly hoping for some sign of gratitude for his effort, but Mauritius remained stone-faced.

Publius folded his hands. "Forget the documents. Perhaps we can find some other sort of incriminating evidence. For instance, I have heard outrageous rumors about this man. They call him a sorcerer of the dark arts, a charmer of snakes and demons, a man who can heal with the touch of his cloak. I've even heard that the man has raised himself from the dead."

Mauritius lifted his head, his interest piqued. "Paul of Tarsus is a healer?"

"According to some. But my point is this: you don't make a man your leader because he trips and falls in the road and then travels around a bit and says some things. There must be more to the story . . . and we have only to find it." He rested his chin on his hand for a moment, then snapped his head back. "What if you could get him to confess to burning Rome?"

Mauritius blinked. "What would he possibly add to what he has already stated at his trial?"

Publius shrugged. "A man on trial will say anything to save his life. But now he has been convicted and will be executed in, what, five days? No man wants to exit the world without boasting of his glorious deeds. Appeal to his arrogance. Appeal to his desire to leave a legacy of greatness."

Mauritius reached for his cup. "You may be right. Let us drink to it."

And they did.

ELEVEN

The Seventeenth Day of Junius

The garden usually soothed Mauritius's troubled spirits, but the dawning of a new day had brought a malignant mass of dark clouds that hovered over the city. Surely a bad omen. He sat on a carved bench beneath a dying tree that stretched skeletal arms toward the somber sky. Irenica had begged him to hire a man to remove the tree, and he had been too busy to heed her request. Now he wished he had. The garden was his only escape from the combined weight of his wife's and daughter's distress, and yet today it brought no comfort or peace.

Shortly after rising, he had sent a slave with a message for Severus: he was to remove Paul of Tarsus from his dungeon, see that he was washed clean, and bring him to this garden so they could talk in more congenial surroundings. But looking at the dark skies overhead, Mauritius realized his garden would not provide the atmosphere for which he had hoped. Still, anything would be an improvement over the prison.

When Severus and the prisoner finally arrived, Mauritius noted that Paul wore a clean tunic, though an old one, and for

191

the first time in weeks he could see the man's skin without a covering layer of grime. The man's beard had been trimmed, his iron fetters replaced with simple rope. No one who saw him would realize they were seeing the infamous Paul of Tarsus, but instead would assume that an old slave was being led from the auction house to his new master.

Mauritius stood as the prisoner entered his garden, not out of respect but because he wanted to stretch his legs. He gestured to the garden path. "Will you walk with me?"

Paul followed, barely keeping up due to his halting, uneven steps.

Mauritius slowed his pace to match Paul's. "I usually come out here," he began, locking his hands behind him, "to find some measure of peace. You cannot see over these garden walls. You cannot see what has become of this great city."

He glanced at the prisoner, expecting a reply, but Paul remained silent.

"I have asked you here because I wanted to tell you something," he continued, shifting his gaze to the pathway. "I misjudged you, Paul of Tarsus. You are more a soldier than a revolutionary. You are a man with much blood on his hands."

Paul lifted his head. "You will get no argument from me, but you speak of sins from a past life. By God's grace my sins have been washed away."

"The sin of destroying Rome in the great fire? The sin of murder? Your God could 'wash away' sins as heinous as these?"

"My sins were wicked indeed—I murdered Christians. I would have killed them all, if I were able. But the blood of Christ can wash any man clean, so long as he is willing to repent."

Mauritius snapped his mouth shut, stunned by the man's bluntness. He waited to see if the prisoner would say anything else. After a brief silence, he moved on and pointed to the stack of pages on the bench where he'd been sitting. "I read your friend's writings. I realize the pages contain only rough notes, but the themes are clear: sin, grace, and mercy. Yet these philosophical scribblings tell me nothing of why these Christians look to you as their leader, or why Nero has singled you out as the chief enemy of Rome."

The corner of Paul's mouth twisted. "I think you already know we were not responsible for the fire."

"Why then would Nero bring such an accusation against you? Rumors about your powers abound in the city streets. Perhaps Nero sees these supernatural powers as a threat?"

Paul shook his head. "I have no powers."

"Are you saying the stories are not true?"

"I do not know which stories you have heard, but many of them *are* true. It is God who works with great power through His faithful ones. His followers have been known to work miracles in His name."

"What sort of miracles?"

"Extraordinary signs and wonders," Paul said. "Handkerchiefs and aprons that touched me have been taken to the sick and their illnesses cured. Evil spirits have departed from the possessed. In Troas, God used me to restore a dead man to life again after he fell from a third-story window."

"And raising yourself from the dead—this is the same type of miracle?"

Paul took a wincing breath. "If I had ever been dead, I assure you I would not be standing here."

Mauritius set that fact aside for later reference. "You have healed people, yet you don't brag about your powers."

"In all my life, I have never said such things to brag. I boast only about my weaknesses so that Christ's power will rest on me."

"Very few men admit weakness. Certainly none boast of it."

"I boast gladly, for God's power is sown in weakness."

Mauritius drew a deep, frustrated breath. This man spoke in riddles that confounded common sense. While he was not about to confess to burning Rome, he freely confessed to killing Christians. Mauritius tried appealing to the man's pride, but the prisoner seemed to have none. And a man without pride certainly harbored no arrogance.

He tried another tack. "I assume you have earned riches, land, and influence among your people? Perhaps these things have aroused Nero's jealousy."

Paul lifted his gaze to the cloud-laden horizon and stared as if he would impress the image onto the back of his eyelids. "I have never taken a single coin for my work in Christ's name. Yet God rewards me—look at that sky. Have you ever seen anything so majestic?"

Mauritius turned his back to the horizon. "Even the temple priests and priestesses earn their living in service to the gods. Why should you be any different?"

"The good news of salvation," Paul said, turning to look Mauritius in the eye, "is free. It was freely given to me, and I give it away in return."

Mauritius folded his arms across his chest and stared at the puzzling prisoner beside him. He had discovered nothing to serve as evidence against this man or his followers, and he could not appeal to human pride when the man was as humble as a servant. "You have certain powers," he started again, "but claim to have no authority of your own. You have done miraculous things, yet you do not seek to enrich yourself. You sound more like a slave than a leader."

"I am a slave . . . one who has been set free."

"We are Roman citizens," Mauritius pointed out. "We are free men."

Paul snorted softly. "All men are a slave to something. The question is—what?"

Mauritius did not respond as Paul's question scratched at his soul. Why did it bother him? He had nothing in common with this Christian, or any other for that matter.

"That Greek," he said, changing the subject. "He risked his life every time he visited. Why would he do that?"

Paul shrugged. "He is writing a book. He believes it is important that people know the certainties of my life. And not only my life, but all those who serve as emissaries of Yeshua the Messiah."

Certainties. The word seemed to hang in the thickening air, and Mauritius felt it mock him. His life had become a series of *uncertainties*, with his daughter dying and his wife furious . . .

"My daughter is sick," he said abruptly. "If I pray to your Christ, will she be healed? If you touch my cloak and I drape it over her, will she be made well?"

Paul looked at him, compassion stirring in his eyes. "I don't know. God's ways are not my ways."

"So you offer me nothing."

"I offer the truth of salvation. I have traveled many miles offering that truth to Jews and Gentiles alike."

"You complicate your life with all of this; the truth is simple. The gods give life and they take it away. In the meantime, we can only hope for their favor by honoring them." Mauritius pointed again to the papyrus sheets on the bench. "The Greek can take his pages; I see no value in them. He will be released soon."

Paul's face creased in a sudden smile. "Thank you. But before

195

I go—the Greek, Luke, is an excellent physician. His talents are unmatched."

Mauritius shook his head. "I will not anger the gods by bringing a Christian into my home." He lifted his hand. "Severus! Take this man away. Return him to the pit."

He turned and studied his garden, where a wet wind moved in the trees beneath a bruised and swollen sky.

—⁓⁓⁓—

Mauritius listened to the doctor's excuses, then followed the man as he left the room.

"Wait," he called, stopping the man in the vestibule. "Why isn't my daughter getting better?"

The doctor's face went pale when he turned and found himself face-to-face with an angry father. "There . . . there is nothing more I can do," he stammered. "The balm was . . . ineffective."

"How is it possible," Mauritius asked, glaring down at the man, "that you can do nothing more? You are supposed to be a good doctor. You are supposed to be the *best*. You certainly are the most expensive physician in Rome."

"I have spoken with others," the man said, his chin jutting forward. "No one has an answer for this condition, and your daughter is not responding to anything I have tried. I have no other ideas. You are welcome to send for another physician if you do not approve of my efforts."

"Please." Mauritius's anger faded, replaced by desperation. "Surely you can think of something else."

The doctor shook his head in dismay. "I have nothing to offer. But you can make another sacrifice. Plead to the gods for her life." He managed a tremulous smile. "Take heart, Prefect,

196

you are a *good man*. The gods can still hear you and do your bidding."

The doctor bowed and left the house, leaving Mauritius alone with his thoughts and his dying daughter.

—ɯ—

Hoping to clear his mind, Mauritius threw a mantle over his tunic and stepped outside. He walked away from his home, away from the prison, away from the responsibilities that had so often prevented his involvement with his family. He had left the responsibilities of parenthood in Irenica's hands, and she handled them well until she encountered a foe she could not charm, manipulate, or bully into obedience.

As for him, he had always enjoyed watching his daughter's life unfold. He adored baby Caelia, even though he was content to watch her from afar. And he was startled by toddling Caelia, who often looked up at him with awe in her eyes. "So big!" she used to say, rising on tiptoes in a futile effort to attain his height. He always picked her up and held her above his head, grinning while she spread her arms as if she could fly.

The girlish Caelia amazed him, especially when she came to him with questions he could not answer. "What lies beyond the Great Sea?" she once asked, studying a map of the Roman Empire. Once when they sat together in the garden, she looked up at the night sky and asked who put the stars there. "The gods," he answered, feeling foolish for not knowing more than that.

Now Caelia stood on the brink of womanhood, and his heart twisted in anguish when he realized he might never see her married, never hold her children, and never hear her gentle farewell when she stood at his deathbed. Surely the gods never meant for children to die before their parents! So why were they ignoring his impassioned pleas?

Jupiter had not answered his prayers. Bona Dea had not heard his pleas. He had offered wine, incense, and life itself—all without result.

Was no god listening to him? Were they deaf, sleeping, or simply ignoring him? Perhaps he had somehow offended a deity; perhaps he had laughed during a ceremony or accidentally drunk from a sacrificial cup of wine.

He stopped and glanced around, realizing he had walked all the way to the river, which shone like crushed diamonds in the light of the rising moon. A good place to bare one's soul.

"If I have offended you," he said, lifting his gaze to the heavens, "forgive me and hear my prayer. My prayer is not selfish—or perhaps it is, for my daughter means everything to me—but I beg you, gods above and below, to hear my prayer and act on my behalf. My wife begs you, I beg you, to hear and act for us. Show us your divine power and prove your worthiness by healing our daughter. Let her rise from her sickbed and be as she was before, beautiful, healthy, and alive!"

No one answered, and nothing moved save the rippling water.

—∽w∽—

Back in his dungeon, Paul sat in the golden glow of torchlight and finished telling the story of his encounter with the prefect. When he had finished, the physician sat with his arms folded around his bent knees and remained silent . . . and thoughtful.

"I told him you were a fine physician," Paul added, "and that your talents were unmatched. I thought he would surely ask you to see his daughter, but the man is nothing if not stubborn."

Luke shook his head. "Is he stubborn . . . or set against Christ?"

Paul shrugged. "Are they not the same thing?"

"Not always." Luke hesitated, and then the words seemed to tumble over his lips. "The first thought that entered my mind after hearing your story was that this Roman does not deserve my help. How could I do him a kindness when he and Rome have brought nothing but suffering to my brothers and sisters?" Luke shook his head. "I confess, my heart wrestles with anger, and the Spirit convicts me with each breath I draw. This is not easy for me, Paul. I know I should look at the lost people around us and feel the love and mercy of Christ flowing through me. Instead I feel rage and a desire for vengeance."

"We are human," Paul said, speaking softly. "Grace, mercy, unconditional love—these do not come naturally given our sinful state. Only through Christ's work in us can we exhibit such virtues." He smiled. "You know this prefect better than I do—"

Luke startled. "How—?"

"And better than you realize," Paul continued. "You once prayed to the gods of Greece just as he prays to the gods of Rome. Think about it—in your account of the Lord's life, why did you write so often of the poor, the outcasts, and the foreigners?"

A frown furrowed Luke's brow. "I . . . I wanted others to understand that God's kingdom is open to all. His mercy extends to everyone."

"*Exactly*. We should never forget what it was like to be lost. Or what joy it was to be found."

Luke stared at Paul a long moment, and then an inner light reached his eyes. "I will live in that joy for the rest of my life . . . and throughout eternity."

"Do not worry, brother," Paul said with a warm smile. "When

the time comes, you will be given the strength to do what is right. Because where sin abounds, grace abounds even more."

"You should get some rest," Luke said, his eyes shadowed with concern. "You have had a busy day."

"Rest?" Paul laughed as he stretched out on the gritty stone floor. "In four days I will enter my eternal rest. But until then, because I respect my doctor, I will try to get a little sleep."

—◆—

In the privacy of his household shrine, Mauritius knelt before a wall filled with the masks of his glorious ancestors. The lararium stood before him, equipped with all the essential tools: an offering of incense burning in the *turibulum*, a heaping portion of salt in the *salinum*, fine wine in the *gutus*, and a flickering oil lamp. In addition, he had commanded a slave to heap sweet cakes on the patera as a special offering.

Everything was intended as a sacrifice to whatever god would answer his prayers. Whoever did his bidding and healed his daughter would have Mauritius's devotion for life.

He had been on his knees for a quarter hour, according to the water clock, and he had received no insight, seen no sign, felt no caress of wind on his cheek. "Are you even there?" he asked, even as his blood ran thick with guilt for the audacity of the question. He knew it was foolhardy to question what every Roman understood to be true, but *why* had none of the gods acted on his behalf? He had done everything a man could do; he had followed every ritual and spent a fortune on sacrifices, salves, physicians, and priests. So why had nothing worked?

He opened his eyes when he inhaled the scent of Irenica's perfume. A moment later he heard the swish of her gown and saw her shadow on the candlelit wall.

"You missed the doctor," he said, his voice flat.

"You told me I should get out for fresh air," she answered. "So I got out."

"Where could you go at this hour?"

She did not answer him, and Mauritius was glad she remained silent. Many wealthy Roman women, especially if they felt slighted by their husbands, visited captive gladiators at night. If Irenica had been at a *ludus*, he did not wish to know about it.

She remained behind him, and Mauritius did not turn, having no particular desire to see her. "There is nothing more the doctor can do." He turned the catch in his voice into a cough and went on. "He will not come here again."

"I am not surprised. She has been sick and silent for nine days now."

Mauritius stood, taking a last look at the masks, the candles, the many sacrifices. "We have things to say . . . but we should not speak here."

"Do you fear the gods will hear your true thoughts?" She threw the words at him. "You have accused me of angering the gods by my vanity. But what of you?"

"Me?"

"I have heard gossip among the wives of the guards. They say you treat this man from Tarsus with gentleness and sympathy. He spits in the face of Rome, and you are kind to him!"

"The man from Tarsus is a Roman citizen," Mauritius explained, struggling to remain calm. "If I have demonstrated any degree of kindness, it springs from the fact that, as a citizen, he is entitled to respect."

"From what springs the kindness of harboring a Greek Christian against the direct orders of your emperor? You should be tried and executed for conspiracy, yet you think *I* have angered the gods?"

Mauritius clenched his fist. "I harbor the Greek doctor because Nero wants Paul of Tarsus healthy enough to be executed in four days!"

"Your daughter is dying and you dare dishonor the gods by your actions. *You* are the one to blame for their disapproval of our offerings. You are to blame for her illness! She does not get better because you show mercy instead of justice to those who are traitors against Rome!"

Mauritius turned away, finding more comfort in the lifeless masks of his ancestors than the anguished countenance of his wife.

"All these years," she continued, the sound of tears in her voice, "you have been busy in the service of the emperor. I remained loyal to you while you were occupied elsewhere, but did you never realize how lonely I was? You don't think I was starving for attention? I had nothing to occupy my time. Nothing." She sniffed. "Then Caelia was born—my precious baby girl. She was my joy, my life while your attention was elsewhere. With her in my life, I knew I would never feel such utter loneliness again, no matter what happened to you. But now loneliness stands again at my door because you refuse to consider your selfish ways."

"*This*," Mauritius seethed, rancor sharpening his voice, "is not my fault."

"It is all your fault!" Irenica shouted. "By witness of all the gods I say her death will be on your head!"

"My head? Have I left our sick child to seek pleasure in the arms of a stranger? Have I lowered myself to pay—?"

"At least," she interrupted, her eyes narrowing, "I spent this night with a Roman and not a Christian or a Greek!"

A surge of rage hit him, a white-hot bolt of lightning that slammed into his chest and blinded him. He lunged toward Irenica, felt his hands encircle her throat, and drove her to the wall where he held her in his grasp like a mortal enemy. With one effort, one sharp twist and jerk, he could snap her neck and end her accusations forever—

"Do it," she said, struggling to breathe beneath his strangling grip. "Save me the trouble for when she dies."

Struck by the desperation in her words, Mauritius released her and backed away, shaken by the depth of his own anger. Irenica slid down the wall and crumpled onto the tile floor, her shoulders shaking in silent sobs.

And in that moment Mauritius realized he was about to lose everything—his daughter, his wife, his position. Perhaps even his life, if he somehow botched the Christian's execution.

He turned on the ball of his foot and left the house.

CHAPTER

TWELVE

The Eighteenth Day of Junius

Cassius stepped into the crowded inn, then caught the inn-keeper's eye. He lifted a brow, and the innkeeper responded by jerking his head toward a small room he reserved for choice customers—or anyone who could pay the required amount.

Cassius lifted the bag he carried and made his way to the room, dodging drunks and the slaves serving drinks. A dingy curtain hung over the doorway, and when he pushed it aside he saw four of his friends, three of them from Aquila's house. They looked up as he entered, their eyes lighting with anticipation.

"Did you get them?" Alban asked.

Cassius nodded. "The finest blades a fat purse can buy."

Nuncio shook his head in pleased surprise. "But where did you get the fat purse?"

Cassius grinned. "Not all who wish to be rid of Nero are poor. Some are wealthy . . . and wish to remain anonymous."

Lichas's eyes widened. "Are they Christians?"

"No, but they support our cause. They believe that our fighting to release Paul and Luke from prison will give others the courage to rise up against Nero. More than one person has mentioned Spartacus—if he could encourage the slaves to rebel, they believe we can encourage the Christians to take a stand against injustice."

"Aye, wouldn't that be something?" Proteus, a grizzled retired veteran, looked up and grinned, his one eye gleaming. "Spartacus defeated the Praetorians and two legions, and all he wanted was for his men to return to their homes."

"Surely we can do more," Cassius said. "Our numbers are increasing every day. With God on our side, we can defeat Nero and take back the city. This place has been filled with evil long enough—it is time to hand it over to those who would do good in the name of Christ."

Nuncio opened his mouth as if to shout, but Cassius held up his hand, reminding his comrades that they must remain quiet. "I know you have risked your lives by venturing out after dark," he whispered, "and you will risk your lives again in this fight. But if we are successful, all of us will be heroes, and the movement to take Rome will begin."

"So," Proteus said, "let us see what you've brought."

Cassius set his bag on the table and opened it. From the bag, he and his men drew weapons—heavy steel swords, iron daggers, and short, blunt sticks of wood. Proteus unsheathed a short blade, unwrapped its leather sheath, and ran his finger along its edge. He lifted his hand, revealing a thin line of blood in his flesh. "Quality craftsmanship." He smiled soberly. "I'd say we are ready."

Cassius nodded. He crossed his arms and looked around the circle of men. "Each of you take a smaller weapon and conceal it on your person—that is in case you are disarmed. Then take a sword and hide it within the folds of your cloak."

He waited until every man had armed himself, then lifted his chin. "Yes, we are ready. It is time."

As one, the men followed Cassius through the crowded inn and out into the night.

---~~~---

Cassius lifted his hand, stopping the men a block from Nero's prison. "All right," he whispered, turning to face them. "Do we need to go over the plan again?"

Proteus grunted. "You and I wait until the guard comes out to meet his replacement, then we take him before the prison door closes."

"You cannot let the door close," Cassius said. "It opens from the inside only, so the plan is ruined if we do not catch that door."

"And after that?" Nuncio asked.

"The three of you keep watch outside the main entry while we get Paul and Luke," Cassius answered. "Once we have them, we will come out the same door to meet you. Then we split up. Nuncio and Alban will give Paul and Luke their cloaks in case someone recognizes them."

"What if there is trouble at the city gate?" Proteus asked. "Some of the Praetorians might know Paul on sight, especially if they were at the trial."

"We can handle them." Cassius rested his hand on the hilt of his sword. "We will do whatever we have to in order to escort Paul and Luke out of the city. Once they are safe, we'll come back and give Aquila and the others the good news. They won't be in such a hurry to leave Rome once they have seen what we can accomplish." He paused to scan the group of men. "Any questions?" When no one spoke, he lifted his fist and nodded.

The five men spread out, creating a circle around the prison building. Alban, Nuncio, and Lichas took up positions near the main entry while Cassius and Proteus waited near the vine-covered doorway Eubulus had described to Aquila.

Cassius ran his hand over his tunic, comforted by the weight of the steel dagger he had hidden beneath the short sleeve. A thrill of fear shot through him at the thought of using it. That fear would quickly turn to exaltation if they accomplished their goal.

"There." Proteus inclined his head toward the hidden entrance. The overhanging vines moved as the door opened. A Praetorian emerged and kicked a rock between the door and its threshold.

Time to act.

Cassius drew a breath and stepped out of the shadows. "You there," he called, smiling as he hurried forward.

The Praetorian stiffened and reached for his sword. "Halt! Come no closer."

"I'm afraid I have lost my way," Cassius said, feigning an expression of helplessness. "If you could point me toward the Forum—"

At that instant Proteus stepped out from behind a column, startling the guard. When the Praetorian whirled to confront Proteus, Cassius pulled the dagger from his sleeve and thrust it between the guard's ribs and twisted it.

Proteus clapped his hand over the wounded man's mouth to smother his cry, then supported the man as he collapsed to the ground.

"Where's his replacement?" Cassius said, glancing around.

"No time to worry about him." Proteus grabbed hold of the man's arms, and together he and Cassius dragged the guard into the prison and closed the door.

"Balbus?" a voice called from around a corner. "I can't believe you're on time for once."

Proteus held his finger over his lips, hiding himself in a nearby shadow.

"Balbus?"

Cassius pressed himself against the wall as the second guard approached. The Praetorian drew his sword when he spied Proteus. "Who are you, and how did you get in here?"

Proteus grinned as Cassius attacked from behind and cut the man's throat.

With both guards lying motionless on the floor, Cassius and Proteus hurried forward to rescue Luke and Paul.

Luke had just entered a shallow doze when noise from above startled him back to wakefulness. He glanced over at Paul, who had begun to snore. "Paul! Did you hear something?"

Paul's eyes flew open just as two silhouetted figures appeared in the round opening above their heads. "Luke! Are you down there?"

Luke recognized the voice. Cassius.

"Quickly," Cassius called. "We'll throw down the rope and pull you up."

Paul looked at Luke, his brows lifting. "Did you know about this?"

"Of course not."

The thick rope fell through the opening, its knotted length landing between Paul and Luke.

"Come!" Cassius said, urgency in his voice. "We do not have much time."

Luke squinted up at the opening. "Did Aquila send you?"

"We come in the name of Christ," Cassius answered.

"Have you hurt anyone?" Paul asked.

"Two dead." Cassius's voice vibrated with thinly veiled pride. "We handled them easily."

Paul frowned as he pushed himself into a standing position. "You would bring violence against the emperor's guards in the name of Christ? You would commit murder in His holy name?"

"Have they not murdered us?" Cassius knelt at the edge of the opening and peered into the dungeon. "The moment we have been waiting for has come. It is time to overthrow this cursed power and return Rome to the people."

"By whose authority do you think Rome *has* power?" Paul asked. "All powers are ordained of God."

Cassius gaped at him a moment, then laughed. "The foul air down there has addled your brain. Nero's evil has nothing to do with God."

Paul glanced at Luke and shook his head. "God is more powerful than Nero. If He wanted Nero out of the way, He would do so."

"He *is*, don't you see? We are going to remove him!"

Luke moved to Paul's side. "I understand the anger you feel, Cassius, but you must trust us—this is not the way. God will bring good even out of Nero's evil. Light will shine even in this darkness."

The young man's voice rose in anger. "If you do not come with us, you will die here and your cause will die with you."

"No, Cassius," Paul said. "Christ has already triumphed over every enemy. You say you come in His name, but it is clear you do not know Him."

In the glow of the torchlight above, Cassius's face flushed.

The ambitious young man would not forgive this . . . and he would never understand.

The older man with Cassius tugged at his sleeve. "We have to go, *now*. We are out of time." He pulled Cassius away.

Then Luke heard a distant door slam. "Two guards dead," he murmured, turning to Paul. "I am sorry for it."

"Hmm." Paul sighed and sank back to the floor. "And we will pay the price for it, no doubt. I would willingly bear the blame if I thought it might bring that man to a place of understanding."

Luke lay back down, resting his head on his hands, but he could not sleep. His thoughts followed Cassius and his companion out into the night. Where would they go? Did they have another plan to incite violence, or would this be the end of their destructive foolishness?

"By the way," Paul said.

"Yes?"

"That part about the light shining in darkness—that was very good."

Luke smiled. "Perhaps I will write it down."

—— ∽∾ ——

Mauritius walked on, his cloak blowing in the wind, the hood pressing against his face, but he did not lift his hand to move it. He walked through the bustling market, past the Temple of Jupiter, through the old gate at the Servian Wall. He walked because he could not remain in his home with an angry wife, a dying daughter, and unresponsive gods. He walked because, as long as he was not home to receive news to the contrary, Caelia still lived.

He did not intend to walk to the prison, but his feet obeyed his regular habit and took him to the place he knew best. He found himself approaching the front door, but rather than advertise that he could not go home, he went around to the side entrance . . . and his pulse quickened when he spotted blood on the paving stones. Immediately he pulled his dagger and moved to the door. It was closed and locked from the inside, as it should have been.

He turned at the sound of footsteps. Euphorbus, the guard scheduled to take the midnight shift, slowed when he saw Mauritius. "Where is—?" he began, but Mauritius silenced him with a swift motion.

Together they went to the front entrance and entered the building. Mauritius looked around, confused by the chamber's ordinary appearance. He gestured to Euphorbus, sending him to check the side door while Mauritius moved to the circular opening and stared into the dungeon below. In the dim circle of light he beheld two figures—sleeping men, by the look of it, though someone might have arranged blankets to look like two bodies—

"Prefect! Over here!"

Mauritius ran forward. There, beside the side door, two Praetorians lay in puddles of blood. He swallowed the lump that had risen in his throat and reached for a torch to survey the scene. He saw nothing out of place, nothing the murderers might have left behind.

Cold sweat broke out on his forehead as he moved toward the dungeon. His pulse quickened when he saw that the rope had been lowered; even now it dangled from the iron hasp in the floor. So his prisoners *had* escaped, and the decoys below were intended to fool a casual observer. A sense of dread shot through him.

If Paul and Luke had escaped, he might as well fall on his own sword, for Nero did not forgive Praetorians who allowed condemned prisoners to vanish, especially those who were as well known as Paul of Tarsus.

He brought the torch closer to the round opening and again peered down at the evidence of his failure, then blinked when he saw movement in the pit. One of the decoys moved, but how could it?

"Euphorbus!"

"Prefect?"

"Descend at once and tell me what you find down there."

Euphorbus's brows wrinkled, but within a moment he was on the rope, carefully sliding his body over the knots, his face twisting in disgust as he lowered himself to the chamber below.

When he reached the bottom, one of the figures sat up and spoke. "Anything wrong, Euphorbus?"

Mauritius felt his stomach sway when he recognized the voice. It was the prisoner, Paul of Tarsus.

—m—

Mauritius sat behind his desk and stared at the prisoners. When he first heard Paul speak, he had been convinced he was seeing an apparition. Yet the men before him were undoubtedly flesh and blood. He did not understand how or why Paul and Luke remained in his prison, but here they were, reeking of filth and as unkempt as they had been when he last saw them.

"So *this*," Mauritius said, not willing for them to see how the events of the last hour had shaken him, "is how my kindness is repaid. Nero's prison is attacked, and two of my guards killed. If I had not come along when I did, you might have been killed, as well."

"Or we might have escaped," the physician pointed out. "But we did not."

"Some people are tempted to take justice into their own hands," Paul said, tugging casually at his beard. "But we had nothing to do with what happened here."

Luke cleared this throat. "It might interest you to know that this is at least the second time Paul has not escaped when given the opportunity. Once, he and his companion Silas were singing hymns to God in prison—"

"In Philippi," Paul interrupted. "You probably know of it, since it is a Roman colony."

"I know it and I care nothing about it!" Mauritius snapped.

Luke shot Paul an irritated glance and continued, "After they had been singing, an earthquake shook the prison doors open. Everyone's fetters fell off."

Mauritius blinked. "Impossible."

"No, no, it happened," Luke said. "The jailer—a lowly man, not an exalted prefect like yourself—was about to kill himself, supposing that all the prisoners had fled. But Paul shouted to him, 'Don't harm yourself! We are all here!' and prevented a tragedy."

Mauritius looked from the Greek to Paul of Tarsus. "I have never heard of an earthquake that could remove a prisoner's chains."

Luke gave him a beatific smile. "Amazing, isn't it? The jailer was so impressed that he called for lights and went down into the dungeon to make sure his prisoners were all present. When he saw they were, he fell on his knees before Paul and Silas and asked, 'Sirs, what must I do to be saved?' And Paul answered, 'Put your trust in the Lord Yeshua and you will be saved—you and your household.'"

Mauritius held up a hand. "That is enough. I can assure you that I am not about to fall to my knees in front of either of you. Neither am I going to call on your Lord Yashiva—"

214

"Yeshua," Paul corrected. "The Messiah."

"—and neither am I going to let you change the subject. No earthquake occurred here tonight, but two men broke into the prison and murdered two of my Praetorians. Now." Mauritius lifted a brow. "You take no responsibility for this?"

"As I said, we had nothing to do—"

"If we *were* responsible," Luke added, "would we be standing in front of you now? Would you not be under guard in Nero's palace, facing his wrath for allowing us to escape?"

Mauritius pressed his lips together. For foreigners, these men knew entirely too much about how the Roman Empire operated. "You seem to know a great deal about our emperor, but you have displayed remarkable ignorance. Your crime against Rome had nothing to do with violence or murder or theft. Yours was a crime of *words*—words meant to defy Nero and the empire. Yet here you stand, still spouting arrogant words."

"Is that how you see it?" Paul said. He looked up, and their eyes met. "I seem to recall being sentenced to die for arson and murder."

Mauritius sputtered, unable to think under the man's steady scrutiny "Yes, of course. That was what the indictment said. But you and I both know"—he lowered his voice—"that you have been in and out of prison for years, not because of what you *did* but because of what you espouse. You urge people to serve your Christ, not the emperor of Rome. You preach, telling them to worship only one God. Yet people are *dying* because of your insistence on this one God."

"I tell people the truth," Paul replied, "and urge them to pray for kings and all who are in authority, so that we may live a peaceful and quiet life in all godliness and respectfulness."

"How can you not see that even with these words now, you

are spitting in the face of the emperor?" Mauritius said. "By such words alone you defy Rome itself. But words cannot destroy empires."

"If our words seem a threat," Paul said, "perhaps it is because they are not mere words. They are truth."

"You keep saying 'truth,' but it is only a truth according to you. If it were the only truth, everyone would believe it."

Luke shook his head. "Not so, Prefect. Christ, who *is* Truth, rose from the dead and yet many do not believe."

"Perhaps they recognize a fabrication for what it is."

Paul smiled. "If Christ has not been raised from the dead, our preaching and our faith are useless."

"And you would sacrifice your life for a useless fiction?" Mauritius rested his arms on his desk. "You harbor no uncertainties at all?"

Paul's smile broadened. "You have seen many things in your time of service to Rome. You have witnessed many executions. So consider this, Prefect, and tell me if it is true: do men die for things they doubt?"

Mauritius turned away, his mind burning with the memory of the evocatus, Jove. The man could easily have pretended to sacrifice to Vesta; he could have hidden his infatuation with this new deity. But he did not. Instead, he was confident in his assertion and willing to die for his conviction that Jesus the Christ was the only living God.

Still, this man Paul could not be right. "You claim you serve a God who is above all other gods, and yet all I see before me is an old man in chains," he said, turning to face the prisoner directly. "The record of your life will be a litany of beatings and filthy prison cells."

Paul hung his head. "I deserve worse. My hands have been

stained with the blood of innocents. My heart has been empty and cold. I once denied Christ every day, and every word on my lips was blasphemy. But Yeshua extends grace to everyone who comes to Him."

"What is this *grace*, and why should a man want it?" Mauritius blew out a breath. "Men want to be rich, not poor. To be powerful, not weak. To have slaves and not be one. These are the things man lives for."

"Do you really believe that?" Luke chuckled. "The next time you walk the streets of Rome, look around, Prefect, and test what you believe. Look at the men with riches and power, then peer behind the façade. Behind the wealth, behind the social standing, you will find men who are miserable, lost, searching for meaning . . . just as you are."

Euphorbus stepped forward, his fist clenched. "Watch your tongue, Greek."

Mauritius stared, unable to shake a feeling that the Greek had looked into his soul. How could the man know that his home, which might appear perfect to a casual observer, was filled with strife, anger, and distress? Caelia's illness and Irenica's anguish were only symptoms of a family who did not know how to live together in peace . . .

"It does not take an intelligent man," Paul added, "to look around and know this world is missing something."

Mauritius stood and narrowed his gaze, determined that these Christians would not examine his soul further. "I am missing nothing," he said, stepping from behind his desk. "Rome has given me everything."

The Greek met his gaze boldly. "What about the love a father feels for his sick daughter?" he asked. "What has Rome offered to ease *that* pain?"

Mauritius's anger, successfully held back a few minutes before, spurred him to punch the physician in the face. As Luke recovered, Mauritius drew his sword and held the blade to the physician's throat. "Another word and I will send you to whatever god you name."

Luke remained perfectly still, not daring to breathe. Mauritius waited until he was certain the Greek would not speak again, then thrust his blade back into its scabbard. "You are right," he said with a sigh, moving toward the window. "My daughter, Caelia, is dying and no one knows why. And the gods . . . they do not answer me."

"There is another way."

Mauritius turned and glared at the old man with burning, reproachful eyes. "You spin your tales of this Christ, but your religion is nothing but a fool's crutch—mindless sentimentality for the weak and the poor, tales to make their pathetic lives endurable until they are buried and forgotten."

He returned to the window where the first pale hints of sunrise had brightened the sill. In two days, at another sunrise, he would lead Paul of Tarsus out to the execution block. The thought of sending the old man to his death brought Mauritius a surge of dark pleasure . . . but then cold, clear reality swept over him in a chilling wave.

Irenica was right. He had been too gentle, too accommodating with these Christians. His attempt to cleanse the Praetorian Guard was only a token effort, especially since he had treated Paul of Tarsus with unmerited tolerance. He had been far too deferential. By allowing the Greek to visit his prisoner, he had demonstrated compassion and pity for foreigners who denied the gods of Rome.

Comprehension seeped through his despair. "Ah," he said,

sensing the truth all at once, "I understand now! My own deceit has angered the gods so much that they refused to heal Caelia."

Luke frowned. "What?"

Mauritius motioned to Euphorbus. "Put the Greek in the holding cell until the cart arrives. Then take him to the Circus so he can die for the enjoyment of my gods—and they can grant me this favor for my daughter's sake."

Euphorbus grabbed Luke's arm and jerked his head toward the door. "Let's go, Greek."

Paul looked from Luke to Mauritius. "You promised to release him!"

"That was before two of my guards were found murdered."

"But we had nothing to do with it. This—this is not the answer, Prefect."

Mauritius gave him a grim smile. "You should have escaped when you had the chance."

The aged apostle turned toward his friend. "Luke! Be strong and of good courage! Fear not, my friend . . ."

Luke followed the guard without complaint. Paul watched them approach the door, then turned pleading eyes on Mauritius. "Prefect, don't do this."

Luke sent a smile winging over his shoulder. "Do not worry. God will make this good, brother."

Mauritius waited until Luke disappeared through the door before turning to Paul. "Now you will see how Rome treats its enemies." He stepped forward, pulled his sword, and slammed the hilt against the side of Paul's head.

The aged apostle went down without a word, and he did not speak again.

CHAPTER
THIRTEEN

Slowly, Paul swam up from unconsciousness, clawing his way through a confusing fog until he reached wakefulness. He lay on stone, hard and cold, and struggled to open his eyes.

He discovered that he was on the stone floor of his cell, his body bent, his head throbbing. The knotted rope had been tied around his waist, so the guards must have lowered him like a sack of rocks . . . and dropped him from a convenient height. Why take pains with a prisoner who would die in two days?

He tried to lift his head, then flinched at a sharp pain near the back of his skull. Resigned to lie where he was, he closed his eyes and breathed in the familiar stench, felt his empty stomach recoil, and sighed beneath the weighty oppression of loneliness.

Alone.

Luke had been taken away. He was probably at the Circus Maximus by now, crowded into a holding cell with other Christians who would be killed for Nero's entertainment. They might be crucified, burned to death with boiling tar, or used as prey for exotic wild animals. But at least they would not die alone. At least they had each other.

"Help me, Yeshua," he whispered, his dry tongue sticking to the roof of his mouth. "You called me as your emissary to the Gentiles, and so I have been. I have met them in Galatia, Troas, Ephesus, Lystra, Salamis, Antioch, Athens, and Pontus. I have spoken to them in homes, inns, on mountains and in pastures. I have listened to them in synagogues and temples. I have heard so many words that at times my ears buzzed with exhaustion.

"But now no one is with me, and the only eyes I see belong to a rat.

"Help me finish the race, Yeshua. I cannot do this without you."

—◌◌◌—

Priscilla lay on her bed, soaking her pillow with tears. She had been weeping since receiving the news, and she could not stop weeping. The news of Luke's transfer from the dungeon to the Circus had dashed her last hope.

Aquila entered and sat on the edge of the bed, his hands by his sides as he stared at nothing. "Cassius and those with him have disappeared," he finally said. "The entire city is on alert. The Praetorians are everywhere."

Priscilla burst into fresh tears, reminded again that men from their community had murdered two guards. "How," she sobbed, "could they take such a risk when our community's departure date is so close?"

Aquila shook his head. "They are confused and selfish men with their own ambitions. I do not expect them to return to us. They are probably already outside of Rome . . . unless they are hiding in hopes of attracting others to their cause."

Sniffing, Priscilla sat up and hugged her bent knees. "I cannot believe Luke is to die tomorrow. I . . . I cannot bear the thought of losing him *and* Paul."

Aquila nodded, his expression morose.

"I only wanted to help this city," Priscilla went on. "But now the stench of death hangs over this place. I used to think Rome glorious, but the glory is gone. Nothing remains here but anger, madness, and evil."

When she reached for a linen handkerchief, Aquila drew her into his arms. "How many more would have died without you, love? Rome will never be completely dark so long as you are here."

They held each other for a moment, and then Priscilla lifted her head. "My heart breaks for the people who cannot leave. For the widows and orphans. I know I cannot help everyone, but Christ asked us to try."

"I know," Aquila whispered.

"I *do* want to stay in Rome, husband." She looked up at him. "But we are stronger together. Where you go, I will go. It is what I promised you when we wed." She pressed her fingertips to his cheek. "When and where you are Gaius, I then and there am Gaia."

"I remember," Aquila said, smiling. "How could I forget? We were married here, in Rome."

"And in Rome I will stay," Priscilla answered, "until you lead me elsewhere."

—⟊⟊⟊—

Luke stepped from the prison cart into an off-loading area at the Circus Maximus, a U-shaped arena that regularly drew thousands of Roman spectators to its contests. Six hundred years earlier, the stone structure had been built for horse racing, but in subsequent centuries the arena was adapted for entertainment featuring gladiators, wild animals, and other athletes. One hundred fifty thousand people could find seats in the stands, and as many as two hundred fifty thousand could watch from the windows of homes and palaces on the Aventine and Palatine Hills.

The sounds of hammers and chisels filled the air as a pair of guards led Luke along a row of shops that encircled the track. Cooks, astrologers, prostitutes, jewelers, and metalworkers all sold their goods or provided services at the Circus. According to reports, the great fire of Rome had begun in these shops.

A wry thought twisted Luke's mouth as he walked between his guards: Christians had little to do with astrologers, prostitutes, or the metalworkers who created images of the Roman gods, so how could anyone believe it was they, Christians, who had started the fire? But reason and logic did not hold much weight when a populace was emotionally overwrought. Nero's anger had fanned the flames of illogic, and the people of the Way were paying the price.

Still, God could bring good even out of this.

Most of the Circus shops had since been rebuilt, though some appeared to be undergoing renovation still. Luke did not have time to peruse the many markets in which Romans could spend their sesterces, for within moments his guards pushed him down a flight of stone steps. Beneath the main concourse, he saw large cages that had obviously been designed to hold beasts of prey but were now filled with men, women, and children, a few of whom he recognized from Aquila's house.

They were *his* people, his brothers and sisters.

Luke's eyes misted as he studied them—nearly thirty, by his count, and all of them looking at him with fear on their faces. Some must have recognized him, for they pointed and whispered to their companions.

"I know you," one of the men called. "You have traveled with Paul. You are Luke, the physician."

Luke said nothing as a guard shoved him into a cell, then locked the iron door.

"Is it true?" a woman in another cell asked when the guards had left. She pressed her face to the bars. "Are you Luke?"

He nodded. "I am."

"Then you have been with Paul," she answered, hope lighting her eyes. "And we all know how Paul worked miracles."

"When it was God's will," Luke answered. "And at this same hour, Paul sits in the dungeon where God has led him."

The flicker of hope faded from her expression.

"Do you know what will happen to us?" another man asked. "They tell us nothing in here."

Luke swallowed hard. "When I climbed out of the wagon, I saw charioteers preparing for races today."

"We heard them." A woman nodded. "The sound of horses pouring into the stadium."

"Tomorrow those horses and drivers will rest." Luke hesitated. "Tomorrow there will be . . . other entertainments. For Nero."

The room erupted into terrified cries. Women pulled their children close and began sobbing while men went pale and silent. Fear dominated the room like a thick fog, and Luke knew he had to say something. But what?

The truth. He could only offer the truth . . . in love.

"Do not be afraid," he said, his gaze settling on the face of a young girl. "There will be pain, but it will last only a moment. And then we will be home in the presence of Christ. I am certain of this truth."

The little girl looked up into his eyes. "You promise?"

He bent, hands on his knees, to her level. "In the name of Jesus, I promise that you will be all right." He smiled at her, then straightened to face the others. "I don't know what you are feeling, brothers and sisters, but I can tell you this—in the past few days I have struggled with my emotions. In my heart I felt there should be revenge for the crimes Rome has committed against those of us who believe in Jesus the Christ. But there is only one way—only one *righteous* way—we can respond to this. Remember what Christ said while on the cross: 'Forgive them, for they do not know what they are doing.'"

"You want us to forgive the Romans who will watch us—out there?" a woman cried.

"It will not be easy." Luke turned until he spotted the woman's anguished face. "Forgiveness always comes at a price, and it is never easy. But Christ gave His life to pay for our sins, and we were just as lost as the Romans 'out there' filling the arena. He paid the price for us . . . and tomorrow we will be able to forgive the Romans because He forgave us."

A man in a nearby cage stepped forward, his knuckles turning white as he gripped the iron bars. "I don't fear for myself, but my children are with me, and my wife. How can I watch—?"

"Do what the Spirit of Christ leads you to do," Luke said. "Be an example of the believer in your speech, conduct, and love. Many Romans have been watching to see how we Christians live. Let us show them how we die."

He looked at the people who watched and waited, looking to him for comfort. "Do not fear what you are about to suffer," he said, softening his voice. "Be faithful until death, and Jesus will give you the crown of life."

One by one, they turned to their loved ones—husbands, wives, children, and friends. Though stained with fatigue and stress, their faces seemed to glow in the shadows of the subterranean chamber as they drew their loved ones close.

Luke sank to his knees in the straw. "Christ taught us to pray, so let us pray together." He clasped his hands and waited as the others knelt with him. "'Our Father in heaven,'" he began, "'sanctified be your name. Your kingdom come, your will be done on earth as it is in heaven.'"

—◊—

In the dark pit of the dungeon, Paul knelt and lifted his voice: "'Give us this day our daily bread. And forgive us our debts as we also have forgiven our debtors.'"

—◊—

In the courtyard of Aquila and Priscilla's house, the small band of believers prayed in unison: "'And lead us not into temptation, but deliver us from the evil one.'"

—◊—

"'For yours,'" Luke prayed, "'is the kingdom and the power and the glory, forever. Amen.'"

When he lifted his head, Luke beheld the same faces, but all traces of fear had vanished. They were sober and flushed with emotion, but instead of uncertainty he beheld assurance—a holy confidence.

"God is good," Luke said, settling down in the straw. "And He is with us."

—◊—

Mauritius stood in the Temple of Jupiter, his hands deep in a bowl of warm blood, his spirit soaring. Surely *this* sacrifice would result in the desired effect. He had sent the Greek to die and confirmed the Jew's execution, so no one, not even Irenica, could accuse him of being soft on blasphemous Christians.

The priest stepped forward and inclined his head. "The signs are favorable. The internal organs are clear."

"Ah. Good."

Mauritius dipped his hands in a basin of clean water and reached for a towel. "Thank you," he said, drying his hands. He pressed two gold coins into the priest's palm. "Here. Thank you again."

Smiling in the calm strength of knowledge, he strode out of the temple and walked toward his villa. Perhaps Caelia would be sitting up when he returned, the glow of health restored to her cheeks. Tomorrow they would laugh at the memory of her illness, and he could confess that he had been blind not to see the truth at once. Irenica would be happy he had finally righted the situation. Tomorrow afternoon, after the games, Nero would hear of the Greek physician's death and be pleased. All would be as it should be, and Mauritius's charmed life would be restored.

He resisted the urge to whistle a jaunty melody. He could not be overconfident, for the gods had a tendency to punish those who took them for granted, but with pulse-pounding certainty he knew he had done the right thing. Soon the entire world would know that Fortuna was again smiling on his household.

He turned the corner, his smile broadening in approval at the sight of his villa. He sighed out of an overflow of good feeling and nodded at a neighbor who stared at him, apparently baffled by Mauritius's obviously cheerful mood.

He had just entered his gate when the front door opened and Irenica's handmaid ran toward him. "Dominus! Come quickly!"

Mauritius's grin froze. The woman was undoubtedly bringing good news, so why wasn't she smiling? Her countenance was tense with alarm, her steps unnaturally quick . . .

"Dominus," she called hoarsely, breathing hard, "you must come at once. Your daughter's life is slipping away!"

He looked at her hands and saw blood.

Surprise siphoned the air from his lungs. He spurred his feet into action and ran to his daughter's bedchamber.

—⚊ꙮ⚊—

Mauritius's wide eyes took in the sickroom with one horrified glance. His daughter lay on the bed, pale and still, while blood drenched the sheets and a profusion of wadded towels. Irenica, her arms and hands stained red, regarded him with panic in her eyes. For an instant he thought she would berate him for some misstep, but he saw nothing in her expression but frantic entreaty.

"She started coughing," she whispered, her voice in tatters. "Then coughing up blood. Please, husband, save her. I cannot lose her. Whatever you must do, do it."

Mauritius braced himself in the doorway as his mind raced. Jupiter had failed him, Bona Dea—all the gods had not only failed to answer but had failed to hear. Who *did* hear? Who had the power to save his only child?

He could think of only one who might help.

The physician. The Greek. The one he had sent away to die at the Circus.

Mauritius whirled around and ran out of the house, calling for a litter.

—⚊ꙮ⚊—

The hired litter dropped him outside the holding area at the Circus Maximus. "Stay here," Mauritius commanded, holding the litter bearers with a stern glance. "I will return in a moment."

He strode past the guards at the entrance to the subterranean cells, took the steps two at a time, and found his way to the section holding the Christians. Standing between two separate cages, he scanned the occupants and felt relief flood over him when he spotted Luke sitting with a group of men.

"Physician!" He gestured to a guard with keys. "On your feet. You are to come with me at once."

"On whose authority," the guard said, "do you—?"

"On my own authority," Mauritius snapped. "I am Prefect Mauritius Gallis. Now open this door!"

The keys seemed to jangle for an eternity as the guard fitted the key into the lock. Mauritius kept his eyes on the guard's hands, afraid he might look up and find the Greek obdurate or rebellious. He had known warriors who refused to cooperate after being sentenced to death. What would he do if the Christian refused to come, or if the others closed ranks around him? He could not punish them with a fate worse than the one they would meet on the morrow.

When he finally did look up, he saw the physician standing quietly on the other side of the iron gate, his expression serene and his hands folded.

"Come." Mauritius resisted the urge to grab the man's arm and drag him up the stairs. "Your services are required."

—⁂—

Without ceremony, Mauritius escorted Luke through the villa and into his daughter's sickroom. Irenica paced on the opposite side of the chamber, but she froze in place when she saw who Mauritius had brought with him. The physician was dirty, his clothing soiled beyond help, and he brought with him a stench that filled the entire villa. Mauritius was used to such things, but Irenica had never inhaled anything more unpleasant than sour milk.

"Who is this?" she asked, her eyes blazing with alarm.

Mauritius ignored her question and turned to the Christian. "Can you help my daughter?"

The Greek did not turn to consider the patient. Instead, he stared at Mauritius, his eyes narrowing. Mauritius could not be sure, but he felt as though he were being weighed and measured, and the physician's decision would somehow depend upon his worthiness.

By all the gods, his daughter was doomed. If this Greek required an apology or recompense, if he demanded his freedom or that of his friend Paul . . .

But the Greek said nothing. He simply nodded, then moved to the sickbed. He knelt on the floor and lifted a corner of Caelia's shirt. "This is not good." He pointed to the swelling and bruising on her side. "This is evidence of bleeding under the skin. Quickly, get me a sharp blade."

Irenica gasped.

"Now!" Luke shot a glance over his shoulder at Mauritius. "Do not waste time."

Mauritius pulled a dagger from his belt and held it, handle out, in the empty space between himself and his prisoner. He could not look at Irenica's face. What would prevent this man from murdering their daughter? Any other condemned criminal would happily take the opportunity to repay a Roman for the pain and suffering they had endured.

Luke placed his hands into a bowl of water and then shook the droplets off. He turned back to Mauritius and met his gaze, and in that moment Mauritius felt the physician silently acknowledge all that had passed between them. "I have already forgiven you for what you have done," the Greek said, his voice low as he held out his hand. "Your daughter's chest is filling with blood. If I do not drain it, she will die."

Mauritius stared at the blade, then placed it in Luke's flat palm. What choice did he have?

He watched, his heart in his throat, as Luke dipped the blade in water. He then sliced into his daughter's chest. "I need a pen and papyrus," he said, his voice calmer.

Irenica hurried away to fetch the items. As Mauritius watched blood flow from the incision, Luke leaned forward to catch his eye. "Do you trust me?"

"Do I have any choice?"

A small smile lifted the corner of Luke's mouth. After Irenica hurried back into the room, Luke took the papyrus and jotted words on it, then gave it to Mauritius. "You will find Aquila and Priscilla at this house. Tell them I sent you for these things and they must be brought to me immediately."

"Are you sure—?" Mauritius began.

Luke cut him off. "I've seen this illness only once before, on the isle of Rhodes. There is much to do if we are going to save your daughter's life."

As blood continued to flow onto the mattress, the Greek stood and washed his hands again. "You are trusting me with your daughter's life, and I am trusting you with the lives of those you will find at that villa. Now"—he turned to Irenica—"I will need more clean water and linens. As soon as you can get them."

Mauritius nodded and hurried out of the house.

—ɯɯ—

Luke heard the slam of the front door and sank to the floor by the girl's bedside. The girl's mother lingered across the room, probably repelled by the foul odor.

"I apologize for my appearance," Luke said, gently wiping the incision area with a folded piece of wet linen. "I have not had an opportunity to bathe in many days."

"Um, do not, uh . . ." The woman spread her hands, unable to find the words. Luke suppressed a smile. He could not blame her for being stunned by his abrupt appearance. He would be socially unacceptable in the eyes of women like the prefect's wife, and his reputation had probably preceded him. If the prefect had told her anything about the men in Nero's prison, she probably thought him the worst sort of miscreant, a threat to civilized people everywhere.

"I, uh, want to thank you for coming," she said, doing her best to fill the awkward silence. "I'm sure you were occupied when Mauritius interrupted."

"I was not so busy," Luke said, bending to peer at his patient's mottled complexion. "Could you bring the lamp closer, please? Or if the smell bothers you, we could place the lamp on a table."

She picked up the oil lamp and brought it to him. "It is no trouble. It is the least I can do to—oh!" She brought her free hand to her nose, then gingerly set the lamp on the table near Luke's side. "There."

"Thank you." He could see more clearly in the light, and already the girl's skin was looking less bruised.

"I need to see to something . . . in the atrium," the woman said, her hand still at her nose. "If you don't mind, I will leave you for a while."

"Enjoy the fresh air," Luke said, his attention on his patient. "Breathe some for me, will you?"

He pressed the linen over the incision, applying pressure to the cut. The excess blood had drained away, and now he had to stop the bleeding. When the blood began to coagulate, he would stitch the wound. But not yet. He would do so after the supplies arrived.

He looked at his bloodstained fingers. Why had God brought him to this place, to this moment? He had always imagined that he studied medicine in order to care for Paul, missionary to the Gentiles. Now, as they neared the end of their lives, he supposed that God wanted him to focus on writing his second book, to leave behind a trustworthy record of how the Way began.

But so much had happened, and time was short. And here he was, using his medical skills again, and on a patient he had not wanted to see. If his flesh had won the battle, he would have remained with his brothers and sisters at the Circus, leaving the Praetorian prefect to deal with the consequences of his own actions.

But he could not let his flesh win, because as Paul often said, they were slaves to Christ. And a slave does not question his master; he obeys.

And what did Christ ask of him? Here, as always, to love.

So he came, reeking of refuse and grime, splashing blood on a noblewoman's tile floor. Tomorrow they would have to empty out this bedchamber and burn incense to clear the air.

But the girl would get well, and the mother would be grateful. As to the prefect . . . only God knew what He had planned for Mauritius.

—◊◊◊—

Mauritius finally found the house he sought on the other side of town, past the Circus and south of the marketplace.

234

Frustrated at the distance and the late hour, he pounded on the door. "Open up! Luke, the physician, has sent me to speak to Aquila and Priscilla. I have come alone!"

He was about to curse himself for daring to hope the door might actually open to him, but after a moment he heard the bolt slide back. The door opened, and there stood Eubulus, the guard who had disappeared from a Praetorian prison cart.

Blinking in astonishment, Mauritius numbly offered the note as proof of his purpose. "Luke has sent me to see Aquila."

The burly guard's brows nearly rose to his hairline, but then he stepped aside and allowed Mauritius to enter the courtyard.

He found himself in a garden that might have once been beautiful. But the hedges were broken and spindly, and the trees bent under the weight of hammocks. Makeshift tents cluttered the open spaces, pots cluttered the fountain, and embers glowed in what must have been cookeries. Instead of offering peace and solitude, this garden obviously offered sanctuary and a hiding place for dozens of Christians.

Mauritius scanned the crowd but recognized no one. "I seek— I have come to ask a favor of a man called Aquila."

The men and women in the garden stared at him. Then an arm lifted and pointed to the upper story of the house. Mauritius flew up the stone steps and walked through an open doorway into a room where two women and three men sat around a table. Apparently he had interrupted some sort of meeting.

All of them gaped when they recognized the Praetorian sword at his side. One woman's eyes widened in a flicker of shock.

"Luke sent me," Mauritius said, holding up the note in Luke's handwriting. "I need your help."

The woman stood, the corners of her mouth tight. "Luke is alive?"

"Yes."

She closed her eyes and breathed deeply, her lips moving in apparent prayer.

"Please." Mauritius set the papyrus on the table. "My daughter, Caelia, is ill. Luke is with her, but he needs these things right away."

The woman opened her eyes. "Tell me what you need."

Mauritius snatched up the note and began to read aloud.

———✠———

When the Roman left, Aquila, Priscilla, and Eubulus huddled by the courtyard gate.

"Do we leave now?" Aquila asked. "Eubulus, perhaps you should. He knows where you are, and he will likely send guards to arrest you again."

"I can pack food and blankets," Priscilla said, ticking off items with her fingers. "We have already packed supplies for several others, so we can send you with one of those bags. We'll find someone else to guide the people to the aqueducts."

"I think we should wait."

Aquila looked up, startled by the big guard's calm tone. "But the risk, especially for you—"

"The prefect is not thinking about me now." A wide smile lit the guard's face. "The man is not unreasonable, and at this moment he is doing something he has never done before. He is trusting a Christian. Why don't we trust him in return?"

Aquila looked at Priscilla, who looked at Eubulus, then shook her head. "We are leaving in two days," she said, her voice a feminine ripple in the evening air. "Why don't we trust the Lord to handle the prefect?"

Aquila wasn't so certain he shared her confidence, but he

squeezed her arm and nodded nonetheless. "Agreed," he said. "We will leave in two days' time."

—∾∾—

Back inside his daughter's bedchamber, Mauritius waited in the shadows, out of the physician's way as Luke took care of his daughter. Irenica stood at Mauritius's side, clinging to his arm and watching the Greek work.

One thing was clear, and Mauritius would never forget it: Paul of Tarsus was right. The Greek was a skilled physician, and he had saved their daughter's life when no one else could.

CHAPTER
FOURTEEN

The Twentieth Day of Junius

Lying on the floor of his prison cell, Paul stared toward the light of a new day and thought about Luke. Of all the men he had ever known—his fellow Jews, apostles, disciples, and kinsmen—Luke had been the most steadfast, the most loyal, and the most temperate. If any man was an embodiment of brotherly love, Luke was.

And unless God willed otherwise, in a few hours Luke would die in the oval arena of the Circus Maximus while the Romans cheered.

"Forgive them, Father, for they do not know what they are doing."

Paul imagined the scene. Luke had never been an exuberant man, never given to wild emotion in joy or sorrow. He tended to keep his feelings inside, sharing them only with people he trusted.

But he would be a rock for the others who would die with him. He would share his heart and his convictions with compassion, and he would give them the courage to face death with honor.

He has done the same for me.

Paul closed his eyes, his heart swelling with emotions no human words could express. The Spirit dwelling inside him groaned, but though he battled loneliness, dread, and fear, Paul would not ask for another hour. He would endure one more day and night, and on the morrow he would rise to face His Savior.

Would he face anyone else?

His recurrent dream had haunted him again last night. He had walked the dusty road to Damascus, and at the hill where he had once been struck down, he had seen a crowd waiting. He knew the faces—Stephen was there, and Nicodemus, and the family he had captured in Jerusalem and sent to prison. Even the little girl.

Paul opened his eyes, preferring the sunlight to the shadowlands. He would spend his remaining hours praising HaShem who was *'El Elyon*, God Most High; *'El Shaddai*, God all-sufficient; *'El 'Olam*, the Everlasting One; *'El Ro'i,* the all-seeing One; and *Yahweh*, the God who is and shall be.

"You are *Yahweh-Tseba'oth*, the God with armies to serve you; *Yahweh-Nissi*, my banner; *Yahweh-Rapha*, my healer; *Yahweh-Rohi*, the God who is my Shepherd; *Yahweh-Jireh*, the God who is my Provider; *Yahweh-Tsadaq*, the Righteous God; and *Yahweh-Shalom*, the God who is peace and who brings peace."

Inexplicably, he thought of Prefect Mauritius Gallis, who would be one of the last people Paul would see with mortal eyes. The prefect did not know peace, nor would he, because even if his daughter improved, he would still have to face Nero and life in this unholy city. The gods of Rome held no power; they were illusions spun by the evil one in order to blind people to the Truth.

240

"Here we are, Adonai"—Paul felt a smile curve his lips—"in the heart of a city that worships more gods than the average man can count, and yet none of their gods are like *you*. None of their gods is righteous, not one has the power to heal, and not one has armies to do his bidding. Only you, Adonai, are exalted in all the earth."

Tomorrow he would see his last sunrise, and then he would lay his head down and close his eyes, ready to return to the third heaven where Yeshua waited for all who trusted Him.

"'So from the west they will fear the Name of Adonai,'" Paul said, reciting a passage from the prophet Isaiah, "'and His glory from the rising of the sun.

"'For He will come like a rushing stream driven along by the *Ruach Adonai*.

"'But a Redeemer will come to Zion, and to those in Jacob who turn from transgression.

"'As for Me, this is My covenant with them,' says Adonai: 'My *Ruach* who is on you, and My words that I have put in your mouth, shall not depart from your mouth, or from the mouth of your offspring, or from the mouth of your children's offspring,' says Adonai, 'from now on and forever.'"

—⁂—

Mauritius bolted upright, as wide awake as if Nero had called his name. He blinked, then remembered where he was: on a dining couch in the atrium where he had gone once it was clear Caelia was improving.

He ran his hands through his hair, trying to throw off the lingering effects of sleep. The sun had already risen, but his servant had not yet come to wake him, so the morning was still young. He had time to check on Caelia.

He rose and went to his daughter's bedchamber. Caelia was sleeping, but naturally so, curled on her side and not in the flat pose of death. Irenica slept on a pallet on the floor, and even in repose her face appeared drawn and weary. But now, thank the gods, the situation in their home would improve.

Finally, Mauritius looked at the Greek. He slept, too, sprawled out in a chair far too small for his long, lean form. His head was tipped back, and from his open mouth came the sounds of snoring. His hands hung at his sides, his legs stretched across the floor, and Mauritius did not have the heart to wake him.

The man had done what no other physician could do. Mauritius had watched in silent awe as the Greek released the pooling blood beneath his daughter's skin. Then he had sewn up the incision with needle and thread, his stitches as neat as an army surgeon's. Afterward he gave Caelia a tea made of herbs obtained from the villa filled with Christians . . .

Mauritius closed his eyes, refusing to consider them further. He was not a perfect man by any means, but he was not so dishonorable as to violate a good man's trust.

He thrust his hands behind his back when the Greek stirred. Mauritius waited until Luke opened his eyes, and then he managed a small smile. "A good day to you."

Luke sat up quickly and leaned forward to examine his patient. "She sleeps still?"

"She is resting," Mauritius said, nodding in approval. "She has not looked so peaceful in days."

The Greek blew out a breath and relaxed. "Good. I am glad . . . I could be of service." He lifted his hands, which were markedly clean compared to the rest of his body, and sighed. "Your daughter should be back to her normal self within the week."

Mauritius dipped his head. "We are grateful."

Luke smiled weakly. "If that is all, I suppose I should be on my way."

"Wait." Mauritius drew a deep breath. "I would like you to remain here for a while yet. I will have my servants draw you a bath and give you clean clothing. But before you go, I would ask you to meet someone in my garden."

"That is kind of you." Luke bowed his head. "And now I am grateful."

Mauritius moved to the hallway and clapped his hands for a slave. An instant later, someone appeared.

"Follow this man," Mauritius told Luke, ignoring the slave's incredulous look, "and enjoy the bath. You should be in no hurry to leave us, for you are welcome here today."

—⁓—

In the underground holding area of the Circus Maximus, sunlight slanted through the windows and touched the sleeping faces of those imprisoned in the animal cages. Children stirred from their mothers' laps, and men looked toward the light and realized that unless God chose to work a miracle, the day of their death had dawned.

From far away, an eerie sound cut through the early morning silence—a shrill cry, followed by a guttural roar. One of the children turned to Miriam, his mother. "What is that sound, Mama?"

She pushed his curly hair from his eyes and tried to smile. "I think," she said, keeping her tone light, "it is a big cat from the jungle. I saw one once, in a triumphal parade." She looked across the cage, caught her husband's eye, and smiled. "We will walk in a triumphal parade, too, when we leave this place to meet Jesus."

Other children began to wake and stir. Miriam greeted each

of them and bade them keep quiet. "No sense in waking the others," she whispered. "Let them sleep for now."

She knew it would take hours for the slaves to prepare for the games. The merchants would arrive at midmorning to set up their shops. By midday the aromas of roasting meat and baking pastries would envelop the arena, making the prisoners' mouths water in anticipation of a meal that would never come.

By midafternoon, the spectators would begin to arrive. Thousands of people would set aside their daily work and set out for the Circus—plebeians and patricians, senators and prostitutes, rich and poor, young and old. Those who came early would amuse themselves in the shops while others scrambled for the best seats. They would bring food in baskets, intending to make a day of the entertainment.

As the sun began to dip toward the west, the procession of athletes and other dignitaries would begin. Many people paid dearly for the honor of walking in a procession at the games, but Miriam could not see the point of it. Most people were still eating or shopping at that time, and many of the figures could not be recognized from the distance of the stands.

After the procession, the trumpeters would lift their instruments and play flourishes to herald the start of the races. Miriam's mouth quirked. Nero himself had actually raced at the Circus. Despite being thrown and having to be reseated in his ten-horse chariot, he was declared the winner. The judges were awarded one million sesterces for their pronouncement.

But today would feature only one race, and it would be run only to satisfy those who craved the sound of thundering hooves. The other drivers and their teams would rest today, and the eager crowd would find entertainment in another sort of spectacle.

Miriam lowered her head and breathed in the lovely scent of

her son. Not even the odor of this animal cage could overpower the perfume of her boy's skin, and not even the knowledge that Nero would be in the stands could dim her anticipation of what lay ahead.

Luke had prepared them well—she was braced for the pain, perhaps even a fleeting panic, but after that she would know Paradise. No matter what awaited them on the arena's sand— gladiators, jungle animals, wild dogs, or fiery crosses—nothing could compare to the joy of being united with the One who had already defeated death.

Hugging her son, she prayed the hours would pass quickly.

———ഝ———

Paul did not know what to expect on his last day in the prison, but he was surprised when a shadow blocked the light from above. He looked up and saw Severus standing next to the opening, the knotted rope in his hand. "Paul of Tarsus, stand."

Paul remained on the floor, amazed to hear his name. Had they decided to execute him a day early?

"Now, prisoner. Stand and make yourself ready to see the prefect."

Slowly, Paul pushed himself off the floor and stepped toward the opening.

An hour later he found himself washed, fed, and wearing a new garment. The iron bracelets had been removed from his wrists, though fetters still weighed heavily on his ankles. Severus said nothing to explain these unexpected actions, and though Paul thought they might be related to Luke's death, he could not determine how exactly.

He alighted from the prison wagon and saw that they had stopped at a beautiful villa.

Severus jerked his head toward the garden gate. "Mauritius Gallis waits to see you inside."

Paul opened the gate and stepped into the garden, then closed his eyes and breathed in the sweet scent of living things—trees, flowers, and moist earth. He had not dared hope he would ever again stand in a garden or walk beneath a blue sky, but here he was . . .

Yahweh-Rohi, my Shepherd, you knew this weary lamb needed to rest in green pastures.

As his heart sang with gratitude, he walked along the path in the walled garden. The path led to a bench, where Mauritius Gallis waited.

Paul studied the prefect as he walked forward. The man sat hunched on the marble seat, his head propped on his fist, his elbow resting on his knee, his eyes focused on something beyond Paul's field of vision.

Was he thinking of Luke and regretting his harsh action? Were these acts of kindness the result of a guilty conscience?

Severus followed and dropped the chain that ran through Paul's fetters.

Paul waited silently for the news that would break his heart.

Mauritius finally looked up. He locked eyes with Paul. "The Greek is alive."

Paul blinked, feeling his knees turn to water. He would have fallen if Severus had not caught him. He sought the prefect's eyes. "Praise God."

"Because of him, my daughter lives. He did not have to save her, but he did."

Paul bowed his head. "Luke knows he did not deserve mercy when he received it, so he extends mercy where others would not."

The prefect shifted his attention to the trees along the garden wall. "He sent me to a villa for supplies, which was filled with your people—people of the Way. He knew I could arrest them, have them all taken to the Circus. Nero would like nothing better than more fodder for his wild beasts."

Paul nodded but said nothing.

Mauritius looked at him and blinked hard. "I sent word to Nero, asking if there had been any change in the status of your execution order. But there has been none—you will die at sunrise tomorrow. I am sorry for it, yet I give you my word that the Greek will be able to accompany you without fear of persecution or reprisal."

Paul clasped his hands. "Thank you, Prefect. That means a great deal to me."

Mauritius leaned forward, his eyes intently focused on Paul's face. "I should be thanking *you*. My wife, my daughter, and I are grateful you told us about Luke. I should have listened to you earlier."

"But you did listen, and God was gracious to you. I hope the experience has shown you something . . . true."

The prefect did not speak for a moment. He seemed to be listening to the wind in the trees, the cooing pigeons. Finally he closed his eyes. "I am sorry for Nero's Circus. I am sorry many of your people will die today."

Paul tilted his head. Was the Spirit working on this man? Perhaps. Yeshua said that no man could come to Him unless His Father drew him. Taking a chance, Paul stepped forward and sat next to the prefect. Mauritius did not react but stared straight ahead.

"Have you ever been sailing?" Paul asked.

Mauritius's nod was barely perceptible. "I have."

"Good." Paul folded his hands. "Imagine yourself looking

247

out at the vast sea. You reach down and put a hand into the water and scoop it up. But almost immediately the water begins to leak through your fingers, and within a few moments your hand is empty."

"Of course," Mauritius answered. "The water is like life."

"Indeed it is. From birth to death, it is continually slipping through our hands. Before we know it, our lives will be gone, along with all we hold dear in this world. Yet the kingdom I seek, the one I live for, is like the sea. Men strive for the cup of water that slips through their fingers, but those who follow Yeshua the Christ live for the endless expanse of sea."

Mauritius remained silent for a moment, then turned his head. "And what—after all this—if I still do not believe in your Christ?"

Paul smiled. "I wasn't trying to convince you. I was simply sharing . . . Truth." He turned to face the Praetorian. "Listen to me, Prefect. Considering the expanse of eternity, I have only moments left, so it is not me who looks at you now, but Christ himself. When He looks at you, He shatters your defenses. And in that moment you understand that you are completely known and completely loved by God." He gentled his tone. "I will pray that moment comes for you soon."

Mauritius drew a deep breath and let it out. He motioned to Severus, who stood waiting at the garden gate.

"I must leave you now," the prefect said, standing. "I have promised to eat with my wife and daughter today, or at least to sit with them for a while. I wish you well, Paul of Tarsus. And I will see you again tomorrow."

—⁓⁓—

Paul watched Mauritius walk away, then turned to look for Severus, but the guard had disappeared. Puzzled and a bit anxious, he stood and waited for someone to claim him. What was this? Had the Lord arranged an escape?

A few minutes passed, and then Luke stepped into the garden. He appeared well rested and, most surprising, was wearing a new tunic and mantle.

"Luke! What? How did—?" Realizing that he was babbling in confusion, Paul hurried forward to embrace his friend. "I have never been so glad to see anyone."

"It is good to see you, too."

Paul squeezed Luke's arms. "It really is you and not an apparition."

"It is. I am alive."

"Thank the Lord." Grinning, Paul pulled away and gestured to the garden around them. "I think we should walk and enjoy this lovely spot while we can."

A flash of humor crossed Luke's face. "Of course. I must say, you look much better in the sunlight."

"I feel better, as well. I feel . . . hopeful."

After walking together in silence for a while, Paul turned toward Luke and smiled. "You saved his daughter."

"Yes. You helped me remember that I did not deserve to have Christ save me."

Laughter floated up from Paul's throat. "They will know us by our love, brother. And not only by our love for each other, but our love for *them*. This is the Way."

Luke nodded, then looked toward the garden wall. "I could hear the cheers of the crowd as I visited the bathhouse. Many of our friends will die today . . . and I will never forget their faces."

"You will see them again soon enough." Paul clasped his hands behind his back. "The trumpets will blow a great welcome when they arrive home. And when they look back, they will remember your courage and the way you comforted them."

He chuckled. "How did you know I talked to them?"

Paul lifted his face to the sky, his senses hungry for more light. "I know you, Luke, so of course you talked to them. And you gave them what they needed."

Luke shook his head. "'In the midst of the flame and the rack,'" he said, using the voice he always employed for quoting others, "'I have seen men not only not groan, that is little; not only not complain, that is little; not only not answer back, that too is little. But I have seen them smile, and smile with a good heart.'" He looked at Paul. "That's what Seneca, Nero's poet, wrote about our brothers and sisters."

Paul hauled his gaze from the sky and returned it to his physician. "God has a plan, even for Rome. And our people bear witness to Christ's power even as they die."

"On the night I first visited," Luke said after a moment's hesitation, "I did not understand why you would not tell our brothers and sisters what to do—whether to stay in Rome or leave. In light of all the trials you have faced, it seemed a simple answer. But now I have learned, perhaps even gained a bit of wisdom. There is only one guiding principle: seek Christ in all things."

"It is all we can do," Paul answered. "If we live, we live for the Lord; and if we die, we die for the Lord. Whether we live or die, we belong to the Lord. We are His slaves, set free to serve Him."

"Is there . . . is there anything I can do for you?" Luke asked.

"Yes." Paul smiled without humor. "If you find yourself in Jerusalem, please find my sister and nephew. Give them my love and tell them I prayed for them right up until the end."

Luke nodded. "I will make a point of it."

"I will have a note for Timothy tomorrow. Will you deliver it to him in Ephesus?"

"Yes."

"And—" Paul bit his lip, trying to think of anything else he might have forgotten. "I have no possessions to give away, unless you count the clothes on my back."

"I think," Luke said, his nose crinkling, "you should keep those."

They walked for several more moments without speaking, and then Luke stopped. "I have an ending for the book," he said.

Paul blinked. "You are going to finish it?"

"Of course. The prefect has returned my notes and granted my freedom. As soon as I am settled in a quiet place, I will finish the writing."

"All right." Paul folded his arms. "What is the ending?"

Luke pressed a hand to his chest. "Paul remained two whole years in his own rented quarters and continued to welcome all who came to him—proclaiming the kingdom of God and teaching about the Lord Yeshua the Messiah with all boldness and without hindrance." He grinned. "You should be very pleased with that."

"I am," Paul said. "But isn't it incomplete? What of my second imprisonment? Of the trial at the Forum, of Nero's verdict, the great fire of Rome, and the darkness of that horrid cell?"

Luke's dark eyes flashed a gentle warning. "I began my telling of these events with Jesus' proclamation to bear witness in Jerusalem and to the ends of the earth. And now the story that began thirty years ago in Jerusalem has come to Rome. If that is not the farthest place we could have imagined . . ."

"You are correct. It is the right ending—it feels complete." Paul studied his friend. "So this is the end." Tears filled Luke's eyes as Paul stepped forward to embrace him. "And yet death is only the beginning," Paul added in a choked voice. "We will soon meet on a new road, of that I am certain. To live is Messiah, and to die is gain."

Luke drew a quavering breath. "I like that."

"So do I."

Paul patted Luke's back, then released him. "Here comes Severus," he said, a catch still in his voice. "I will say farewell now and see you in the morning."

"Bright and early." Luke gave him a warm smile. "I'll be there."

Aquila and Priscilla lingered in the courtyard, embracing those who stood with their earthly belongings in their arms. Herodion, Rufus, and a handful of other Christians in the community were staying behind, while Aquila and Priscilla, along with some others, would leave as soon as they said their farewells.

Priscilla had said her private farewells last night, after the house had stilled and the courtyard had quieted, save for the churr of insects. She had moved through her bedroom, running her hand along the plastered walls, saying good-bye to the space she had decorated and loved. She walked through the kitchen area, quietly stacking her clay pots and putting her wooden spoons into a jar. Herodion's and Rufus's wives would be cooking here, and Priscilla prayed the Lord would bless them.

She tiptoed into the garden and stroked the young fig tree that had not yet borne fruit. Let others eat from it when it had grown, but she would always treasure the joy of nurturing it from seedling to tree. She stood beneath the sprawling canopy of a terebinth and looked up at the stars—those she would take with her on every step of the journey ahead. Let those who remained enjoy the tree and rest in its shade. She and Aquila would find another terebinth, one with shade for tired travelers who needed to hear that a Savior promised to give them rest.

She made her way back to the big bed where she and Aquila had slept night after night. The place where they had loved, prayed, and sometimes disagreed. Let another couple sleep in this bed, let them be dominus and domina of this house, and let them glorify Christ together.

With a heart too full for words, she had lain down to sleep, knowing she would have to wake in the morning and not look back.

Now Priscilla held her friends tightly, knowing she might not see them again until heaven. She took extra time saying good-bye to Fania, Herodion's wife. "Don't forget your promise," she whispered in Fania's ear. "Visit Moria as often as you can. Make sure she and her baby are doing well—and pray for the salvation of their master."

"We will," Fania promised. "Some of the other women are going to help me. We will make sure Moria does not feel alone. Some of the men have said they will look for Carmine, too. Once we learn where he lives with his new master, we will keep an eye on him."

Finally, Priscilla picked up the bag she had packed and followed Aquila to the gate. They would leave their house for the community. They would pledge their prayers for those who believed Christ wanted them to stay and be salt in a decaying culture and light in a dark empire. Staying meant risking their lives every day, but, like Paul, they had decided they were slaves to Christ and meant to be about His work in Rome.

At home with Irenica and Caelia, Mauritius sat in his chair and watched his little family as they laughed and enjoyed each other's company. Caelia seemed to grow stronger with every passing hour, and even in the dancing firelight he could see that color had returned to her cheeks. Irenica looked lovely, too, now that the lines of stress and despair had vanished from her countenance. She had been grateful to him for bringing the Greek to their home and following his unexpected instructions.

The wonder of it all, Mauritius reflected, was that the Greek had healed his daughter not with mischief or "Christian magic," but with something far more unexpected—mercy and compassion, even for an enemy.

And that, Mauritius realized, was rarely witnessed in Rome.

—⁂—

The sun was lowering toward the western horizon as Aquila opened the courtyard gate. With Priscilla by his side, he stood and watched as those who were leaving departed in groups of three and four. "Go with God," he murmured as each group moved down the stairs.

He studied their faces as they set out. Most of them were wide-eyed and tense, worried about walking the city streets unobserved. This first part of the journey would be the most dangerous, so Aquila tried to put them at ease so they wouldn't draw unwanted attention.

Priscilla must have understood his unspoken intention, because she gave each group a bright smile, though her eyes shone with unshed tears. The evidence of heartsickness and exhaustion had disappeared from her face, and he prayed the others would take courage and comfort from her brave example.

"Mingle with the crowds," he said as the others went out.

"Do not draw any attention to yourselves. Do not walk too quickly or too slowly."

When the last group had gone, he closed the courtyard gate and waved a final good-bye to Herodion, Rufus, and their wives. Then he drew Priscilla into his arms, a move that caught her by surprise.

"What is this?" she asked, smiling.

"It is gratitude." He pressed his lips to her temple. "I could not do this without you."

She said nothing, but rested her head on his chest for a moment. They stood together in the hush of the alley until the setting sun gilded the stones and filled the crevices with shadows.

"We'd better go," Aquila finally said.

Priscilla nodded and began descending the steps to the street.

They mingled with the crowds of people going home for the night, walking among pedestrians and donkey carts until they reached Palatine Hill. There they looked around to see if they could spot any others from the community, but Aquila saw no one. He turned to Priscilla with a question in his eyes, and she shook her head.

"Good," he said. "They have all passed this way already."

At Palatine Hill they skirted the emperor's new palace and walked until they reached the few remaining residences of the patrician families. They knocked at the house with the blue door, where a servant stepped out and led them to a walled garden. There, between the stones of a waterfall, Aquila spotted the tunnel that led to the aqueduct. He thanked the servant and entered the tunnel, extending his hand to help Priscilla walk on the uneven stones.

Though the aqueduct was no longer in use, a small stream still flowed along its bottom. They walked while staying to the edge, moving away from the sounds of the city. Darkness deepened as they walked, and Aquila felt a moment's panic—what if they got lost in here?

Soon, though, he spied a crack in the stone wall and saw the silver sheen of moonlight on the stones. When he and Priscilla reached the opening, they found themselves outside the city, in a field littered with large rocks and wildflowers. Ahead they could see small camps, makeshift tents, and the glow of cook fires.

"It's our group!" Priscilla's voice vibrated with joy. "We've caught up to them."

They lengthened their strides and before long joined the others. After a quick head count, Aquila determined that all the travelers were present. They had lost no one on their way out of the city.

"Tomorrow," he said, slipping his arm around Priscilla's shoulders, "we will break up into groups and travel separately until we reach Ephesus. But for tonight, we will stay together and pray for our brother Paul, who faces the executioner at sunrise."

He squeezed Priscilla's shoulder and went to help Eubulus set up another tent. After they had completed their task, he looked for his wife and found her sitting on a rock, her eyes fixed on the stone walls and gleaming villas of Rome in the distance.

He sat beside her. "You are not missing the city already, are you?"

She laughed softly. "The city? Not yet. The people? I think I shall always miss them. Especially Luke and Paul." Her voice broke, and Aquila reached for her hand. "Paul would not want you to be overcome with sorrow. He would remind us that we will see him again soon."

She nodded. "I know."

"'What is your life?'" Aquila said, quoting the apostle James.

"'For you are a vapor that appears for a little while and then vanishes.'"

"But not forever," Priscilla said, her eyes misting as she stared at the city. "Not forever."

—⁓—

As golden torchlight flickered through the opening in the ceiling of Paul's dungeon, Luke sat across from his friend with a hamper between them. With Mauritius's permission, he had brought provisions from the prefect's house.

Aware that the hour was growing late, he pulled several items from the basket.

"This," he said, lifting a cup and a jug of wine, "represents the Lord's blood, which was poured out for us. We drink this to remember His sacrifice."

He poured wine into the cup and gave it to Paul, who drank and then bowed his head. Luke shared the cup as well, then set it aside as he recalled the immense suffering, pain, and humiliation Jesus had endured on the execution stake.

"Amen," he said. He pulled a flat loaf from the hamper, broke it into two pieces, and handed one to Paul. "And this," he went on, "represents Christ's body, which was broken for us. We eat this to remember His sacrifice."

Silently they ate, recalling the body that was bruised and bloodied for the sins of the world. When they finished eating, they prayed for courage, strength, and faithfulness unto death.

With their prayers concluded, Luke embraced his friend and mentor, promising once more to join him at sunrise on the morrow.

FIFTEEN

The Twenty-First Day of Junius

Paul stared at the rope as it descended from the round opening overhead. Its length coiled on the floor like a snake. Had any prisoner ever refused to grab hold of it, knowing that doing so meant he was about to die? Or were they always ready to do anything or face anyone to escape from this horrible pit?

He was ready to go. He placed his foot into the loop and clung tightly to the thick cord. "Pull!" he called. Then he rose from darkness into the gloom of early dawn.

Severus extended a muscular arm and pulled him into the upper chamber. Mauritius sat at his desk, his eyes heavy-lidded. Torches pushed at the darkness, for the sun had not yet shown itself.

"Prisoner Paul of Tarsus," Mauritius said, his voice flat and perfunctory, "is there anything you wish to say before you walk outside?"

Paul knew what awaited him on the other side of the door—a chopping block, an ax, and his executioner. He looked around, and soon his grateful eyes found what they sought: Luke. Breathless and red-eyed, he stepped into the room.

"You almost missed me," Paul said. "Another ten minutes and—"

"I will ask again," Mauritius interrupted. "Paul of Tarsus, do you wish to say anything before we go?"

Paul pulled a folded letter from his tunic and held it out. "If you will permit me, I would like to give this letter to Luke. With your permission, he will deliver it to my friend Timothy in Ephesus."

Mauritius nodded. "Permission granted."

"One more thing." Paul gave the prefect an apologetic smile. "I would like for Luke to read a marked portion of the letter aloud as we . . . play our parts out there. The letter says everything I want to say."

And everything I want you to hear.

"Permission granted," Mauritius replied, looking away.

Luke's brow had furrowed, yet he took the unsealed letter, unfolded it, and found the portion marked with a symbol. He caught Paul's eye. "I will read it."

"Thank you."

Severus opened the heavy wooden door, and Paul stepped out into the small courtyard. Overhead, the stars had begun to fade behind a sky of dark blue. A faint glow on the eastern horizon indicated where the sun would soon rise. The soft light was enough, however, to reveal everything he expected to see—stump, ax, executioner, and a basket. He hadn't considered the need for a basket, but the Romans could be remarkably fastidious.

He walked over to the executioner and positioned himself before the chopping block as Luke raised the letter and began to read. For an instant Paul feared the light would not be bright enough for Luke's aging eyes, but then the eastern sky began to glow pink.

"'For I am already being poured out like a drink offering,'" Luke read, "'and the time of my departure has come.'"

Paul closed his eyes as the executioner pressed his head to the block, exposing his neck. The apostle smiled at the sound of Luke's voice. The inspiration to have Luke read had surely come from the Holy Spirit. The words were fitting and would settle into Mauritius's heart.

"'I have fought the good fight, I have finished the course, I have kept the faith.'"

Reading aloud would also give Luke something to do, apart from the grievous task of watching a friend die.

"'In the future,'" Luke read on, "'there is reserved for me a crown of righteousness, which the Lord, the righteous Judge, will award to me on that day—and not to me only, but also to everyone who has longed for His appearing.'"

Paul heard the blade whistle through the air . . . and then he opened his eyes.

———～✕✕～———

He is standing on a hilltop near the Damascus road, and the people who have visited him in innumerable night visions are waiting. Their eyes seek his, and then, to his amazement, their somber expressions melt into enthusiastic smiles. They reach out to him, patting him, squeezing his shoulders, and their rubs and pats and robust embraces do not hurt, nor does his twisted back. For the first time in years, he straightens his spine and lifts his arms over his head. He is healed! Renewed!

He lifts his gaze to the faces in the crowd—Stephen, Peter,

James, and John Mark! Friends who have gone on ahead of him are waiting to welcome him, to lead him to the One he met on this same road so many years ago.

The crowd parts, and just as he did that first time, Paul falls to his knees in the sand. Before him stands Yeshua, the Christ who has guided him all these years. The same Christ who has comforted him, who set him on a path of discovery, adventure, suffering, and glory. The Christ who promised to welcome him into Paradise, and to tell him . . .

"Well done, my good and faithful servant." The glow of Yeshua's smile warms Paul's bones down to the marrow. "Well done, my friend. Welcome home."

INTERVIEW WITH THE AUTHOR

I'm always asked how much of a novel is fact and how much fiction, especially when a story is based on historical events. So I've addressed a few topics introduced in this novel in the hope that you'll appreciate a fuller understanding of the time in which Luke and Paul lived.

1. **Was Paul actually executed because Nero believed he incited the great fire of Rome?**
   I could find no historical evidence directly supporting the idea that Paul was accused of inciting arson, but Nero did blame Christians for the fire. Since Paul was reported to be a leader among the new sect, the notion that Paul was blamed for such a destructive fire is not an unreasonable assumption, especially since we don't know exactly when Paul was executed. Many believe he died in June, AD 68.

2. **The film portrays Paul's prison as large, whereas you describe it as a hole in the ground. Why the difference?**
   Filmmakers often use visual shorthand to convey information. They show a stone building with prisoners and the

263

viewer automatically understands it is a prison, so there's no need for the writer or director to spend time explaining details that aren't important to the story. But a novelist has the luxury of employing more words. Therefore, I could more easily explain Paul's prison. In doing my research to write the novel—which came *after* the movie—I learned that this prison, known as the *Carcer* in Paul's day (the root for *incarceration*), consisted of two chambers hewn out of rock, one above the other. It was located in the heart of Rome near the Roman Forum and was used only for the detainment of prisoners and occasional executions.

Ancient Rome had no police force other than the Praetorian Guard and no pressing need for a jail. The emperor made laws in (sometimes forced) cooperation with the Senate, but not all of those laws would make sense to a twenty-first century individual. The Romans didn't base their laws on a morality derived from a Judeo-Christian ethic. Roman laws had more to do with what was beneficial for Rome and Romans.

Furthermore, each *paterfamilias*, or head of the household, was the voice of Roman law in his own family. A man could flog his slaves or his wife or his children to death, and no one would arrest him. Unwanted babies were frequently left outside for wild animals to devour, and slaves were used as their masters saw fit. Adultery was common, prostitution legal, and crimes such as stealing were quickly punished. Even an adult child was not free from his father's authority until the father died.

On the other hand, in Rome it was illegal to wear clothing that implied one belonged to a higher social class than one actually did, to spend more than an aristocrat might

spend on a banquet (lest you shame the aristocracy), and
to hide if the emperor put your name on a list of those
who needed to die so that their property could be sold to
help pay the empire's debts.

The Romans had no great need of prisons, except for the
occasional holding cell for those who awaited the emperor's
verdict. Paul and Peter both spent time in an underground
vault about twenty-one feet in diameter, accessible only
by a hole in the twelve-foot ceiling. It was a truly hellish
place. Sallust, who died in 34 BC, described it as "exceed-
ing dark, unsavory, and able to craze any man's senses."*

3. **I've always understood that the apostle was called Saul
(or Sha'ul) before his conversion and was called Paul
afterward. True?**
Not exactly. Sha'ul is the apostle's Hebrew name, so in
Jewish circles and with his Jewish friends he was probably
called Sha'ul even after his conversion. Paul was the name
he used among Romans, and he was probably known as
Paul as a child growing up in Tarsus. But since he became
viewed as the "apostle to the Gentiles," it is fitting he
would be best known as Paul.

Luke writes, "But Sha'ul, who is also Paul, filled with the
Ruach ha-Kodesh, fixed his gaze on him . . ." (Acts 13:9).

4. **Did Paul really witness the young Jesus talking to the
scribes and chief priests in the Temple?**
I don't know. It's unclear how old Paul was when he died,
so I guessed at his age and put his timeline alongside

* Sallust, *The Conspiracy of Catiline*, p. 55.

Christ's. Paul was a student at the Temple as a young man, so he certainly could have witnessed this event. Still, we have no recorded evidence of such an encounter.

5. **Did Paul know Stephen as a youth? And did he associate with Nicodemus?**
I believe it's safe to say yes to both questions. Nicodemus was an esteemed member of the Sanhedrin, and Paul probably would have known him at least by reputation. And if Stephen and Paul were about the same age, they might have studied at the Temple together. The Sanhedrin was more than a court—it was also a religious school where young men went to study the written and Oral Law.

6. **What is the Oral Law?**
Most Jews believe the Oral Law is composed of everything Moses learned from God on Sinai that was never written, but transmitted orally to his successors. The Oral Law also includes edicts, ordinances, and teachings from the sages throughout the generations, along with laws extrapolated from Torah verses. The Oral Law has since been written into the Talmud and Mishnah.

Karaite Judaism does not accept the Oral Law and considers the form of Judaism commonly practiced today as "Talmudism," not authentic Judaism. They base their beliefs on Deuteronomy 4:2: "You must not add to the word that I am commanding you or take away from it—in order to keep the mitzvot of Adonai your God that I am commanding you."

7. Did Nero really light the streets of Rome with Christians as they burned to death on crosses? And did he torture and kill them at the Circus Maximus?
Yes to both questions.

8. How long did Nero rule?
Nero ruled from AD 54–68, committing suicide not long after Paul was executed. The notorious emperor stabbed himself after being tried and condemned to death in absentia by the Senate. One of the empire's most brutal leaders, he was the first Roman emperor to take his own life.

Though he tried to kill all the Christians in Rome, within a short time after his death the church in Rome was thriving, made stronger by persecution. St. Peter's Basilica stands today on the very spot where Christians were tortured in the Circus of Nero.

9. How did Luke die?
We don't know for certain, but apparently he did not die in Rome. He wrote the New Testament books of Luke and Acts, which together make up more than one quarter of the New Testament. If he was Greek and a Gentile (some believe he was a Hellenized Jew), then he was the only Gentile among the Spirit-inspired writers of the Bible.

References

Aquinas, Thomas. *Summa Theologica*. Trans. Fathers of the English Dominican Province. London: Burns, Oates & Washbourne.

Betz, Hans Dieter. "Paul (Person)." Ed. David Noel Freedman. *The Anchor Yale Bible Dictionary*. New York: Doubleday, 1992. 186–201.

Burk, Denny. "Was the Apostle Paul Married?" 8/30/11, http://www.denny burk.com/was-the-apostle-paul-married/, accessed 11/24/17.

Cottrell, Jack. *Romans*. Vol. 2. Joplin, MO: College Press Pub. Co., 1996.

Dunnam, Maxie D., and Lloyd J. Ogilvie. *Galatians / Ephesians / Philippians / Colossians / Philemon*. Vol. 31. Nashville, TN: Thomas Nelson Publishers, 1982.

"Eight Things You May Not Know about the Praetorian Guard," http ://www.history.com/news/history-lists/8-things-you-may-not-know -about-the-praetorian-guard, accessed 12/4/17.

Elwell, Walter A., and Philip Wesley Comfort. *Tyndale Bible Dictionary*. Carol Stream, IL: Tyndale House Publishers, 2001. 543.

Fiensy, David A. *New Testament Introduction*. Joplin, MO: College Press Pub. Co., 1997.

Fruchtenbaum, Arnold G. *The Footsteps of the Messiah: A Study of the Sequence of Prophetic Events*. Rev. ed. Tustin, CA: Ariel Ministries, 2003.

Fruchtenbaum, Arnold G. *The Messianic Bible Study Collection*. Vol. 107. Tustin, CA: Ariel Ministries, 1983.

Hayford, Jack W. *Hayford's Bible Handbook*. Nashville, TN; Atlanta, GA; London; Vancouver: Thomas Nelson Publishers, 1995.

Kurian, George Thomas. *Nelson's New Christian Dictionary: The Authoritative Resource on the Christian World.* Nashville, TN: Thomas Nelson Publishers, 2001.

Lampe, Peter. "Prisca (Person)." Ed. David Noel Freedman. *The Anchor Yale Bible Dictionary.* New York: Doubleday, 1992. 467–468.

McGee, J. Vernon. *Thru the Bible Commentary.* electronic ed. Vol. 5. Nashville, TN: Thomas Nelson Publishers, 1997.

Mehr, Assaph. "How Did Ancient Romans Identify Themselves?" Quora, 9/3/15, https://www.quora.com/How-did-Roman-citizens-identify-themselves-as-citizens-during-the-first-century-AD, accessed 11/27/17.

Melick, Richard R. *Philippians, Colossians, Philemon.* Vol. 32. Nashville, TN: Broadman & Holman Publishers, 1991.

Miller, Stephen M. *How to Get into the Bible.* Nashville, TN: Thomas Nelson Publishers, 1998.

Mills, M. S. *Colossians: A Study Guide to Paul's Epistle to the Saints at Colossae.* Dallas: 3E Ministries, 1993.

Morgan, Robert J. *On This Day: 365 Amazing and Inspiring Stories about Saints, Martyrs & Heroes.* electronic ed. Nashville, TN: Thomas Nelson Publishers, 1997.

Myers, Allen C. *The Eerdmans Bible Dictionary.* Grand Rapids, MI: Eerdmans Publishing Co., 1987. 684.

"Nero Persecutes the Christians, 64 A.D.," EyeWitness to History, www.eyewitnesstohistory.com (2000).

O'Toole, Robert F. "Paul's Nephew." Ed. David Noel Freedman. *The Anchor Yale Bible Dictionary.* New York: Doubleday, 1992. 201–202.

Pfeiffer, Charles F., and Howard Frederic Vos. *The Wycliffe Historical Geography of Bible Lands.* Chicago, IL: Moody Press, 1996.

Platner, Samuel Ball. "Castra Praetoria." http://penelope.uchicago.edu/Thayer/E/Gazetteer/Places/Europe/Italy/Lazio/Roma/Rome/_Texts/PLATOP*/Castra_Praetoria.html, accessed 12/20/17.

Plümacher, Eckhard. "Luke (Person): Luke as Historian." Ed. David Noel Freedman. Trans. Dennis Martin. *The Anchor Yale Bible Dictionary.* New York: Doubleday, 1992. 397–420.

"Ranks in the Praetorian Guard," https://trello.com/c/6Gd2U8Ub/30-rank-descriptions, accessed 12/4/17.

Reasoner, Mark. *Roman Imperial Texts: A Sourcebook*. Minneapolis, MN: Fortress Press, 2013.

Richards, Larry. *Every Man in the Bible*. Nashville, TN: Thomas Nelson Publishers, 1999.

Richards, Sue Poorman, and Larry Richards. *Every Woman in the Bible*. Nashville, TN: Thomas Nelson Publishers, 1999.

Robertson, A. T. *Word Pictures in the New Testament*. Nashville, TN: Broadman Press, 1933.

Schreiner, Thomas R. *1, 2 Peter, Jude*. Vol. 37. Nashville, TN: Broadman & Holman Publishers, 2003.

Stern, David H. *Jewish New Testament: A Translation of the New Testament that Expresses Its Jewishness*. 1st ed. Jerusalem, Israel; Clarksville, MD, USA: Jewish New Testament Publications, 1989.

"Surgical Instruments from Ancient Rome," University of Virginia, http://exhibits.hsl.virginia.edu/romansurgical/, accessed 11/16/17.

"Template and Guidelines for Domestic Roman Sacrifice," Religio Romana, http://www.novaroma.org/religio_romana/DomesticSacrifice Template.html.

Townsend, John T. "Education: Greco-Roman Period." Ed. David Noel Freedman. *The Anchor Yale Bible Dictionary*. New York: Doubleday, 1992. 312–315.

Vincent, Marvin Richardson. *Word Studies in the New Testament*. Vol. 1. New York: Charles Scribner's Sons, 1887.

Vos, Howard Frederic. *Nelson's New Illustrated Bible Manners & Customs: How the People of the Bible Really Lived*. Nashville, TN: Thomas Nelson Publishers, 1999.

"What is Karaism?" The Karaite Korner, http://www.karaite-korner.org/main.shtml, accessed 12/15/17.

"What is the Oral Law?" http://www.chabad.org/library/article_cdo/aid/2056/jewish/The-Oral-Law.htm, accessed 12/15/17.

"Writing Implements and Materials," http://romanatoz.blogspot.com/2011/03/writing-instruments-and-materials.html, accessed 12/4/17.

Youngblood, Ronald F., F. F. Bruce, and R. K. Harrison, eds. *Nelson's New Illustrated Bible Dictionary*. Nashville, TN: Thomas Nelson Publishers, 1995.

Angela Hunt has published more than one hundred books, with sales nearing five million copies worldwide. She's the *New York Times* bestselling author of *The Tale of Three Trees*, *The Note*, and *The Nativity Story*. Angela's novels have won or been nominated for several prestigious industry awards, such as the RITA Award, the Christy Award, the ECPA Christian Book Award, and the HOLT Medallion Award. Romantic Times Book Club presented her with a Lifetime Achievement Award in 2006. She holds both a doctorate in Biblical Studies and a Th.D. degree. Angela and her husband live in Florida, along with their mastiffs. For a complete list of the author's books, visit angelahuntbooks.com.